PRIMEVAL

EXTINCTION EVENT

PRIMEVAL

EXTINCTION EVENT

DAN ABNETT

TITAN BOOKS

Primeval: Extinction Event
ISBN: 9780857680624

Published by
Titan Books
A division of
Titan Publishing Group Ltd
144 Southwark St
London
SE1 0UP

First edition January 2011
1 3 5 7 9 10 8 6 4 2

Primeval © 2009 Impossible Pictures.
Cover imagery: Belukha mountain 4506m, Altai, Russia © Shutterstock. Vicious Dinosaur
© Shutterstock.

Visit our website:
www.titanbooks.com

Did you enjoy this book? We love to hear from our readers. Please email us at
readerfeedback@titanemail.com or write to us at Reader Feedback at the above address.

To receive advance information, news, competitions, and exclusive Titan offers online, please
sign-up for the Titan newsletter on our website: www.titanbooks.com

A CIP catalogue record for this title is available from the British Library.

Printed and bound in Great Britain by CPI Group UK Ltd.

For Ray

ONE

The advance camp was an assortment of canvas prefabs erected a few hundred yards from the river. After hours, you could hear the fast-flowing water chuckling and gurgling like a gleeful baby.

It wasn't a bad place to be, if you didn't mind being nowhere. The closest town, which wasn't much more than an oblast station, was three hours drive east, six if the day was warm and the track turned to mud.

The camp sat against a screen of grey conifers that hid the mossy, misty depths of the forest. A patch of ground was being cleared to make a landing strip, but it was slow work.

Technically, it was early summer, but this far north summer had only managed to give the region the limpest of embraces. The nights were still long, and the brief days were watery and cool, with hazy white skies that turned the broad tracts of forest and the hills beyond into brooding watercolour studies.

Walking up from the latrines to the north end of the camp, Dima tamped a filterless cigarette against the side of its packet. He wasn't going to smoke it, but the habit kept his hands busy.

The commanding officer had restricted smoking privileges inside the camp, and it was prohibited on open forest patrols. To Dima, this was another symptom of the progressive Westernisation of Russian culture. He'd read about it in one of his sister's glossy magazines. Smoking was banned in the West; you couldn't even light up in bars. Drinking was frowned on, too. Men were transforming into what they called "metrosexual" creatures, all tanned and toned and depilated, with a sudden interest in childcare and macrobiotics.

It made him laugh. When signs of this creeping decay showed up in the Russian Army, then it was time to man the barricades.

He played with the fat cigarette. The old habit would die hard in him and he was proud of it. In the eyes of the West, he would be seen as a dinosaur, a throwback, a primitive beast from the distant past, out-evolved and threatened with extinction.

The reason he didn't light it actually had nothing to do with the CO's orders. Cigarettes were a scarce commodity at the advance camp, and there was no local store or bar to buy them from. A man guarded his supply, and rationed it carefully. There was no way of telling how long the deployment was going to last.

Routine manoeuvres, that's what they had all been told — an unscheduled training exercise in the deep woods of the Krasnoyarsk Krai, six weeks minimum, maybe more. Dima had hoped that the spring might see his unit off on a more recreational deployment, perhaps on the Baltic. Instead they got months in the damp and drizzle of Siberia.

Still, the prefabs were heated, the food was good and plentiful, and the regimen none too arduous. He quite liked the woods. He liked the peace, the stillness, the endless nature of the forest. Sometimes, on patrol, he could lose himself. It felt as if the trees stretched away from him in all directions, including time.

He liked the way the stillness could be broken by sudden, bright bird song: clear notes, rasps, the band-saw buzzing of woodpeckers. There were other sounds too, from deep in the woods, grunts and squeals made by animals he had not yet identified.

A human cry broke the air.

Someone in the camp had shouted. Dima turned and caught sight of a 4x4 coming down the loop track through the trees. Its top was down, and its headlamps were switched on to combat the overcast gloom, even though it was late morning. Dima stuffed the cigarette back into the packet and jogged over to the side of the track, the folded skeleton stock of his AK-74 bumping against his shoulder.

He raised his hand in a friendly challenge. The approaching 4x4 dropped a gear and began to slow down. There were four men aboard: an army regular at the wheel and three troopers in black BDUs and field caps. The trio wore no insignia or unit marks, and no expressions on their faces. Their Bergens and cased weapons were piled in the back of the vehicle behind them.

Dima felt a pinch of anxiety.

Aye, aye, what's this now? These men aren't regulars. He knew exactly what they looked like. *Voiska Spetsialnoye Nasranie*, that's what they damned well looked like. Troops of Special Purpose. What were they doing here? Suddenly the deployment didn't feel so much like a routine training exercise. Top brass pulled that kind of stunt all the time. A man got deployed, and then found out it was the real deal.

The 4x4 halted beside him.

"Morning," he said, waiting for them to identify themselves so he could allow them to pass.

"I've got to get these boys to the CO," the driver said.

"That shouldn't be a problem," Dima responded easily.

11

The man in the passenger seat fixed him with a caustic gaze. The guy had deep scars running straight down from the corners of his mouth that reminded Dima of the chin-joints of wooden ventriloquist dummies.

"You know who we are?" he asked Dima belligerently. His accent was strong, maybe Rostov or the Urals.

"Yeah, I think so," Dima replied, trying to keep it light.

"Then do us a favour," the man said, and he made a little gesture with his hand that suggested he was brushing Dima out of his way, like a scatter of cake crumbs.

Dima heard a sharp whistle. He looked over his shoulder. Several men had emerged from the camp's prefabs, and one of them was Zvegin, the CO's adjutant. Zvegin waved impatiently. He forked his fingers into his mouth and blew another shrill whistle.

Dima took a breath.

"On you go then," he said.

The driver thumped the gears and squirmed the 4x4 away down the rutted, wet track as if he was on a tight clock.

Dima watched them go. What was this all about? Spetsnaz. There was going to be trouble, he could feel it in his gut.

He wandered away from the track and into the trees, turning things over in his head. The firs were solemn and grey, and seemed sympathetic. *They* didn't mind if he took five and smoked a cigarette.

So he lit up. His feet were damp. The forest floor was covered in needle litter and little browned scraps of pine cone that looked like spent ammunition. Rocks were caked with lichen as pale as verdigris. Birds piped and chattered in the vaults of the wood. There were black spruce and fir, and enduring larch, and the occasional broadleaf. Daylight, as muffled and white as snow, sank through the canopy overhead.

He inhaled. *God damn the West and its emasculating trends.* Few things could match a drag on a filterless cigarette, and fewer still could compete with that experience in the great outdoors. Fresh air seemed to magnify the flavour.

As he continued to smoke, Dima gradually realised that the wood had become very quiet. The birds had stopped calling. He couldn't even hear the occasional crack and pistol shot of the stirring trees. He felt unaccountably guilty about the cigarette in his hand, as if the stink of it had forced nature into disapproving silence. The smell of the smoke was certainly pungent. It carried in the cold, damp air.

Dima hoped to hell the CO couldn't smell it down in the camp.

He pinched the ash off the half-smoked cigarette and put the offending butt in his top pocket. Then he turned.

It was simply standing behind him. It was just *there*, as tall and as solid and as motionless as the trees. He wondered — in the very little space of time left for wondering — how something so entirely huge could have approached without him hearing anything.

It was such a shock to turn and find it standing there that he forgot to be terrified.

Then Dima began to remember very quickly. He reached for his AK, fumbling with the strap like a raw recruit.

The creature snapped forward to take him. It moved with a speed that something so big had no business being capable of. Its jaws opened.

He saw teeth, and a gape a metre wide.

TWO

It was going to be bad.

Central London, a weekday lunchtime, fine weather, crowded streets; the factors did not add up well. Whenever the ADD — the anomaly detector — painted a contact anywhere near a population centre, the team moved with particular urgency. Today, the contact point was slap bang in the middle of the biggest population centre around.

"Let's hope it's something small and fluffy," James Lester said, sitting in the back of the sleek black SUV as it attempted to edge through the dense traffic. "Something from a quieter moment in history. Something cute. Perhaps something furry with big eyes. Or something pretty and bird-like. I don't know, something —"

"Vegetarian?" Jenny suggested.

Lester turned to look at her.

"Vegetarian would be good," he agreed. "Vegetarian would be excellent."

Jenny Lewis returned her attention to the laptop that was open on her knees.

"Cover story?" Lester asked.

"Just the basic shape for the press release," she replied, "so we can rush it out as soon as the incident's been contained."

Lester pulled out his mobile and tried a number. Then he made a face.

"Cutter's not picking up. Why doesn't that surprise me? Far be it from him to keep us in the loop."

"He's probably got his hands full," Jenny offered, still typing.

Lester leaned forward, and raised his voice.

"Can we get through this?" he asked the driver. "Can we *try*? We're not even on Charing Cross Road."

"It's a bit stuck, sir," the driver replied.

Lester made a slightly pained expression and sat back. Jenny looked up.

"If it doesn't start moving soon, I'm going to get out and walk," she said. Lester didn't look too enamoured of that idea.

"It's Oxford Street," she continued. "The contact was right on Oxford Street. That's got to be less than 300 yards from here. I —"

"Damn," the driver exclaimed emphatically.

Suddenly, there were people all around them, a rushing tide of people pushing and threading through the stationary traffic. They were moving fast, in panic, in fear. There was a commotion of agitated voices, shouting and yelling. Lester's vehicle rocked as the flow of bodies bumped and shoved past it. Hundreds of people — shoppers, tourists, city workers — were pouring back down Charing Cross Road from the direction of Oxford Street.

"Oh God," Lester sighed.

"I think that pretty much answers the question," Jenny said.

"What?"

"It's not vegetarian."

***

"Hold on," Cutter told them.

"No no no no no!" Connor pleaded from the passenger seat next to him.

The road was blocked. Hastily abandoned cars littered the street, and floods of people were swarming towards them. Cutter swung the wheel, and the big silver pick-up mounted the curb at speed. He kept one palm flat on the horn, encouraging people to get out of his way.

"Try not to kill anyone!" Abby called out from the back.

"Particularly, like, us!" Connor added.

Nick Cutter's expression was grim. He didn't reply. He kept his hand on the horn, and his foot on the accelerator. The pick-up blasted down the pavement. He had to jink the wheel to avoid an old man who seemed too dazed to get out of the way, and the pick-up's bull bars clipped a litter bin and sent it flying across the road.

"Was that a person? Oh God, did we just hit someone?" Connor asked. He had his hands over his eyes.

"No, we didn't," Cutter muttered. He wrenched on the wheel, and bumped them off the pavement and across a zebra crossing. He spun the wheel sharply again, and began to drive down Oxford Street on the wrong side of the road.

Two black Land Rovers with tinted windows followed Cutter's pick-up in a tight, obedient formation. Every wild turn and illegal manoeuvre Cutter made, the Land Rovers stuck right with him, following him down the pavement and across the zebra crossing in a high-speed convoy, nose to tail.

The crowds of fleeing civilians began to thin. Within moments only an occasional straggler fled past, sprinting in the opposite direction. Oxford Street — in the middle of a weekday lunchtime

— had emptied. It looked like the four-minute warning had sounded. Buses, taxies, and the odd private car choked the street in both directions, but they were all empty. Some had been left with their doors open and their engines running. That spoke of an alarming haste to leave. There were abandoned bicycles, scattered bags of shopping, even a discarded set of golf-sale sandwich boards.

"How close?" Cutter asked.

"I couldn't say," Connor replied.

"Would you be able to say if you opened your eyes and looked at the detector?"

"Probably," Connor agreed. He opened his eyes. They were back in the middle of the road, travelling down the centre line between the queues of cars and buses. Connor didn't think their wing mirrors were long for this world.

"Um, island," he said, pointing.

"I see it," Cutter snapped, and he brutally swerved the pick-up around the traffic island without losing speed. "Detector?"

Lurching in the passenger seat of the thundering pick-up, Connor studied the display on the portable detector.

"Okay, less than a hundred metres now," Connor said.

"Stop!" Abby cried.

Cutter hit the brakes and brought the pick-up to a juddering halt. The two black Land Rovers behind it braked savagely. The leading Land Rover turned out and came to a halt beside Cutter's pick-up.

The Land Rover's side window whirred down, revealing Hemple's frowning face.

"Professor?" he asked.

Cutter nodded ahead, as if that said it all. Then he got out of the vehicle. Abby took two CO2 pistols and two air-pump rifles out of the pick-up's weapons case and loaded them, then she and Connor followed him.

Hemple touched his radio headset.

"Bone Idol is moving. Switching to feet. Go, *go*!"

The ARC's armed response alpha team executed a rapid dismount from the Land Rovers. There were six of them — including Jake Hemple — all dressed in black battledress and stab vests, and brandishing a variety of ultra-modern assault weapons. Before joining the ARC, every single one of them had been something seriously heavy in the services: SAS, paras, commando.

"Bone Idol?" Cutter asked, glancing at Hemple as they strode forward. "Really?"

Hemple shrugged.

"I don't make the code names up, Professor."

"Who does?"

"I would imagine that would be Miss Lewis," Hemple replied.

"Yes, I imagine it would," Cutter said, glaring ahead.

"Do I have a code name?" Connor asked eagerly.

"Yes," Hemple responded.

Ahead of them, the abandoned traffic had been rearranged. Several cars seemed to have been shunted out of line, forming a fairly effective roadblock across the street. Abby handed a CO2 pistol and an air-pump rifle to Cutter. He tucked the pistol into his belt and checked the rifle's pump pressure.

Hemple raised his right fist and signalled his team forward. They skirted between the jumbled cars, crab-walking with their weapons aimed tight to their cheeks. Hemple and three of the others carried MP53s. Jenkins and Mason had Benelli MI Super 90 semi-automatic shotguns.

Cutter and Abby led the way, with Connor in tow, keeping his eyes on the portable detector. Hemple fanned his fire team out so that all three of the principals were in sight and covered at any time. He'd been working with the ARC long enough to know that things could hit the fan on an average day just as messily as they could in Basra or Helmand. He'd seen things, things his old oppos in 22 Regiment would never believe in a million years.

A million? Make that *millions*.

The shame of it was, Hemple wasn't allowed to talk about any of it.

It was an odd job to wind up in, that was for sure. Here they were, walking down the middle of Oxford Street, armed to the gills, trouble-shooting for three oddball civilians.

There was Connor, a tall and gangly lad with shaving issues. He was a joker, a whizz-kid, a computer nerd... or was he a computer geek? Hemple wasn't sure. There was Abby Maitland, petite and very pretty with her bob of white-blonde hair. Every time they went out on a call, she displayed a serious devotion to her work that would put most servicemen to shame.

Then there was the professor, Nick Cutter, clean-shaven with light, unruly hair, mean and moody, driven and brilliant. Like all brilliant men, he wasn't an easy ride. Hemple admired him, but he didn't get him at all. Cutter had a bitter, wounded air about him, as if he'd lost too much already and was damned if he was going to let anything else slip away.

Cutter was leading the way through the stranded traffic. With his cargo trousers, his faded, green army jacket and his rifle, he looked for all the world like a great white hunter stalking big game on the veldt.

Hemple wondered exactly *how* big the day's game was going to be.

"Wow, that's not right," Connor said.

They were coming up on a black cab in the middle of the road ahead of them. The cab had been rammed with such force it had been flipped over onto its side. It lay in a starburst of chipped windscreen glass. Connor stooped and peered in through the shattered window.

"Just look for the anomaly," Cutter said. "We must be right on it."

There was a brief, deep snorting sound from somewhere nearby. Cutter took off at once, and Abby and Connor went with him as if they were tied to him with string.

Hemple waved his men after them.

Cutter ran to the next corner and skidded to a halt, looking around rapidly. The others came up behind him.

"Anything?" Abby asked.

Cutter shook his head.

"Can you still hear it?"

"No," Cutter said, "it's gone. I can smell something though."

"Oh, nice!" Connor exclaimed. He'd stepped off the pavement and planted his right foot in a spatter of wet dung. "Oh, my shoe! Oh, that's nasty!"

Cutter came over and bent down to examine the fecal matter.

"It's fresh," Connor moaned, "though not in every sense of the word. Look at my shoe! That's a brand-new pair of Vans, and they're ruined!" He started to scrape his sole against the kerb.

"Well, Professor, did you find some useful... er... *excrement*?" Hemple asked, standing over Cutter.

"Oh, it smells *really* bad!" Connor complained. He found some discarded napkins and began to wipe off the offending fecal matter.

"Uh, yeah," Cutter said to Hemple. "From the volume of the

scat, it looks as if we're dealing with a pretty big creature."

"I guessed that from the overturned taxi," Hemple said.

"True," Cutter replied. "As for the consistency..."

"Yes, let's examine that in detail," Hemple suggested with a wry smile.

Cutter looked up and beckoned over Abby.

"What do you think?" he asked her.

"I can't be sure," she said, crouching down to look more closely, "but I'd say we're looking for an omnivore. Not a discriminating one, either. There's a lot of bone matter ground up in this, and undigested bark. All sorts of things."

"So?"

Abby stood up and looked around.

"I don't know. A giant pig?" she suggested.

"A giant pig," Hemple echoed doubtfully.

"Well, it's not an exact science," she protested.

"And it smells! Science smells!" Connor groaned, still wiping his shoe.

"We've got to spread out," Cutter said.

"I'd be happier if we stayed as one group," Hemple countered.

"I'd be happier if this wasn't happening at all," Cutter replied. "We've got to find this creature quick smart. It's big, it's aggravated, and it's not fussy about what it takes a bite out of. It may not even be on Oxford Street any more. It could have gone off down a side road. It could have gone anywhere."

Hemple sighed.

"I need Connor and Abby to find the anomaly and lock down its location," Cutter told him.

"Mason? Redfern? Stay with them." Hemple turned to the others. "Rest of you are with me and the prof."

***

Cutter and the four soldiers moved away down the street. Cutter looked back over his shoulder.

"The anomaly," he urged, "quickly, please."

Connor nodded and with a final wipe he turned his attention back to the detector.

"Where do we start?" Mason asked, the big shotgun propped across his shoulder.

Connor slowly turned in a circle, standing on the spot, holding the detector up.

"We're right on top of it. This way."

He moved towards the nearest shops. Mason swung in behind him, his shotgun lowered to a cover position. The other soldier, Redfern, had his MP53 pulled up tight against his chest.

"After you, miss," he said to Abby. "And stay where I can see you."

Cutter walked another thirty yards down the street, with Hemple and his men in tow. They passed two more vehicles — a BT van and another black cab — that had been struck and damaged. Both vehicles looked as though someone had gone at them angrily with a battering ram.

Cutter thought he heard the deep, ragged snorting noise again.

Jenkins turned to the left sharply, aiming his shotgun.

"Contact!" he barked.

"Hold your fire!" Hemple countered. He ran forward. There was a woman crumpled up in the doorway of a shoe shop. Her hair was bedraggled, and the front of her coat was soaked in blood.

"Dammit!" Cutter growled, moving beside Hemple and bending over her.

"Miss? It's okay," Hemple said softly. "You're going to be okay."

The woman didn't reply. Her face was pale and she was staring at nothing. Her whole body was trembling very slightly.

"She's in shock," Cutter said. He reached in and gently moved her coat aside. There was no sign of injury.

"That's not her blood," Cutter confirmed. Parts of her coat were damp with something other than blood. Cutter touched the patches and sniffed his fingertips.

"That's got to be saliva," he said. "Smells pretty rank."

"What did you see? Miss? What did you see?"

The woman was virtually catatonic. She didn't respond to Hemple.

"Sir!" one of the team shouted.

Hemple and Cutter got up.

"Stay with her," Hemple told Jenkins. "Keep talking to her." Jenkins nodded, and knelt down in the doorway beside the woman.

Cutter and Hemple hurried to catch up with the other two men. They'd come to a halt beside a single-decker bus. As he approached, Cutter saw what they were standing over, and turned his head aside in anger and disappointment.

"We've got two dead here," Garney, one of the two squad members, said. He gestured to the body at his feet, and to another one nearby. "There's another one over by the kerb."

"Oh God," Cutter murmured.

"I can't work out if they've been bitten or trampled to death," Murdoch, the other trooper, said.

"Or both," Garney suggested.

It was a fearful, mangled mess. There was blood right across the road, and it had spattered up the side of the bus and all over the white plastic traffic bollards on a nearby island. Deep impact dents showed where the side of the bus had been struck several times. Some of the side windows were broken.

Cutter made himself look at the bodies. This is what it meant when he didn't get his job done — death, horrible, undeserved, violent death; innocent people caught in harm's way, their normal, everyday lives ended, cut off. He wondered who the victims were. What had they been doing? Had they been shopping, or on their lunch breaks, or heading for an early showing at the cinema? What had they been planning for the rest of their day, their week?

Their lives?

Who was going to miss them when they didn't come home?

Cutter swallowed hard. Anger swirled impotently inside him. How many more was it going to have to be?

He closed his eyes, and saw Stephen's face.

He heard a deep, snorting noise.

Cutter opened his eyes. He listened hard. He glanced at Hemple and the two troopers, his expression fixed, and motioned them to follow him.

Thirty yards away, behind a Fed Ex van, something large was moving around. They could hear it snuffling and grunting. Over the top of the van, Cutter glimpsed a fleshy, humped back, thick with dark bristles. It was big, all right, whatever it was. He could smell its ripe, pungent odour.

He advanced more slowly now, the rifle in one hand, his other hand open and raised at his side, emphasising caution.

The thing behind the van moved again. They could hear what sounded like hooves clopping on the asphalt.

"Steady," Cutter whispered. "I want to get the first shot. I want it alive, if possible."

"After what it did to those people?" Garney said, a look of shock on his face.

"I want it *alive*," Cutter repeated.

He took another step.

His mobile started to ring.

Cutter hit 'reject call' as quickly as he could, glancing down. On the mobile's screen, the caller ID read 'Jenny Lewis'.

But he hadn't been fast enough. The creature had heard. There was a violent, ugly snort from behind the Fed Ex van, and something struck the side of the vehicle so hard that it rocked down on its shocks. Then whatever it was started moving away, and quickly. They heard it crunching into vehicles. They heard the hoof-like clatter on the road surface.

"Come on!" Cutter yelled.

With the soldiers at his heels, he started to chase after it.

"He's still not answering," Jenny snapped. She glanced at Lester. He was leaning back in his seat, his head resting on one hand in a pose that oozed listless tedium. He was drumming the fingers of his other hand on his armrest.

Outside, the street had become quieter. The mad rush of people had passed by. Drivers were getting out of the jammed cars to look around. A few of them were leaving their vehicles and hurrying away to follow the crowd. But even though the people were gone, their vehicles still sat in the way.

"I'm not just going to sit here," she said. "Are you coming?"

Lester shifted in his seat.

"I'll coordinate from here," he said.

"Fine," she replied, getting out of the car and slamming the door.

Lester wound down his window as she began to stride away.

"Jenny?" he called.

"Yes?" she said, turning back.

"Try not to get eaten or anything."

"I'll do my best," she responded, then she spun and marched off between the rows of halted cars towards Oxford Street.

As she walked, she pulled out her mobile and tried Cutter again.

Abby looked at Connor.

"In here?" she asked, doubtfully.

"That's what it's telling me," he replied, carefully studying the detector's display.

They were facing the entrance of a small arthouse cinema, a tall-fronted building sandwiched between a mini-market and a budget travel office. The marquee board promised some European arthouse classic, the sort of film Connor would gnaw his own leg off to escape.

"Keep behind me," Mason said. He led the way in with the shotgun ready. Abby and Connor followed, and Redfern brought up the rear.

The lobby was small and dark. There was no one around. It took a moment for their eyes to adapt from the bright sunlight in the street. A spinner full of leaflets had been knocked over near the concessions, and the ticket office door was open, as if someone had left in a hurry. They could hear the soundtrack and dialogue of the movie booming from the theatre next door.

"We're right on it," Connor said, reading the display on his portable detector.

"Can you smell that?" Abby asked.

"More dung," Redfern noted.

"I suppose." She nodded.

With Mason in the lead, they pushed open the swing doors of the cinema. The amplified sound and jumping blue-grey flicker of the screen washed over them. There was another light too, a softer light. Connor felt the magnetic tug on all things metal.

They stepped into the cinema.

It was very dark. The silhouettes of the seat backs looked like rows of molars. A gamine Sixties ingenue gazed soulfully out of the black-and-white world of the film, while a man spoke French off-camera.

Off to the left there was a hole that had once been a side door. Something large had gone that way, and just beyond they saw the dim impression of daylight, indicating the route the creature had taken to the street.

The anomaly floated in front of the screen, like a scintillating, multifaceted jewel catching, like sunlight, on a patch of rippled water.

"Bingo!" Connor said, triumphantly.

"What was that noise?" Abby asked, looking around.

"Where has it got to?" Hemple demanded, running up.

"Wait, wait," Cutter whispered. They kept their heads down, and threaded between the abandoned vehicles. They saw a scraped fender or a dented wing every few yards. Chips of headlamp glass dusted the ground.

"I think it's stopped running," Cutter said, raising his rifle.

Hemple signalled to his men to circle in around them.

They were close. Cutter could hear the creature breathing. The respiration was deep and bovine. The ripe smell hung in the air.

Cutter took another step.

It came at them.

A car smashed aside, turning violently end to end. The beast was the size of a rhino, a colossal thing with terrible power and weight in its deep, humped body. Its head was a freak-show photo-fit of pinched, squinting eyes, flaring nostrils, bristled cheeks, and a giant, long-snouted mouth full of spittle and ugly, discoloured teeth the size of tent pegs. Its noxious breath assaulted them like a chemical weapon.

Hemple swore.

"What did Abby tell you?" Cutter murmured. "Giant pig."

He aimed his rifle.

The beast began to charge them.

It was going to be bad.

THREE

The anomaly seemed to flare and pulse. It was exhibiting some kind of inherent instability Connor hadn't seen before.

He saw the soldiers struggling to manage their weapons in the fluctuating magnetic wash. Even with gun furniture and sights deliberately switched out for plastics, the metal fabric of all ARC weapons was vulnerable to anomaly magnetics.

The mag field was affecting the cinema's projector too. The movie was running slow. Frames were lingering in the blue and white glare of the big screen, and the French voices had slowed to deep, treacly bass notes.

"Call Cutter," Connor said to Abby. "Tell him we've got it."

Abby took out her mobile and tapped a speed-dial number, but she was distracted. The phone — a slim model with a metal cover — shot out of her hand and disappeared into the anomaly.

"Nice one," Connor said, rummaging in his pocket to find his own mobile.

"Didn't you hear that?" Abby asked, looking behind them. "There's that sound again."

"It's just the soundtrack." Connor responded, and he held his phone out to her.

Abby shook her head.

"No —" she began.

Then she saw it, and so did Connor. There was something in the gloomy cinema with them. It was hidden in the shadows to the left of the screen, but Connor could tell it was big — and agitated. It exhaled, and a wave of bad air washed over them.

"Back up, real slow," Redfern hissed.

"Do as he said," Mason added, raising the shotgun.

In the darkness of the deserted movie theatre, something that sounded like the demon-god of all swine snorted and began to move towards them.

It was a ton and a half of gristle, bone and meat, with a skull a metre long, and a monstrously short fuse.

"It's an Entelodon!" Professor Cutter shouted.

But Jake Hemple didn't bother committing it to memory. From his professional perspective, the fact that the thing charging at him possessed a scientific label had little or no bearing on anything. Knowing what it was called — or where it sat on evolution's great family tree — wouldn't keep it from killing him, and this giant pig-thing promised a particularly horrible death.

He had seen the bodies in the street.

So, the name didn't matter. All that mattered was its size, its power, and the speed at which its screaming, snorting snout full of teeth was closing.

Hemple thought about squeezing off a shot, but he remembered Cutter's counter-intuitive instruction to keep the thing alive, even though it wasn't showing signs of extending the same courtesy to them.

"Professor..." he growled.

Cutter stared at the oncoming monster with a mix of alarm and admiration. Certain creatures, even a grossly ugly one like this, managed to be truly impressive in their singularity of purpose.

The Entelodon was a massive, foraging waste disposal system from the mud pools of the Asian Cenozoic, 35 million years ago. Everything about it was made to endure. Its bones and body mass were huge and heavy, built to soak up trauma and physical punishment. Indeed, its great gargoyle face was ridged and split with old, half-healed scars where it had engaged with others of its kind in brawls over food or mating rights, evidence Cutter had seen in the fossil records many times. Its thick, enameled teeth were worn and broken in places from grinding down bone and bark, and its deep neck muscles gave it a hell of a bite. No part of a kill would be wasted. Everything would get pulped and passed down into an iron-clad stomach that could digest anything.

The Entelodon was created to survive by any basic means.

Part of its arsenal for survival was its astonishing aggression. It came from a world where it had very little to fear apart from a bigger, meaner Entelodon. That upbringing meant that it wasn't going to back down.

Cutter had the rifle aimed right at it. He wanted to hit it in the flank or the hunched back, where there was some meat and the dose would have maximum effect. The thing's head, which formed most of the target, was thickly boned, and there was a danger of the dart simply bouncing off.

He heard Hemple saying his name. He heard Murdoch and Garney swearing as they started backwards. He smelled the landfill stench of the Entelodon's breath.

He twisted and shot a dart into the black bristled flesh at the top of its neck.

Still it came on.

He pumped the rifle furiously, and put a second dart in its left shoulder.

His plan had been for the creature to fall at his feet in a drug-induced coma before it could plough him down like a runaway freight car. Suddenly he realised that no one had explained this to the Entelodon.

Its jaws opened wide to display brown teeth sticking out like a hippo's tusks. Its long, repellant tongue was the colour of blancmange, and it quivered as a pressurised snort burst from its gullet.

It wasn't even slowing down.

Hemple barged Cutter sideways, tackling him like a rugby player. Locked together, they slammed over the bonnet of a late model Lexus that stood beside them, and rolled off the other side, barely vacating their location as the Entelodon hit.

The demon pig crunched into the side of the Lexus and did about six grand's worth of damage to the door panels. The side windows burst in sprays of glass chips, and the car shifted several feet to one side.

Hemple and Cutter had landed on the road. The right-hand side of the car bumped into them as it was shunted around.

The Entelodon struck again, head down, butting into the obstacle, refusing to give in. Tyres dry-squealed as the Lexus was rammed sideways. Hemple began to rise.

"Drop!" Cutter yelled at him.

They both rolled flat. A third shunt slid the battered Lexus over their heads and shoulders. They found themselves looking up into the oil-sweet blackness of the car's underside.

The demon pig knocked the car again, and then Murdoch and Garney began yelling at it to draw it away from Cutter and their chief. It swung aside and began to stomp in their direction, indifferently spattering dung in its wake.

Cutter and Hemple clambered out from under the wrecked car. The pig had its back to them. Cutter loaded another dart.

"Let me take the shot," Hemple said, brandishing his MP53.

Cutter shook his head.

"Fat lot of good that's done so far," Hemple responded, and he nodded at the pump rifle.

"That thing's got a hell of a constitution," Cutter said. "It's used to shrugging off just about anything that goes into its system. It's metabolising the drug faster than most creatures its size. We just need a wee bit more."

The pig had gone for Murdoch. He ran clear as it crashed into the works van he'd been using as cover. Its canines ripped the skin of the van's cargo space like tinfoil.

Cutter fired the rifle, and put the third dart into the pig's rump. It rotated, stamping, as if it was executing a clumsy three-point turn, and gazed balefully at Cutter and Hemple. It barked and snorted, and began to canter towards them again, head-butting a Mini out of its way.

"Oh good," Hemple said, "I see you've got its attention again."

Connor didn't need to be told to run. The glimpse he'd got of what was coming out of the cinema's darkness was pretty persuasive. They all bolted for the lobby.

Abby fired her dart rifle in the confusion, but there was no way of telling if she'd hit anything. In fact, Connor wasn't sure of anything any more, including where she was.

He made it into the foyer, and glanced over his shoulder. No

Abby, no Mason, no Redfern, but there was a hell of a lot of snorting and bellowing coming his way.

The swing-doors exploded open with such force that one of the arrestor springs broke. Something that looked to Connor like a cross between a water buffalo, a mastiff, and an alligator thundered into the lobby area, spit drooling from its preposterously unpleasant mouth. The thing had the build of a hyena, with hunched shoulders, long forelimbs and shorter hindquarters, but it seemed to have hooves, and it squealed like a stag boar with anger management issues.

Connor said something colourful and sprinted towards the nearest door. The street exit was out of the question. He knew he'd never make it. The pig from hell was as big as a truck, but it could move like nobody's business. Connor headed for a closer option.

He made it into the gents' in a time that wouldn't have discredited Usain Bolt. The pig was right behind him. Connor slammed the toilet door in its face, but it splintered clean through it with an almighty crash, and pursued him inside.

The pig's hooves slithered on the tiled floor, fighting for purchase, and it skidded sideways into the toilet stalls, comprehensively demolishing the first three in a row. Doors and partitions shredded under its bulk as it thrashed. Water gushed from ruptured cisterns and broken toilet bowls. Connor raced across the room and started pulling himself through a small, frosted glass window — the only other exit.

The pig lunged at him.

Connor pushed off from some pipework with his feet and posted himself through the window. The massive jaws snapped shut on nothing, just inches from his ankles.

Outside, in the alley behind the cinema, Connor fell head-first and landed on his back under the men's room window on a deep pile of refuse sacks. He looked up in time to shield his face with his arms as the pig's head smashed through the toilet window, spraying broken glass and splinters of frame into the alley.

His mobile started to ring. Under the circumstances, he decided to let voicemail take the call.

He rolled off the sacks onto his feet, and got his breath back, realising that he was safe enough. The pig's head was fearsome, and it was making a lot of noise, but there was no way it was going to get the rest of its body through the window. The angle made it impossible for the creature to attain any momentum.

Abruptly, it withdrew.

Connor hesitated, and then got back up on the rubbish bags to peer in. The toilet was a mess, but there was no sign of his pursuer. He hoisted himself back in through the window, being careful to avoid the rim of broken glass, and dropped down onto the rapidly flooding tiles.

"Abby?" he called softly. "Fellas?"

He splished gingerly across the tiles to the caved-in door and glanced out into the lobby.

"Abby?"

"Shhh!" Abby replied, rising slowly into view from behind the ticket desk. Mason and Redfern were near the street door, moving slowly and warily.

"It's gone out into the street," Abby mouthed.

Connor nodded. He could see it now, through what was left of the tinted, back-printed plate glass of the cinema's entrance, a huge black shape snuffling on the pavement outside. Abby edged forwards, fitting a fresh dart into her rifle.

Connor's mobile rang again.

Cutter gazed down at the mighty Entelodon. It lay on its side beside the wreck of the Lexus, its ribs juddering up and down, and what approximated a snore ripping in and out of its throat.

"I told you, we just had to give it time," Cutter said to Hemple. "I knew the tranks would knock it down eventually."

Hemple shrugged, but didn't seem convinced. His look said, *God made MP53s for a reason, and surely this is one of them.*

"We're going to need chains and tackle, and something like a forklift," Cutter said. He had his phone to his ear. "I want to get it back through the anomaly before it wakes up."

Hemple nodded and called out instructions to Garney and Murdoch. They moved to comply.

"I'm hoping Connor's found the anomaly," Cutter remarked, still listening to his phone. "He's not picking up." He dialed again.

Connor answered almost immediately.

"Little busy!" he yelped.

"What?" Cutter asked. "Have you found the anomaly yet?"

The noises on the other end of the line became garbled. Cutter heard shouting, crashing and what sounded like a gun discharging.

"Connor? Connor, what's going on?"

Connor came back on.

"We've found it, Professor!" he yelled.

"The anomaly?"

"No! Well, yes, that too! But we've found the creature! It's here!"

"No, it's here," Cutter replied. "We just brought it down."

"No, it's *here*!" Connor gabbled. "It's right here! Outside the cinema."

Cutter looked at Hemple.

"There are two of them," he said.

FOUR

Jenny picked her way along Oxford Street, edging between the abandoned cars. It was alarmingly quiet, and she was beginning to regret leaving the comparative safety of Lester's SUV.

She had tried Cutter's phone several more times. She hoped the reason he wasn't answering was bad reception, although it was Central London and the chances of there being any gaps in signal coverage were zero.

She didn't really want to consider the alternatives, though.

Perhaps the anomaly is interfering with mobile reception, she told herself. However random this theory, it was reassuring. She kept reiterating it to herself.

The emptiness of Oxford Street was eerie. It reminded her of a film she'd gone to see, a horror film where everyone turned into zombies and the streets of London were deserted. The scenes had been haunting.

This was somehow worse, not just because it was real, but because it was so *normally* abnormal. The scene hadn't been artfully decorated by some acclaimed set dresser, nor had the emptiness and abandonment been contrived by Hollywood designers. It was simply *empty*, clumsily empty, unromantically empty. It was desolate and frightening in a terrible, prosaic way.

She found Cutter's pick-up and the alpha team Land Rovers. The sensation of relief surprised her. She never thought she'd be so grateful to see a motor vehicle.

Then she realised there was no sign of Cutter or the team.

She hesitated. There was *something*, though. She'd heard something that wasn't the breeze stirring the litter, or the beep of the pedestrian crossings running through their automatic cycles. Something was moving.

Jenny thought she heard what sounded like a sniff or a snort, the sort of nasty grunt a pig would make. Involuntarily she shuddered. She'd had a great uncle who'd owned a farm and raised Wessex Saddlebacks. They had been completely horrid, vicious brutes, and when she'd been a little girl they'd absolutely terrified her.

She looked around now. The light breeze was wafting a smell to her — a really foul smell, like bad drains. She hooked her lip in distaste.

She thought she heard the snort again.

Her phone purred softly in her hand. She answered it before the vibration could become a ring tone.

"Jenny?" It was Cutter.

"Cutter? Where are you?" she began, more stridently than she meant to.

"Lower your voice," he said gently. "Please. Where are you?"

"Where are *you*, more like? I've been calling and calling and —"

"Jenny, where are you?"

His tone was disarmingly quiet.

"I'm on Oxford Street," she said, her voice lowered as instructed.

"*Where* on Oxford Street?"

"I just passed your truck."

"Can you go back towards it?"

"I suppose. What's going on?"

"Jenny, just head back towards my truck, please," Cutter said. "Do it quietly. Don't run."

Jenny turned. Her heart was pounding.

She began to walk back towards the silver pick-up, glancing from side to side as she went. Her eyes were wide. Her imagination was suddenly seeing all sorts of things in the lengthening shadows of the afternoon.

"What's going on?" she whispered as she walked. "Cutter, what's going on? What is it?"

"I think it's an Entelodon," Cutter said. His voice was so soft and calm, it sounded like he was making idle, after-dinner conversation.

"And what's that?"

"It's bad news. You at the truck yet?"

"Nearly," she replied. She paused. "Did you hear that?"

"Hear what?"

Jenny looked around, the mobile pressed to her ear.

"A snort," she said. "A grunt. A grunt like the biggest, meanest pig you ever met. What does an... an..."

"Entelodon?"

"Yes. What does one of those sound like?"

"Like the biggest, meanest pig you ever met," Cutter said.

"I had to ask."

"You at the truck now?"

"Yes," she replied.

"Get in. Quick as you can. Do it nice and quiet. Don't slam the door."

Keeping the phone to her ear, Jenny opened the driver's door of the pick-up. She slid inside and pulled the door shut. As an afterthought, she pushed the button down on the central locking and it engaged with a loud clunk.

"What was that?" Cutter asked.

"I just locked the doors," she told him.

"Okay," he replied.

"What?"

"Well, nothing. Doesn't matter."

"What?"

"An Entelodon won't open a car door using the handle. What I mean is, locking the door's pretty academic."

"Because if it wants to get in, it will?" Jenny asked.

"Yes."

"Once again, I had to ask," she said. She sat bolt upright in the driver's seat and stared out of the window. "Where are you, Nick?"

"I'm coming," he said. "I'm close. Just stay put. We'll be right there."

"Okay." The word dried in her throat. Out of the corner of her eye, she'd glimpsed movement in the rear view mirror. She looked up. There was nothing visible there. She checked the wing mirrors, but the angle was bad. She didn't dare turn her head.

Something came up alongside the pick-up, moving from behind. It drew level with the driver's door. Jenny froze.

"Jenny?" Cutter's voice said from the phone.

She let out a tiny, paralysed *meep*.

"Jenny? Are you still there?"

Its head, a metre long, was level with the window. It was right beside her. She sat, frozen and stiff-backed, facing straight ahead, not daring to move a muscle; her eyes swiveled hard to the right. Even with the door firmly closed, she could smell the reek of it, like the aroma of her great uncle's farm, magnified a thousand times by nightmare.

The skin of its face was scarred and mottled. Bristles, thick and black like beetle legs, sprouted in clumps around the ragged, tufted ears. The flesh around the eyes and brow was a florid pink that darkened to a puce colour around the ears and the heavy jowls. The teeth were as large and as yellow-black as overripe bananas. Some of the wounds on its cheeks and lips were fresh enough to still be scabbed or weeping.

Its eye, the one eye she could see, was a malevolent, glassy black ball half-hidden by folds of pink skin.

It snorted. Aspirated saliva and condensation filmed the outside of the driver's window.

"Jenny? Are you there?"

"I'm not exactly on my own," she said into the phone in a tiny, fragile voice.

"Is it there? Jenny, is it there?"

"Mm-hmm."

"Hold on. Just be still. Sit still."

The Entelodon swung its head and nosed the wheel arch of the pick-up. Jenny whimpered slightly as the vehicle rocked. It began to sniff at the door and the window. Its rank breath came in quick, panting snorts. Gobbets of cloudy saliva spattered the window with each huff and began to ooze down the glass. There was a thin, high-pitched squeal as the edge of one of its canines dragged slowly across the window.

It rumbled, deep in its belly, and then shook its head.

Jenny swallowed hard.

The Entelodon curled back its lips and closed its jaws around the driver's door mirror. The jaws squeezed shut.

The pick-up juddered a little as the Entelodon chewed the

mirror off. Jenny heard it crack and splinter. Chunks of toughened glass fell out of the giant pig's mouth. As its head pulled away, just out of sight, it plucked a length of electrical cable out of the mangled mirror stump. The cable trailed from its teeth.

"Please hurry," she whispered. Turning ever so slightly, she risked a look out of the window.

The Entelodon was looking right back in at her. Its eyes looked like tiny dots of polished anthracite coal, as if they were the product of millions of years of geological transmutation. Jenny tried to stifle a yelp, but it came out anyway.

The Entelodon snorted. More saliva aspirated up the window. The nostrils flared. It thrust its snout against the door, and then banged again, harder.

The pick-up jolted.

The Entelodon head-butted.

Jenny heard the door panel dent. The next blow cracked the window. She cried out in terror and began to scramble across to the passenger side.

"Stay still! Stay still!" Cutter called.

"I'm not just going to sit here!" she yelled back.

The Entelodon drove its head into the driver's door with much greater force, honking and squealing like a hog at feeding time. The window shattered and blew glass at her. She threw open the passenger door and scrambled out.

As she rushed across the street, she glanced back over her shoulder. The Entelodon dragged its head back out of the mangled driver's door and shook its neck. It could see her — or smell her. It rose up a little on its powerful front legs and turned to the side to trot around the pick-up and come at her. She started to run. It broke into a canter, and began bellowing like a fog horn.

Jenny turned and without stopping hurled her mobile at it. The phone bounced off its snout, causing it to come to a halt. The Entelodon bent to sniff the phone. It rolled its huge head on one side so it could scoop the phone up in the V of its jaws. Then it began to crunch.

Jenny kept running. She heard its hooves striking the ground as it moved again, heard its dreadful snorting.

"Jenny!"

She looked up. Cutter was standing on a car ahead of her. He had his gas-powered rifle in his hands. He didn't have to tell her how useless the weapon was going to be in the current circumstances.

"Come on!" he yelled at her. "Run!" Hemple stood nearby.

She needed no encouragement. She ran. It was right behind her.

Cutter looked over at Hemple.

"No choice. Do it," he said.

Alpha team opened fire. Jenny screamed at the roar of gunfire. The high velocity munitions tore into the huge omnivore and puffed clouds of red mist into the air. The multiple impacts stopped it in its tracks and shredded huge chunks of bloody meat off its stumbling body.

It managed a few last, uneven steps, its ancient blood streaming out onto the asphalt of Oxford Street. It whined and gurgled, its snorts and squeals drowning in blood.

Cutter leapt off the car and grabbed Jenny. He wrapped his arms around her and pulled her clear.

Hemple stepped forwards, raised his MP53, and fired a last burst that put the demon pig down forever.

FIVE

Abby hurried up the ramp towards Lester's office. It was late evening.

The glass-walled room grandly overlooked the main operations area of the Anomaly Research Centre, and a combined murmur of human voices and electronic noise rose from the consoles and workstations below her. The Oxford Street incident had been the most public yet, and a lot of very clever people with extremely high national security clearances were going to be working long into the night tidying it up.

Tidying it up... and covering it up.

But the cover-up wasn't Abby's remit. She was as highly cleared as any of the ARC personnel, but her area of expertise lay with the animals. More often than not, they were monsters, but they were always victims too, victims of the anomalies that cast them into an alien world in which they were not intended to exist. This afternoon, they'd had to kill one. She hated that, and it always sat really badly with Cutter.

Abby approached the door of the office. Through the glass,

she could see Cutter, Jenny and Jake Hemple waiting in front of Lester's desk, while Lester sat back and skim-read an interim report.

He dropped the report onto his blotter and sat back with his arms folded.

"So... thank heavens for automatic weapons, then?" he said.

Cutter smiled humourlessly. He'd been around the block with James Lester too many times to rise to the bait. Lester's interests and priorities were so far removed from his that it wasn't even funny.

"We took the kill out of necessity, sir," Hemple said. "All other options had been explored and exhausted."

"Took you a while, though, Hemple," Lester observed.

"We were mindful of Professor Cutter's desire to keep the specimens alive."

Lester glanced at Cutter.

"The creature didn't deserve to be shot," Cutter said.

"It had killed people, Cutter," Lester said firmly, then he sighed. "Three, wasn't it? Three people?"

Jenny nodded.

"It was just doing what it does," Cutter said evenly. "It was probably scared, too."

"And so, I should imagine, were the people it ate." Lester stared at Cutter. "Thankfully, Jenny wasn't one of them."

"Jenny didn't deserve to get eaten any more than the Entelodon deserved to get shot," Cutter said. "It was a no-win situation. I made the best call I could."

"Thank you so much," Jenny said. Abby could hear the withering scorn in her tone and she pulled a face. *Nice going, Cutter.*

"The live specimen was delivered back through the anomaly before it closed," Hemple said briskly. "Now we're cleaning up the area."

"But it's out, isn't it?" Lester inquired.

"Very much so," Jenny said. "There was an extremely high volume of witnesses and word of mouth is like wildfire. We can usually control it with misinformation, but dozens of people had cameras on their mobiles, and many more were tourists with videos and still cameras. On top of that, there was a local news team filming a segment at the location when the event occurred. There's footage on all the news channels, and the Internet's lousy with clips and downloads.

"It's big. It's gone global."

"And what do you propose to do about that?" Lester asked, his emotions unreadable.

"We can't cover it the way we normally do," Jenny replied. "It's too big to deny. I'm working to change the rules and spin the story. There *were* monsters loose on Oxford Street today, but they were new generation animatronics built for a movie. It was all special effects. Nobody really died. It was publicity gone wrong, a spectacularly misguided promotional stunt."

"I thought all those monster shows these days used CGI," Lester pointed out.

"I think I can sell animatronics in the circumstances," Jenny said. "The whole story will be an 'and finally...' by the end of the week." She sounded businesslike to Abby. Jenny was very good at her job, and if she said a story would go away, then it would go away. But Abby could hear a slight catch in her voice. She'd had a tough day and a very close call. She was keeping going to get the job done, but as soon as it was over, the shock would catch up with her and she'd crash.

"Good," Lester nodded. "That's good. We can run with that. We'll need to set up a fake production company to take the rap, maybe a trailer or two, a website..."

"Already in work," Jenny jumped in. "I've got press announcements written and ready. Horrified by the recklessness of the publicity stunt, some of the film's principal financial backers will pull out tomorrow morning. The production will fold on Friday afternoon. End of story."

"What about the people who *did* die?" Cutter asked quietly.

Jenny looked at him.

"You know very well what we do when there's a fatality. The families will be informed and compensated. We usually say it's a traffic accident."

"Don't you think they deserve better?" Cutter looked Jenny in the eye. "If something, God forbid, had happened to you today, wouldn't you have wanted your mum or dad to know the truth?"

"Let's see," Jenny replied. "I was devoured by a prehistoric pig in broad daylight on Oxford Street, or I was knocked down by a bendy bus on Tottenham Court Road? I think I know which set of mental images would help most with the grieving process."

Cutter shrugged and looked away. Lester finally noticed Abby hovering in the office doorway.

"Can we help you?" he asked.

"I need Cutter, when you're finished," Abby replied with a friendly smile.

"Oh, I'm done," Lester said with a wave of his hands.

Cutter walked over to join Abby.

"What's up?"

"Connor's got something," she said. "He wants you to take a look."

Cutter and Abby headed swiftly down the ramp, side by side. Jenny and Hemple left the office behind them.

"You okay?" Hemple asked her quietly.

"I'm fine. A little shaken." She gazed down the ramp at the figures pulling ahead of them. "Nice to know I'm in a no-win situation."

"I don't think Cutter meant it quite the way it came out," Hemple said.

"I'm sure he didn't," Jenny replied, as if she believed precisely the opposite. "He tortures himself when innocent bystanders are caught up in things, and he hates the cover-ups, and yet sometimes he seems to care more about the creatures than people. The efforts he goes to in order to keep them alive and safe."

"He's a riddle, all right," Hemple agreed.

"He's never exactly liked me," Jenny said. "Apparently, I remind him of someone."

"Like an ex-girlfriend, you mean?"

She shook her head.

"It's rather more complicated than that. It would be, of course. It involves Nick Cutter." She glanced at Hemple and smiled.

"Thank you, anyway. You saved my life this afternoon."

"It's my job," Hemple replied. "And, anyway, I got to shoot a monster." He grinned. "I mean, honestly, I'm a monster hunter. I can't believe this job, it's like a childhood dream come true."

"You are joking, aren't you?"

"No," he said. Then he pursed his lips. "Well, a little, maybe. When I was a kid, I wanted to battle dinosaurs and mammoths and giant lizards. What kid didn't? Too many corny movies, probably. And look at me now, I've got my own machine gun and a ready supply of monsters."

She laughed.

"Trouble is, the professor does like to keep them alive," Hemple continued, "so my opportunities for heroism are strictly limited. Luckily, you got yourself into a bit of bother today and there was nothing else for it but to lock and load."

"Glad to be of service," she mocked.

"Seriously," he added, "that's what we're here for, to look after you. All of you. No matter what the prof says, team safety is paramount. I know there was a fatality just before I joined the ARC."

"Stephen," Jenny murmured quietly.

"Cutter blames himself for that, doesn't he?" Hemple asked. "I mean, that's why he's so conflicted."

"Sometimes," Jenny said, "I honestly have no idea what really drives Nick Cutter."

"Shoot," Cutter said. Then he chuckled softly.

Connor looked up from his workstation in the middle of the main ARC chamber as Cutter and Abby joined him. He had the mobile detector he'd been carrying that afternoon, and he'd hooked it up to the main ADD network.

"Something funny?" Connor asked.

"I'll say," Cutter replied, sniffing.

Abby wrinkled her nose.

"Have you changed your shoes since you stepped in that stuff earlier?" she asked.

Connor frowned and looked down at his feet.

"Oh, no. I forgot. I knew there was something." He grinned at them and pulled a gagging face. "I wondered what the pong was."

"Uh, euw," Abby said.

"Apart from excrement, what have you got?" Cutter prompted.

"Ah, well, yes," Connor said, turning back to the monitors enthusiastically. "We were all a bit carried away with the screaming and the running away this afternoon to notice, but there was a bunch of well-strange things about the anomaly."

"Define 'well-strange'?"

"Some kind of integral instability," Connor replied, pointing to various coloured graphics on the flatscreen display. "The magnetic field was all over the place... see? It's all spiking in the weirdest way. Here, right? And also here… and here."

Cutter leaned in to study the screen intently.

"Could be some sort of interference," Connor added.

"From what?" Abby asked.

"I've actually got no idea," Connor admitted, his teeth gritted, "but it's a theory."

"Could it be a system glitch?" Cutter suggested.

"Well, yes, it could," Connor said. "I did, like, drop the detector in the cinema a little bit."

"Was that when you were running away and screaming?" Abby teased.

"About that time, yes," Connor agreed.

"But you wouldn't have called me in if it was a system glitch, would you?" Cutter asked softly.

Connor grinned.

"I ran a diagnostic on the handset to make sure it was undamaged, first. Then I checked the data recorder for errors. Then I compared the readings to the last three anomaly incidents we've dealt with. *Then* I called you in."

"Good work," Cutter nodded. "Go on."

Connor tapped some commands into the keyboard, and punched up three sets of graphics that overlaid the display on the monitor.

"It's nothing like as pronounced as the incident today, but in hindsight you can see the same thing in the last few readings.

There wasn't enough to spot it before. Instability and spiking. Eccentricity. See?"

"I see," Cutter said.

"This is a whole new thing," Connor continued. "It looks like the anomalies are becoming more energetic and less stable. If it continues to graph like this, within a month we're going to have... well, I don't know what we're going to have, actually. But I don't think it's going to be good."

"Neither do I," Cutter said.

In the small hours of the morning, a skeleton staff manned the ARC watch stations and the ADD. The place was quiet. Staff had gone home, or were catching forty winks in the readiness dorms.

Cutter skulked in his laboratory. Anglepoise lamps formed pools of light in the small, cluttered space, illuminating scattered books, notepads, crates of fossils, equipment pods and partly assembled scientific models. Most of those had come straight out of Cutter's head, and looked — to the uninitiated — like haphazard nests of string, duct tape, wire and rods.

Cutter had never liked his new lab at the ARC much. It was smaller and far more functional than his space at the university. He could hardly complain about the facilities on tap, of course, but there had been a sort of personality to the university workspace, a character. He'd known where things were. He'd invested time there, and his belongings and specimens had accumulated in layers, laid down organically like sediment.

The ARC lab was just clutter. He hadn't even moved into it himself, not exactly, not that he could remember.

There had been a hiccup in time, a little speed bump. Cutter had no idea how it had happened, or where, but the evidence was all around him. He didn't belong to this version of the world, or rather it didn't belong to him. He'd gone through an anomaly and something had altered, had reset. When he'd come back, the world had undergone a subtle transformation. Suddenly Lester's operation had increased in size and clout. Suddenly there was a place called the ARC, a bleeding-edge facility purpose-built to tackle the anomalies. Suddenly he had a lab there, and he'd quit his university place.

Suddenly there was no Claudia Brown, just a woman called Jenny Lewis, who looked just like Claudia.

It was by far the most disconcerting thing that had ever happened to Nick Cutter. Holes in time? Encounters with primeval creatures? He could cope with that, but the subtle shift of everything, the alteration of history, *that* spooked him. He wondered if it was actually the world that had changed, or just him.

More than anything else, it had taught him how dangerous the game they were playing had become. One slip, one false move, and history got rewritten and realities got remade. What would happen if you made a really big error? Would history change so much it couldn't survive? Would time collapse? Could they trigger, without even realising it, an extinction-scale event?

Cutter adjusted one of the lamps, and leafed through the notebooks on his desk. He studied drawing after drawing, diagram after diagram. The answer lay with the anomalies, but the more he learned about them, the more he recognised that he *didn't* know. With his help, Connor had devised and built the ADD system, which had allowed them to detect and trace anomaly occurrences. He hadn't been able to determine their frequency, pattern, or energetic mechanism, and he certainly hadn't fathomed out what was causing them. No wonder really, because it wasn't his field at all. A zoologist, he'd been brought in to help deal with the creatures, but the creatures weren't the real problem. You didn't need a PhD in zoology to see that.

The real problem was what was bringing the creatures through time. And now Connor was saying that it was getting worse.

Cutter swivelled his chair around and resumed work on his latest chart. He was attempting to map the anomalies based on where they'd appeared in the present and what time periods they linked to, but there was only so much you could do with a Biro and pieces of graph paper. Perhaps a bigger model would help.

Perhaps a bigger lab.

"Working late?"

He looked up. Jenny was standing in the doorway.

"Just, uhm," he began. "There never seems to be enough time to get things done."

She nodded.

"How about you?" he asked.

"Oh, just working the cover story through. Making sure it sticks. Keeping an eye on the news feeds. You know, I think I've taken the heat out of it."

"Well, that's good."

"You don't think that."

He laughed.

"No, I don't. I think keeping it from the world is just making things worse. I'm not banging on about free speech, you understand. Maybe it's better that the public doesn't know what's going on. But we're working in complete isolation. We should be sharing what we know with the global scientific community, and seeing what they've got."

"You think other people are working on this?" she asked.

Cutter shrugged.

"It's entirely possible. I hope so. I hope someone out there has got a better clue about this than I have."

"You have the detector," she countered. "We can track these things, deal with each incident —"

"That's not enough. That's just firefighting. We need to find the cause. I can't explain how important it is."

She stepped into the lab.

"Try," she said.

He sighed.

"You think I was off with you earlier. You think I didn't care if you got hurt. You and Lester and a whole bunch of others can't understand why I try so hard to keep these creatures alive."

"You have a natural respect for living creatures," she offered.

"Yes, but it's not that." He picked up a piece of graph paper, looked at it, and tossed it back onto the bench. "I don't know what happens every time we kill one. I don't know what effect that has on history. One little change could mean everything."

"We've all read Ray Bradbury, Nick," Jenny said.

"Well, I've *lived* it. I saw things change, Jenny."

"Like me, you mean? Like Claudia?"

He nodded ruefully, knowing they'd gone over this before.

"I didn't dream a different world, I woke up in one. I don't want it to happen again. I don't want it to be worse next time."

"Worse?"

He subtly changed the subject.

"The anomalies seem to be following some kind of pattern, though I can't figure out what it might be. I've got a nasty feeling that, before long, catching some prehistoric monster that's popped through a hole in time is going to be the least of our problems."

"So what do you suggest?" she asked.

"I don't know. That little jaunt we took to Peru, that proved this isn't a local phenomenon; it's global. Who knows what other people in other countries are finding out. We should be pooling our knowledge, especially about the anomalies."

Jenny smiled.

"Well, if there are any other operations like ours out there, I don't know about them." She paused. "Of course, I wouldn't, though, would I?"

"What?"

"Well, it's very likely they'd have someone like me — that they'd be keeping their work secret, too, isn't it?"

SIX

"Okay," Connor said, "what was that?"

"What was what?" Abby asked.

"It went under there." Connor pointed at a row of cheap, do-it-yourself shelves stacked with catering drums of cooking oil.

"What did it look like?"

"It was smallish, and it was moving," he said.

Abby glanced at him doubtfully.

Connor shrugged. "That's all I've got."

She knelt down and peered under the shelves, then jerked back slightly. There was something under there all right. She could see movement in the shadows, and she could hear a sort of soft, chittering noise.

"It sounds a bit like Rex," she said.

"So, lizard, then," Connor said, slightly reassured. "For a moment there, I thought something, you know, creepy and/or crawly."

Abby pulled on a long-cuffed handler's gauntlet and reached under the shelf. "I think it's definitely a lizard. I —

"Ow!"

The creature, a small, slender reptile with a beautiful colouration like old laburnum leaves, shot out from under the shelving. It came out on all fours, but as it cleared the shelves, it raised its narrow body up on its hind legs and accelerated across the floor.

"Door! Connor, the door!" Abby yelled.

Connor made a dive for the storeroom door, but he was too slow. The sprinting reptile shot between his feet and out into the corridor.

"Sorry."

Abby examined her gauntlet. The tip of the index finger had been ripped through.

"It's got some teeth on it," she said.

"And some legs," Connor agreed. "Any idea what it was?"

"I didn't get a good enough look at it," Abby said, checking for blood. There wasn't any.

"It's a primitive Archosaur," Cutter said from the doorway behind them. "Maybe something like Euparkeria."

"An Early Triassic reptile?" Abby queried.

Cutter nodded.

"You got a look at it?" Connor asked.

"It passed me in the hall, and I spotted another couple of them in the restaurant."

"We're going to need box-traps," Abby said, heading for the door.

"I think so," Cutter agreed.

"What about the anomaly?" Connor asked. "There has to be one around here."

Cutter handed him the detector.

"It's in the carwash next door," he said. "Can you take some readings and keep an eye on it?"

***

They went outside, and Cutter helped Abby unload four box-traps from the back of the truck. Connor made a few delicate adjustments to the detector, and began to wander in the direction of the automated carwash that stood on the other side of the service station concourse.

It was mid-morning, and the summer sun was hot. The site — a petrol station, a couple of shops and a cafeteria — served a busy dual carriage-way. Hemple and a couple of his men, dressed in black fatigues but with their weapons discretely locked up in their Land Rovers, were gently moving onlookers back and coning off the station forecourt. Traffic had backed up along the slip road, and there was some irritated honking.

"Something up with the pumps," Mason told a lorry driver as Connor walked past, "we can't let anybody in."

"How long?" the driver asked, squinting down from his cab.

However long it takes to round up God knows how many fast-moving, sharp-toothed Basal Archosaurs, mate, Connor thought.

Most of the traffic seemed content to pull around and head off up the slip road and back to the main carriageway. Some lingered, rubber-necking, curious to know what was going on. As he strolled along, Connor saw a mum with four young kids in a red car, all watching him like prairie dogs. The members of a university rugby team waved noisily from their minibus. Two men in a blue SUV stared at him, and glanced away when he looked back.

Connor reached the carwash. He could feel the static charge in the air, the ant-scurry tingle on his skin. He could smell damp concrete and spilled detergent as he ducked in under one of the rollers of green plastic fronds and entered the main wash area. A couple of Archosaurs were skittering between the raised wheel triggers on the floor.

The anomaly, a comparatively small one, crackled and writhed in the air at the far end of the bay. Pearlescent colours flickered across the ripples of its aperture, and he could feel its magnetic pull. His hair stood up a little. Fronds of thin, blue electricity crackled around the edges of the phenomenon, clambering along the spars and roof struts of the carwash like the creepers of a trailing plant.

He adjusted the detector and began the data record.

It was the third anomaly they'd encountered in the two weeks since the incident on Oxford Street. Like all the others, it wasn't conforming to the energetic patterns they had become used to.

"It's like the others, isn't it?"

Connor glanced over his shoulder and saw Cutter looking at it.

"Yeah," he replied.

"I wonder what's doing that," Cutter murmured. "I wonder what it means."

"It's definitely an electromagnetic variance," Connor said. "Oh, by the way, there are a couple more of those little dudes loose in here."

"I saw them." Cutter continued to stare at the anomaly, as if he expected it to suddenly crack and give up its secrets.

"See what your analysis picks up," he said to Connor. "We can only hope."

"Okay."

"When we're done here, I want to swing by the university," Cutter said, turning to leave.

"You haven't been back there in ages," Connor said, looking surprised.

"No, I haven't," Cutter said. "I left a lot of stuff there in storage, so I want to check through it. There might be something we can use. Maybe some notes I took in the early days that I haven't looked back at. And it's just down the road, so we may as well."

Connor nodded. Of all the team members, he was most aware of the professor's claim that time had been revised, but even he didn't realise how deep that unease went. Cutter didn't want to alarm him by explaining that he had no idea what he might have left at his old rooms in the Central Metropolitan University, or even who'd packed his stuff up and moved it to the lab at the ARC.

He *certainly* didn't want to alarm Connor by telling him his most fervent wish: that there might be notes or files at the university of genuine value of which he had no memory — because they had been written by a different Nick Cutter.

The service station anomaly closed just after two in the afternoon, about half an hour after Abby and Cutter had released the last of the trapped Euparkeria back through it into their own world. The blister of light crackled, flickered and died away, taking the static tang out of the air and letting tension out of all the metal objects in the vicinity.

"Do you want us to come with you?" Hemple asked as they loaded up the trucks.

"No need," Cutter replied, and he gestured to Connor and Abby. "I'll take these two with me in case there's any heavy lifting to do. We'll see you back at the ARC tonight."

Fifteen minutes later, his truck pulled away from the forecourt. Traffic was already being allowed back into the service station.

A woman, sitting in a car parked on the hard shoulder of the slip road, watched him drive away. She had been following him for a few days, watching him, torn between the desire to warn him and the realisation that even if she did, there was nothing he could do.

Her name was Helen Cutter.

SEVEN

The porter remembered Professor Cutter, and asked how he'd been keeping. Cutter kept his answer brief but polite, and when the porter raised the barrier he drove into the campus.

It had turned into a fine afternoon. The red-brick, modern research faculty was flanked by plane and beech trees and framed by lawns, perfect as an architect's model. Students lounged about on the grass, talking, reading, and playing frisbee, or hid from the sun in the shade of the trees.

Connor and Abby were chatting away in the back of the truck. As he drove up to the herringbone parking, Cutter felt an odd sense of nostalgia he hadn't anticipated. The university felt so *familiar*. It reminded him of simpler times and less demanding work, but it also seemed peculiarly distant, as if it lay in some distant era, millions of years away.

He wondered if that was just his imagination, or if something in his mind had altered, and changed his memories with it.

A young woman in the bursar's office informed him that per his instructions, his rooms had not been assigned to another academic, and were still locked up pretty much as he'd left them. It seemed the fellows were hoping that Professor Cutter might return to his tenure as soon as his secondment to the government was done.

"Some of your things have been boxed up and put in store six," the young woman said, checking the manifest. She fetched him the keys. "Fossils, mostly. Can you sign the keys back in before you leave?"

He promised to do so.

His name plate had been slid out of the frame on the door. Nevertheless, Cutter found it immediately. He unlocked his office and went in, with Connor and Abby close behind him.

There was a slight but not unpleasant smell of unused air. No one had been in the room for some time, and the windows had been kept closed. Most of the furniture had been covered in dust-sheets, and books had been taken off some of the shelves and loaded into boxes.

Abby opened the windows that looked out over the lawns.

"Where do we start?" Connor asked.

"Why don't you take Abby down to store six and see what they've put in there," Cutter said, tossing the storeroom keys to Connor. "Then swing by the canteen and get us three big coffees, eh?"

"What are we looking for, exactly?" Abby inquired.

Cutter shrugged. "I'll know it if I see it," he said, but then he saw the panicked look on Connor's face. "For the moment, look for anything that relates to the phenomena we've encountered most recently, however distant the relationship might be."

They left the room, and he began to look around. Just standing there, he realised that — more than anything else — the place reminded him of Helen. It reminded him of the pain of losing his wife, and the greater pain of discovering that she was still alive and that she'd hidden her existence from him. It was just one of her many betrayals.

Cutter didn't know her any more, he realised. He didn't know what she *was*, and he certainly didn't know what she might be capable of doing.

He was terribly afraid, however, that, wherever she was, she knew the answers to all the questions he needed to ask. Perhaps it was the thought of her that had brought him back to the university.

Perhaps he was wasting his time.

Connor hurried across the campus parking lot with three large coffees in carry-out cups. There were only a few vehicles parked in the herringbone next to the professor's truck, but one of them was a blue SUV with two men sitting in it.

Still walking, Connor did a slight double-take, remembering the slip road of the service station that morning, remembering two men in a blue SUV, who'd looked away when he'd glanced at them.

The driver's door of the SUV opened, and one of them got out.

"Afternoon," Connor said hesitantly.

Cutter sorted through the contents of the desk drawer, and then shut it again. He turned to the filing cabinets.

There was a noise in the doorway of the office.

"Took your time with that coffee," he said over his shoulder. He looked up and saw a figure in the doorway.

Only, it wasn't Connor.

The man was about thirty-five and clean-shaven, with straw-blond hair and very serious eyes. The moment Cutter saw him, he knew the man wasn't British. There was something Eastern European about his haircut and the style of his jeans and bomber jacket. When he spoke, his slight accent confirmed Cutter's instincts.

"Professor Nicholas Cutter?"

"Yes," Cutter replied. He wondered if the man was from HR or the bursary.

"I hope, a moment of your time?" The man stepped into the room. Cutter could smell a cheap cologne that had been rather extravagantly applied.

"Actually, I'm not really here," Cutter answered with a polite smile and a dismissive gesture. "I'm just stopping by to pick something up."

"It is important," the man insisted. Was that hint of accent Polish? Czech? No, *Russian*.

"I'm sorry," Cutter said, maintaining his smile but wishing the guy would take the hint. "I'm a bit busy. If you want an appointment, though, you can contact the faculty office and they'll get in touch with me. I'm sure we can arrange something."

"That would take a while," the man said, "and involve official channels."

"I know, but I'm really pushed for time today."

"Pushed for time," the man repeated. He smiled and nodded. "Yes. I am also Nicholas, you know," he said.

"I'm sorry?"

"Nicholas. Or Nikolai, to be correct. My name is Nikolai Medyevin."

Cutter thought for a moment.

"Medyevin?" he asked. "Wait, did you lead the excavation of the Hadrosaur group in Russia a few years ago?"

"Yes, I did," the man said, and he nodded. "I am flattered that you know of it."

"It was a pretty major dig," Cutter said, "and the results were very impressive. I got to see some of the adult specimens when the preparators were working on them at Imperial."

"Yeah, there was generally great results," the man replied. "Strong evidence of family grouping dynamics, and good examples of gender dimorphism. Plus, of course, the quality of preservation."

"It was really good work," Cutter said. He stepped towards the man and held out his hand. "I'm sorry if I came over as rude. I've got a lot on my plate at the moment. It's a pleasure to meet you, Doctor Medyevin."

Medyevin shook Cutter's hand.

"And to meet you at last, Professor Cutter."

"So what can I do for you?" Cutter asked, and then he paused. "Wait a minute," he said, "how did you know I was here?"

Medyevin shrugged slightly, but didn't reply.

"I haven't worked here for months," Cutter continued. Frowning, he took a step away from his visitor. "I haven't *been* here for months, and I only just popped in this afternoon on the off-chance. How could you possibly have known I was here?"

"We perhaps might call it opportunistic, Professor," Medyevin replied.

"What does that mean?"

"It means that security is a great deal lighter here than it is at the ARC," Medyevin explained.

He glanced to his left as Connor and Abby came into the room. Both of them looked oddly stiff and awkward. There was a man behind them. Like Medyevin, he was dressed in jeans and a brown leather bomber jacket, but he was considerably bigger than the slim palaeontologist. He had brown hair, cut short, hard eyes and a generous mouth. Curious, deep scars ran down from the corners of his mouth.

Cutter turned to his co-workers.

"What's going on?" he asked them.

Neither Connor nor Abby replied, but they both stared at him with furious, anxious eyes.

"I said, 'What's going on?'"

"They have been instructed not to speak or to make any abrupt movement," the man standing behind them said. His voice was lower than Medyevin's, and his accent was a great deal thicker.

Cutter laughed, but there was no humour in it.

"I think that's up to them, don't you?"

"Please, Professor," Medyevin said.

Abby stared at Cutter. There was something imploring about her expression. Very quietly, but very clearly, she said, "He's got a gun."

Cutter started as if he'd been slapped. Looking down, he saw the small, black automatic pistol that Medyevin's companion was holding. It was pointing directly at Abby, level with the small of her back. It was so obvious, so glaring, he couldn't believe he hadn't seen it the moment they came into the room.

He hadn't seen it because it was too ridiculous, too outrageous. A scar-faced Russian thug with a gun. It was like something out of a bad spy film.

"I think you'd better put that away so we can get this sorted out," Cutter said gently. "I think we've got our wires crossed. You don't come in here waving a pistol and threatening friends of mine."

"I think that's up to me," the man with the gun said with deliberate irony.

"Professor Cutter," Medyevin began, "we need —"

Cutter raised an index finger sharply.

"No. Shut up. I don't care what you need. This is not acceptable. Tell him to put that gun away and get out. You can stay. Then maybe, *maybe*, we can talk like civilised people."

Medyevin looked uncomfortable.

"I'm afraid, Professor Cutter, I don't get to tell Koshkin what to do. He has authority. So I urge you to cooperate."

The man with the scarred mouth looked straight at Cutter and spoke again.

"Doctor Medyevin has explained the situation to you. He has suggested that you cooperate. Do you need me to reinforce how serious this is?" He raised the pistol and rested it against the back of Connor's head.

Connor murmured uncomfortably, and stood stiff as a board.

"Which one?" the gunman asked. "The boy or the girl? Which one will make the point most effectively?"

Cutter froze in horror.

"I'm sorry, Professor," Medyevin said. "This is not how I would have done things."

EIGHT

"When you say 'missing', what do you mean exactly?" Lester asked.

"Professor Cutter was due in at eight this morning," Hemple said. "We were going to run a debrief."

"And the other two?"

"Abby and Connor were expected in at the same time," Hemple answered.

Lester frowned. He was still on his first coffee of the morning. What Hemple was telling him sounded like a problem, but it didn't sound like the *usual* sort of problem.

They both looked up as Jenny entered Lester's office.

"No answer from their mobiles or land lines," she said, "so I've sent HR round to their homes."

"They're just late for work, aren't they?" Lester said, impatiently. He really wasn't in the mood. "Or it's a phone thing?"

"Unlikely," Jenny replied.

Lester sighed. Cutter was a constant thorn in his side, and now he was even managing to be difficult by *not* being present.

There had been many occasions in the previous few months when James Lester would have cheerfully paid real money for Cutter to disappear. Even that, it seemed, did not make the problem go away.

"When did we last see them?" Lester asked.

"About two-thirty yesterday, at the anomaly site," Hemple said.

"Nothing since?"

"The three of them were heading to the university," Hemple replied.

Jenny's phone rang and she turned away to take the call.

"It's not like Cutter to be unreliable," Hemple said to Lester.

Lester raised his eyebrows significantly.

"There's very little I wouldn't put past Professor Cutter," he responded. "He has a willful, maverick streak that seems designed to aggravate me. What's more, the other two are devoted to him. He could easily lead them both astray. But it doesn't feel like that." He looked down at his desk.

"No, it doesn't," Hemple agreed.

Jenny turned back to face them, slipping her phone back into her bag.

"There's no one at Nick's place, or the flat. Abby's Mini's still in the car park outside, but Nick's truck is unaccounted for."

"Contact the university," Lester said. "Perhaps they will have some idea of where our missing children have gone."

Cutter had signed in at the porter's lodge the previous afternoon, but he hadn't signed out again. According to the official record, he was still on the campus.

"There was a young lady and a lad with him," the porter told Jenny. "I didn't see them leave, either."

Cutter had also signed out several sets of keys that hadn't been returned.

Jenny caught up with Hemple in the car park.

"I've found the truck," he said. "It's just over there. It's locked, and the kit seems to be onboard, as far as I can see."

There was no one in Cutter's old rooms, but the door had just been pulled to.

"Maybe he met an old friend or a colleague?" Hemple suggested. "We should take some time and ask around the campus."

"He'd have called us," Jenny replied, firmly. "He'd have let us know he was going somewhere."

Hemple was looking out of the office windows into the car park.

"What is it?" Jenny asked.

He pointed.

"They've got CCTV."

"Okay, here's the sequence," Hemple said, cueing the tape. Jenny leaned in over his shoulder to look at the screen. The porter had droned on about 'written permission' and 'privacy issues', but she'd flashed him her very important looking credentials and shooed him out of the lodge's monitor room. Then Lester had called so she'd been forced to let Hemple examine the footage and line it up for her to view while she updated her impatient boss on their progress.

On the screen, the previous afternoon ran by at high speed in muted colours. Cars came and went in jerky spurts, looking like toys on the screen.

"Watch the time code," Hemple instructed. "Here's when they arrive. They get out. And they go inside. Okay, now keep an eye on this vehicle. It pulls in about three minutes after them. Blue SUV."

"It looks grey," Jenny said.

Hemple took his finger off the cue. The picture blinked, returned to normal speed, and restored its colour balance.

"Blue," he said.

"Okay."

He began to jog the tape on again.

"There are two guys in the SUV," he told her, "and they sit there for about five minutes."

"Faces?"

"Not clearly. I'm sure our kit back at the ARC could wash things a lot cleaner. I did get a number off the SUV, though. Anyway, here comes Connor, leaving the building."

Connor crossed the screen, right to left, his accelerated pace comically resembling a silent movie star.

"Another five minutes, and back he comes," Hemple continued.

Connor reappeared, carrying cardboard coffee cups. He crossed the screen left to right. One of the men suddenly got out of the SUV and followed him off-screen. After a minute or two, the second man got out of the SUV and walked off in the same direction.

"Now another ten minutes," Hemple said, speeding up the image even more, "and this happens."

He slowed the video again, and a group of figures entered the screen from the right-hand side. Cutter, Connor and Abby were walking close together just ahead of the two men. They came up to the SUV, and the smaller of the two opened the side door. Cutter, Connor and Abby got inside.

Jenny peered closely at the screen.

"Look at their body language," she said. "None of them is exactly happy about getting in."

The two men got into the SUV as well, and it pulled away, moving out of the picture.

"Four-oh-seven," Hemple said, reading the time code. "We can check the gate log to see who signed out, but I'm guessing it will be a fake ID."

"Why?" Jenny turned to look at him.

Hemple wound the recording back and the SUV obediently reversed back into the picture and the parking space. He reached the point where Cutter, Connor and Abby were getting into the vehicle, and nudged the tape to and fro until he could pick out one tiny moment and freeze it.

Jenny stared at the image. Connor was already aboard the SUV, and Abby was pulling herself in. Cutter, beside her, was looking back at the larger of the two men, who had raised his right hand to issue some instruction. There was something in his hand, a fuzzy black speck.

Despite the grainy quality of the picture, Jenny knew it was a gun.

NINE

He woke with a start in the middle of a thunderstorm.

He had no proper sense of place or time. He felt sick, as if he was suffering a terrible hangover, and his limbs ached. He was cold. He could smell metal and fuel. The world was dark, and it rocked and swam like a boat in heavy weather. Constant thunder boomed, a roaring in his ears that wouldn't stop.

He heard voices behind the thunder, smelled sweat and cheap cologne behind the engine fumes. He was sitting on a hard metal bucket seat. His hands were cuffed together with a plastic tie that had been looped to the seat rim. He was blindfolded.

"Where am I?" he asked, raising his voice against the thundering roar.

He heard voices again, but they were indistinct. Hands removed his blindfold, and he blinked at the light.

The spare metal cargo hold of a military aircraft surrounded him. Illumination came from small bulkhead lights. Everything was spartan and utilitarian.

Abby and Connor were cuffed to bucket seats on the hold wall facing him. They both looked pale and scared, and neither of them seemed entirely awake.

"Are you okay?" Cutter asked them.

Connor nodded, even though he looked like he was about to puke extravagantly.

"They drugged us," Abby said groggily. There was a grubby mark on her left cheek. Her eyes were absolutely afraid.

"Yeah," Cutter said. He remembered the needle going into his arm, and had the vague impression of riotously bad dreams. He wasn't sure what they'd been shot full of, or how long they'd been out, but it explained the horrible sense of dehydration and nausea.

"We'll be okay," he told Abby calmly. She nodded.

The aircraft bucked and lurched, making the nausea far harder to manage. Cutter looked around. The man with the scarred face was sitting near the front of the cabin. Medyevin occupied a bucket seat beside Cutter. He was fidgeting with the blindfolds he'd removed from the three passengers.

"How are you, Professor?" he asked anxiously.

"I've been drugged, and cuffed to a metal seat for God knows how long," Cutter replied tersely. "How do you *think* I am?"

"I would imagine bilious and uncomfortable," Medyevin replied.

"You missed out angry," Cutter snapped. "Besides, it was a rhetorical question."

Medyevin nodded. He was clearly uneasy.

"I think you should tell me what's going on," Cutter said.

"Shortly. We —"

"Now," Cutter insisted. "I'm not playing games any more. This is kidnap. This is not in any way acceptable."

"Professor, the circumstances —"

"That maniac threatened my friends with a gun," Cutter growled. "Whatever you want from me, there was no need to bring them into this. There was no need to use them to manipulate me."

"Koshkin approaches problems in a very direct way," Medyevin replied. "He likes to accomplish things in the most efficient manner."

"And he requires my cooperation."

"Yes."

"You require my cooperation."

"We will explain as soon —"

Cutter stared at him.

"You have a creature incursion, don't you?" he said.

Medyevin started.

"What?"

"I'm not stupid, Doctor," Cutter said. "What else would this be about?"

The aircraft plunged abruptly, and the thunder grew louder. Cutter felt his stomach flip, and realised that the constant, pounding thunder was the noise of propeller blades. The descent transition didn't feel like that of a fixed-wing aircraft at all. It wasn't a plane — they were riding in a big helicopter, probably a twin-rotored machine. There were small portals high up in the hold walls: glazed slits that let in thin, dirty light.

Was it daylight? Cutter wondered. Where were they? How far had they come?

The forward hatch of the hold opened, and an older man leaned through and spoke a few words to the scar-faced man. The older man was wearing a black roll-neck sweater and wire-framed glasses. A fringe of silver hair edged his bald head.

The man with the scars, Koshkin, listened and nodded, and then got to his feet. The older man ducked back out and closed the hatch behind him. Koshkin came down the middle of the hold, bracing one hand on an overhead rail. His face was expressionless, except for a vague hint of satisfaction.

He spoke to Medyevin in Russian.

"What did he say?" Cutter asked.

"I said we're ten minutes out. We're on approach," Koshkin said directly to Cutter.

"Approach to where?" Cutter demanded.

Koshkin grinned and didn't reply. It was hard to maintain a conversation while competing with the wind and the rotor-chop. He didn't look as if he cared to supply any answers, regardless.

"I hope there's an airport there," Cutter added.

"Why?" Koshkin asked.

"Because you're going to put me, Abby and Connor on a flight straight back home," Cutter stated.

"Professor Cutter," Koshkin replied, "I thought we'd already established that you were in no position to make demands."

"Uncuff us," Cutter told him.

"Again —" Koshkin began, and he looked vaguely amused.

"Uncuff us. Give us some water. Water at the very least. Threaten us or hurt us, you'll get zero cooperation from me. Refuse us basic levels of comfort or sustenance, you'll get zero cooperation from me. Do we both understand the position we're in now?"

Koshkin's vague amusement vanished from his face. He glared down, and Medyevin shot Cutter a look of deep alarm. Cutter knew that Medyevin thought he'd just crossed a line no one in their right mind would want to cross.

Koshkin reached into his pocket and pulled out a clasp knife that opened to reveal a saw-edged blade four inches long. He turned towards Abby.

What have I done? Cutter thought.

Koshkin jerked the blade, but all he cut was the plastic tie that was clamping Abby's hands. Cutter breathed out, and saw the tension go out of Medyevin's shoulders, too.

The Russian thug sliced Connor's cuffs away and turned to deal with Cutter. While he did so, Connor and Abby began rubbing the circulation back into their wrists.

Koshkin leaned in to release Cutter's hand. For a second, however, he let the toothed edge of the blade rest against the side of Cutter's throat.

"I understand cooperation, Professor," he whispered, "but do not push what cannot be pushed." He took the blade away from Cutter's neck and cut the cuffs.

Cutter didn't return his gaze. He got up and crossed the cabin to join Connor and Abby.

"Five minutes!" Koshkin called out. He put the clasp knife away and walked back down the hold. Medyevin unzipped a sports bag and handed plastic drinking bottles to Cutter, Connor and Abby.

"A solution of sugars and essential salts," he said. "It should help with the aftereffects of the drug."

"What did you shoot us with?" Cutter wanted to know.

"I don't know," Medyevin shrugged. "It was something Koshkin had. I'm just a palaeontologist."

"No," Cutter said, taking a sip from his bottle. "At the very least, you're a kidnapper, Doctor."

Medyevin looked uneasy.

"This is a complicated situation," he said. He glanced down the length of the hold at Koshkin, who had returned to his seat.

Then, despite the covering roar of the rotors, he dropped his voice.

"I tried to warn you. You must be careful. *Cautious.* The word is cautious. Koshkin is a very ruthless man. He is a soldier. Uhm, Spetsnaz. Do you know that meaning?"

Connor whistled.

"That's like Russian special forces. Russian SAS."

Medyevin nodded.

"Special forces, yes. Koshkin has the role of, uhm, special advisor to this situation. It gives him an authority that outweighs the authority of the scientific group."

"Why is that?" Cutter asked.

"The situation has become a military matter," Medyevin replied.

"What *is* the situation?" Abby looked confused.

"Take a wild guess," Cutter told her.

The aircraft was descending fast. The noise of the hammering rotors changed pitch. Medyevin took his seat on the other side of the hold.

"You both okay?" Cutter asked Connor and Abby.

"Yeah," Connor replied, "I just feel like I might be sick, but other than that, just fine."

"I just don't understand what's going on," Abby said.

"They've come to us because they need our help," Cutter explained, "and there's only one area we specialise in that would make that worthwhile."

"Really?" she asked.

He nodded.

"After Madre de Dios we should have known this was coming," he added. "I think we're about to find out that we're not the only ones trying to deal with this problem."

"But how did they know about us?" Abby asked. "How did they know about *you*?"

"That's a good question," Cutter said. "I've no idea, but I imagine we'll find out."

"This is like a rendition," Connor said. "We've been... rendered? Rendited?"

"Whichever," Cutter replied, "that's *exactly* what it's like. Now listen to me. I will not let them hurt you, and I will get us all out of this. If they want our cooperation — if they want *my* cooperation in particular — they're going to have to bend over backwards. No more guns, no more threats."

Connor looked at his watch.

"Any idea how far we've come?" he asked. "My watch says 8.15. Is that morning or evening? Have we been knocked out all night?"

"A little longer than that," Cutter said. "Check the date."

Connor looked at his watch again. His eyes widened.

"Oh my God," he said. "I've lost two days."

The military chopper came in to land. Cutter, Connor and Abby felt the rock and sway as the big bird descended and settled in. The heavy rotors were thumping the air, part whip crack, part thunderbolt.

With a final and quite violent bump, they were down. Koshkin got up and wrenched open the hold's side hatch, which rolled back with a clatter on metal runners. The sound of the rotors poured in, but immediately began to diminish.

Stale, yellowish daylight poured into the hold.

"Get up!" Koshkin ordered.

Medyevin was already up. Cutter, Connor and Abby got

to their feet. Above the exhaust fumes, Cutter could smell wet ground and conifers.

They moved to the hatch and clambered out. The huge twin rotors of the heavy helicopter were still chopping overhead.

They climbed down into a twilight that could only be dawn. The sky was yellow from a pale sun that was not quite risen. Morning mist hung in the air, and it was cold and damp. Everything seemed a little under-nourished and starved for light.

They'd come down on a makeshift landing strip near some woods. Off the strip, through the mist, they could see accommodation tents and several military vehicles. On the other side, two large military freight planes were parked off the landing area and beside them sat a vespine helicopter gunship. All three aircraft were lashed down.

Outside the immediate camp, they could see deeper forest shrouded in a soft, yellow mist. Ground crew and military personnel were approaching the cargo chopper.

"Where is this?" Connor looked around, puzzled. "We're miles from anywhere, aren't we? Is this Scotland?"

Koshkin glanced over his shoulder at Connor and grinned.

"Welcome to Sibir," he said.

"Where?"

"Siberia," Cutter said.

TEN

They were left waiting at the side of the airstrip for ten minutes. The morning air was cold, and before long all three of the ARC personnel were shivering. There was a mist that, in places, made it difficult to see.

Ground crew moved in to handle the helicopter. Soldiers in brown camo-pattern uniforms and blue berets loitered nearby, smoking cigarettes and ostensibly watching the 'visitors'. Assault rifles were slung casually over their shoulders on straps.

They seemed particularly intrigued by Abby.

Medyevin and Koshkin had gone over to talk to an officer. As Cutter watched, they began to gesture, and voices were raised. The conversation appeared to become quite complicated.

The older man with the wire-framed glasses emerged from the helicopter and presented them with three woollen greatcoats. The coats were brown, and very large, and had clearly seen long years of service.

"Please to use," he said.

Cutter took the coats and passed one to Abby and one to

Connor. He hung the third over his shoulder, but both Abby and Connor pulled theirs on against the chill.

"Siberia?" Connor muttered. "Siberia."

"No matter how much you keep saying that word, it isn't going to get any less real," Cutter said.

"I know, but *Siberia*? Come on."

Cutter glanced at Abby.

"What are you thinking about?" he asked.

She looked him in the eye.

"Just wondering," she said.

"Wondering what?"

"They want our help," Abby said. "I think you must be right about what they want our help for. We could look on the positive side, and see this as an opportunity."

"We could indeed," Cutter agreed.

"Opportunity for what?" Connor asked.

"To learn," Abby explained. "To find out what other people know. To see what they've discovered and how they deal with the whole thing. And we don't have Lester here to wrap us in red tape, either."

Connor nodded.

"I just wonder…" Abby went on.

"What?"

"If we cooperate and we help them, what will they do with us when they don't need our help any more?"

Medyevin walked over to join them.

"What happens now?" Cutter asked.

"They're arranging transport, to take you to the advance camp."

"Where's that?"

"About one hour and half away. This is just the dispersal site."

"There's a problem, isn't there?" Cutter questioned.

"What do you mean?"

"Koshkin was giving that officer what for. He wasn't happy about something."

Medyevin nodded.

"The advance camp should have sent transport here to meet us. It was arranged, but it's late."

After another five minutes, two open-topped 4x4s painted olive green drove up the landing strip with their headlamps on against the mist. The drivers, two regular soldiers, got out and left the engines running.

Koshkin got behind the wheel of the first 4x4 and indicated that Cutter should ride beside him. Medyevin climbed into the back, and a soldier with an AK-74 got in next to him.

The older man with the wire-framed glasses took the driving seat of the other 4x4, with Abby next to him and Connor in the back alongside a second young soldier.

Without ceremony, Koshkin put the vehicle in gear and pulled away. The other 4x4 roared after him.

They bounced through the dispersal site camp, past Russian troopers eating breakfast and looking bored, and joined a track at the edge of the forest. It was rutted and treacherous, and, despite the headlamps, visibility was poor under the trees. Nevertheless, Koshkin drove aggressively. It seemed to Cutter as if he was trying to prove something, some macho credential, by driving too fast.

Cutter found it amusing.

The 4x4s blasted along the trail, hissing up spray from the mud, and occasionally squirming and foundering through deeper slicks and badly trenched bends. The forest that enclosed them was magnificent and a little melancholy. The heavy mist, like yellow smoke, diminished all sense of distance, and flattened out the sound of their engines as it was cast back to them. The trees were vigilant black shapes, straight and silent, old and stoic.

He saw the odd bird dart overhead or between trees at the edge of the track. Sometimes, little pockets of clarity flew by, small breaks in the fog that revealed clearings and woodland spaces like mysterious grottos: archways of trees, emerald and black, floors of wet earth and robust undergrowth, and shafts of wan light sloping down from the broken roof of foliage. To Cutter's eyes they looked like primeval places, like the forests that had stood before man's arrival.

He wondered what they would find out here. He wondered what the Russians were so afraid of that they had travelled thousands of miles to kidnap a British scientist.

"How long has your problem been going on?" he asked.

Koshkin concentrated on the track ahead, shifting down hard.

"You'll be briefed," he said.

"Why not save a little time? How long?"

Koshkin kept his eyes on the road and remained silent for a moment.

"Two years," he admitted. His hands turned the wheel in sharp, jerky movements to match the turns of the trail. Cutter held on to the edge of his seat.

"Perhaps longer than two," Medyevin said, leaning forward from the back. It seemed that Koshkin's admission had given him clearance to speak. "Reports go back for some time, but they're not confirmed."

"The forests have always been full of stories," Koshkin said dismissively, "and most of them are the product of farmers who spend too much time drinking."

"But some of the stories are true?" Cutter pressed.

"They are now," Medyevin agreed.

"Two years is a long time for one area," Cutter said.

"The area is large," Medyevin explained.

"Even so. Is it a pattern of anomalies, or have you observed one that has a greater transitionary dynamic than usual?"

"What is he talking about?" Koshkin asked Medyevin over his shoulder.

Medyevin looked at Cutter.

"I'm sorry, Professor. Greater transitionary what?"

"I mean the anomalies staying open and active for longer than usual. Most aperture activity I've observed lasts a few hours maximum. I've known a couple that have remained transitional for days. But months or years — that would be new to me."

Medyevin shook his head.

"Again, you lose me. Please explain 'anomaly'."

"Well, I don't know what you call them. The doorways. The holes in time."

"Holes in time," Medyevin echoed, as if the notion was utterly new to him. "You think time has holes in it?"

Cutter was about to respond when Koshkin hit the brakes hard and the 4x4 slid to a halt, its back wheels turning out slightly in the mire. The other 4x4 also came to a violent halt to avoid crashing into them. Cutter was thrown forward in his seat by the sudden jolt.

He braced himself and looked up.

They'd come around a tight bend to find a man walking down the middle of the trackway. Koshkin had only just managed to avoid running him down. He was a soldier, dressed in camos, an overcoat and a green helmet worn over a pile undercap. He had his back to them and seemed completely oblivious to their presence.

Koshkin's 4x4 had stalled. As he attempted to restart it, he swore in Russian and yelled at the soldier.

The soldier in the middle of the road didn't reply.

He didn't even look around.

Cutter knew instinctively that something was wrong with him. Koshkin yelled again, and then got down out of the 4x4 and strode towards the lone soldier. Cutter dismounted, too. The trooper in the back seat called out and began to raise his AK to stop Cutter, but Medyevin shut him up with a look and a gesture.

He was a few steps behind Koshkin when the man reached the soldier. Koshkin continued to shout angrily in Russian.

"I think he's in shock," Cutter said.

Koshkin looked back, noticing him for the first time.

"What?"

"Look, he doesn't even know we're here," Cutter said.

The soldier was quite young, and his face was pale and pinched. His uniform was spattered with mud, and he looked like he'd spent quite some time crawling across the ground. His eyes were glazed with an empty stare. There was no sign of his weapon.

"He's only wearing one boot," Cutter pointed out.

Koshkin planted himself in front of the soldier and spoke directly into his face. The soldier gently tried to look past the big Spetsnaz officer, as if Koshkin were a tree that was blocking the view.

"What's he looking at?" Koshkin asked.

Medyevin joined them.

"I know him," he said. "It's Sukhenkiy, from the advance camp."

"Sukhenkiy?" Koshkin said to the dazed soldier. He added a question or an order in Russian.

"Wait a minute," Cutter said. "That's not just mud on his clothes."

"What?" Medyevin asked.

"He's soaked in blood." Cutter touched part of the man's coat and his hand came away sticky and red.

"He's staring at something," Medyevin said.

"He's looking *for* something," Cutter corrected. "He's watching for something." He turned to his fellow scientist. "Ask him what he's looking for."

Before Medyevin could oblige, Koshkin slapped the soldier across the face. The force of the blow knocked the soldier onto his back.

"There's no need for any of that!" Cutter snapped at Koshkin as he and Medyevin helped the soldier back onto his feet.

"Is there not?" Koshkin asked belligerently. He gestured at the soldier. The slap seemed to have shaken Sukhenkiy out of his reverie. He was blinking at them, as if he'd suddenly woken up from a deep sleep and couldn't recall where he was. He started to speak, quietly but urgently, almost gabbling to Medyevin and gesturing at the woods ahead of them.

"What's he saying?" Cutter demanded.

"He keeps repeating a name," Koshkin said.

"What name?" Cutter prompted.

Koshkin sighed.

"Baba Yaga," he replied.

ELEVEN

Once he started, Sukhenkiy wouldn't stop talking. Even though he was speaking Russian, Cutter could read the soldier's manic tone.

"He was sent out from the advance camp to meet us," Medyevin reported. "Him and two others in a truck. They were supposed to pick us up from the landing base."

"What happened?" Cutter asked.

"Baba Yaga!" Sukhenkiy announced. He began to walk away along the muddy track. The misty forest seemed to loom ominously on either side of him.

"Baba Yaga, that's folklore, isn't it?" Cutter noted. "A witch in the woods?"

Medyevin nodded.

"So, what does he mean?"

"It's just what the men have started to call it, these last few months. No one's seen it properly, but we think it's the thing doing the bulk of the killing."

"Killing what?"

"The other animals. And men."

"Men?"

"We've lost quite a few," Medyevin said. "Several months ago, we lost three men on a forest patrol. A fourth survived. He was deranged with fear. The shock made him so ill, we were forced to ship him out of the zone to a mental hospital in Surgut. He saw what killed the others. He glimpsed it, anyway. He saw its legs, giant legs, and he kept calling it Baba Yaga."

"After the witch?"

"I think, more properly, after the witch's house, Professor Cutter," Medyevin explained. "In the old hearth stories, Baba Yaga lived in a house that walked around on a pair of giant legs, the legs of a bird, as you would call, a chicken."

Cutter watched Trooper Sukhenkiy shambling away from them along the forest track.

"What period, Doctor?" he asked.

"What are you asking me, Professor?"

"The monsters that are causing you your problems here, the creatures, what geological period do you estimate they are from?"

"I would say," Medyevin replied carefully, "they are Late Cretaceous."

Cutter looked at him. Medyevin managed a thin smile.

"Yes, Professor, I believe we have both made an educated guess about what Baba Yaga might be." He wiped some moisture from his eyes.

It had begun to rain. A fine, unpleasantly penetrating drizzle pattered down through the tree cover. Cutter glanced back at the vehicles. Both of the soldiers had dismounted, and were waiting by the track with their assault rifles ready. Abby and Connor were sitting anxiously in the second 4x4 with the older man.

Koshkin said something to Medyevin.

"He says we should get Sukhenkiy into the vehicle with us and press on for the advance camp," Medyevin explained.

"Well, we can't leave him out here," Cutter agreed. They followed Koshkin down the trail towards the young trooper.

"What creatures have you actually seen?" Cutter asked Medyevin as they walked. "You must be basing your geological time estimate on something."

"Actually, we've seen quite a variety of erratics," Medyevin said. "That's what we have labelled the anachronistic organisms. Some small forms, including mammalians, as well as birds, but predominately Ceratopsians and duck-bills."

"You just referred to those in the plural," Cutter said.

Medyevin looked at him.

"I don't think you've begun to grasp the scale of this, Professor," he said.

Koshkin called out. He'd spotted the truck that the advance camp had sent to meet them. It was lying on its side about twenty yards from the trail in a large patch of churned up undergrowth. A canvas-topped army carrier, it looked like it had been in a collision with a train. It was mangled, and the cab had been ripped open by huge shearing forces of some unknown origin.

There was no sign of the two men who'd been travelling with Sukhenkiy, but there was a lot of blood. Cutter could smell it through the deep musky odour of the forest.

"I think we should keep moving," he suggested.

Medyevin agreed.

Sukhenkiy was still gabbling.

"He says it flipped the truck off the road into the treeline," Medyevin translated. "He was thrown out of the back, and managed to scramble into hiding, otherwise Baba Yaga would have got him too."

"No kidding." Cutter peered at the wreckage. He could see

what looked like bite marks. They were colossal.

Sukhenkiy stopped talking.

The forest seemed very quiet without the chatter of his voice. The soldier stared out through the trees and the mist, and Cutter realised that a sudden, distinctly unnatural silence had descended. Bird calls, and other forest sounds — like the knocks and scurries of insects and rodents — had all fallen off. Cutter had barely been aware of them in the background before, but he was *keenly* aware of their absence. It was basic bushcraft — skills that Stephen had taught him.

There was something out there.

He peered around, and stared in the direction Sukhenkiy was looking, but he couldn't see anything except the ghost shapes his imagination was conjuring in the drifting mist. He was tired, and his nerves were already worn through. The vicing tension of the moment made him see monsters in the woodland shadows, giant things with giant mouths lurking behind the black Siberian trees on giant chicken legs.

The forest seemed to close in. He could feel something, something huge and close; something watching them.

Why couldn't he see it?

Why couldn't he hear it or *smell* it?

Koshkin could feel it too. He pulled out his pistol, the one he had used to threaten Abby and Connor.

Fat lot of use that's going to be, Cutter thought grimly.

"What happened to the birdsong?" Koshkin asked.

Medyevin shushed him. Sukhenkiy began to cry.

Cutter was painfully conscious of the man's wracking sobs. Then he heard something else. He heard a thump. He *felt* a thump. He felt it travel through the ground, as though — close by — something very large and very heavy had just taken a step.

Then he felt it again, something big, yet as light on its feet as it could be, something stalking through the trees.

Where's it going to come from? he wondered. *Which direction? Which way is the attack coming from?*

He turned slowly in the drizzle, rainwater dripping off him, braced, watching every angle.

Then all hell broke loose.

TWELVE

At first, there was thunder, far louder and more concussive than the heavy rotors of the transport helicopter.

The ground began to shake so hard that Cutter thought a major earthquake had begun.

Then a stampede of duck-bill dinosaurs exploded out of the forest. The adults were huge, three-and-a-half-ton creatures, each well over twelve metres long. Juveniles flocked amongst them. They were all running on their hind legs with their bodies down and their thick, dagger-shaped tails held out straight behind them. Mud spatter and divots of loam kicked up under their trampling feet. The creatures were crestless, with long, wide beaks. Beautiful dark stripes dappled down their pale-green hides from the spine ridge.

Cutter stared at them.

There was another sound besides the thunder of their charge, a kind of trumpeting, a riot of explosive blasts that hooted at random like a brass band performing some atonal modern piece. The blasts weren't simply loud — Cutter could feel the physical shock of them in his diaphragm and his sinuses, as if they were pulses of audible sound mixed with something outside the range of human hearing. They reminded him of the odd, booming notes generated by an emu's neck sack.

The creatures were calling as they ran. Soft-tissue acoustic sacs in the elaborate nasal openings of their skulls were producing sounds that reached frequencies well inside the infrasonic register. The calls were probably signals of panic and alarm.

Battered by the cacophony, he stumbled backwards and grabbed ahold of a tree trunk for support. He gazed in awe at the sight in front of him. Medyevin and Koshkin followed him, getting clear of the creature's course.

Sukhenkiy turned and fled.

The herd ploughed on, bolting. Tree trunks splintered and fractured under glancing impacts. Smaller trees were crushed down or uprooted altogether by the thundering giants. The air filled with sap spray and drifting clouds of leaf fragments. There was so much power, so much weight, so much bone and muscle. It was like a dinosaur flash flood, a dinosaur avalanche.

It only took thirty seconds for the creatures to pass by. Cutter estimated about three-dozen creatures, but that was just a guess. The herd cut right across the track and vanished into the forest on the left-hand side, leaving a broad swathe of destroyed vegetation in its wake. Shredded leaves fluttered in the air behind them, along with the fading rumble of their passage and the echo of their odd, hooting calls.

Cutter wiped sap and rainwater from his face and stood blinking. He looked over at Medyevin. The doctor couldn't hide an excited smile, and Cutter knew just what he was experiencing.

"Duck-bills," Cutter said. Medyevin nodded eagerly.

"Anatotitans?" Cutter asked.

"I think so, yes," Medyevin replied.

"A whole herd of them." Cutter laughed in wonder. "Just incredible."

"You begin, I think, to appreciate the scale of our situation," Medyevin said.

Connor and Abby came running up from the vehicles, followed by the soldiers and the older man. The Russians looked stunned, but the other two had excitement written across their faces.

"That was amazing!" Connor yelled.

"I know," Cutter said, and he grinned.

"That sound they made," Abby said, her voice incredulous.

"Infrasonic acoustics, I think," Cutter explained. "You could really feel it." His racing pulse was beginning to return to normal. He looked around.

"Just before that stampede," he said, "I think something was circling us."

"Like what?" Koshkin asked.

"A predator, I'd wager," Cutter said. "Whatever took out your truck. It may also have been what spooked the Anatotitans."

"Has it gone?" Koshkin looked around.

"Shall we stay here and find out?" Cutter asked.

"Get back in the vehicles," Koshkin ordered. Cutter hesitated.

"What about Sukhenkiy?"

Koshkin shrugged.

"He's a damned fool, and Baba Yaga can have him."

Forty-five minutes later, the two 4x4s drove down the forest track into the advance camp. Cutter saw a number of huts, canvas prefabs, and tents clustered in the gloomy clearing. Lamps were in use, even though it was long past dawn and the sun was up.

The deep shadow of the forest seemed to stain the daylight with a primordial darkness.

Koshkin drew up outside the main tent structure. Gaggles of soldiers regarded them with curiosity, but smartened up when they caught Koshkin's look. He barked a few orders and some of them hurried away.

"In here," Koshkin told Cutter. Cutter waited for Abby and Connor to catch up with him and entered the main tent.

It was a canvas longhouse with a walk-board floor. The tent's large internal space had been divided into separate rooms by canvas walls. They glimpsed a radio room, and a room full of pinboards on which hung charts and enlarged aerial photos. Koshkin led them through into a large workspace where several people in military battledress uniforms were grouped around laptops set out on benches. They turned as Koshkin and Medyevin brought Cutter and his friends in.

One of them was a woman. Her face was youthful and strong, though she had to be in her sixties. The lines there and the bleached steel of her hair appeared to be due to a lifetime spent labouring in the open air, rather than old age. She was wearing puzzle-pattern BDUs that had evidently been intended for a man. Wide turn-ups in the legs and sleeves accommodated her shorter, rounder frame. The men around her were all at least a head taller. Her hair was pinned up in a bun, and she had a pair of bifocal glasses on a cord around her neck.

She lifted the glasses, put them on, and peered at Cutter.

"Hello, Nicky," she said.

THIRTEEN

"Who is she?" Abby asked.

At Koshkin's instruction, Abby and Connor had been escorted from the longhouse and taken to the mess tent across the muddy yard. They were placed under the supervision of a skinny young soldier called Vols, who had a smattering of English. Vols was wearing dark, leaf-pattern camouflage and a net-covered helmet, like all the regular army troopers in the camp, and he carried a machine gun over his shoulder. He seemed very serious, and mindful of his duties, and was obviously trying very hard to cultivate a moustache that would make him look more mature.

Connor and Abby trudged across the yard behind him, huddled deep in their outsized, secondhand greatcoats like children playing at dressing up. They kept looking over their shoulders. They could see Cutter back in the main room of the longhouse, through the screen windows. He was still talking to the woman.

"He seems to know her," Connor said, swatting at a mosquito, then another.

"Or she seems to know him."

"Yeah."

"She called him 'Nicky'," Abby said. "I mean, he's not a Nicky. He's just not a Nicky."

"We'd never call him Nicky," Connor agreed.

"We wouldn't. It'd be wrong. At what point in the past was he ever a Nicky?"

"I can't imagine."

"But she called him Nicky like it was perfectly normal."

"I know. Weird," Connor said.

Abby glanced at him, her face buried in the collar folds of the giant overcoat. He saw her look.

"Okay, in the grand scheme of everything else that's happening to us," he admitted, "not that weird. Not kidnapped by Russian spies weird. Not rendited to Siberia weird. Not stampede of Anatotitans weird."

Vols brought them to the door of the mess tent, and held it open in a touchingly formal manner.

"Into be here," he told them.

"Inside?" Abby asked.

"Inside, da!" Vols nodded, and then he realised he was smiling too warmly at the blonde girl, and tried to make his face solemn again.

They went inside. There were rows of tables and benches, and a steamy kitchen area at the far end, where two army cooks in whites were clattering pots and talking loudly to each other. The mess tent windows were screened with thick drapes of mosquito netting. Connor had noticed the density of tiny insects fuming the air, especially now they were near a river. He was sure he'd been bitten already. He didn't care.

He could smell food.

The drug-induced nausea they had all been suffering was slowly being eclipsed by a fearsome appetite.

Small groups of soldiers sat at the tables, eating and chatting. They were off-duty, dressed in T-shirts or unbuttoned jackets. They watched the newcomers enter, as Vols clumsily slung his AK over his right shoulder and took off his helmet and pile undercap as if he were entering church. The undercap had given him comical hat hair. Abby bit her lips so as not to laugh.

"This way is be," Vols told them, indicating the serving area. The cooks had seen them, and stood waiting with ladles.

"I'm starving," Abby admitted to Connor.

"Me, too," Connor said. He smiled and nodded at the watching soldiers.

They were served generous helpings of meat and vegetable stew in broad enamel bowls, along with dark bread, a mug of soup and a mug of strong black coffee from a samovar. They sat at a table with Vols and started to eat.

"It's tasty," Abby said as she ate hungrily.

"It's *great*," Connor agreed, his mouth full.

"Be good?" Vols asked.

"It's *very* be good," Connor told him.

Vols wasn't eating. He had taken out a notebook and started to compose a list as he sat with them.

The other soldiers in the mess tent were still watching them. A trio sitting at the nearest table took particular interest. One of them, a handsome, cocky-looking man with dark hair and blue eyes, tilted his chair back on its back legs and looked at Abby.

"Hello," he said.

"Mm, hello," Abby responded through a mouthful of stew.

"How are you doing?" the man asked. His friends were watching him and whispering to one another.

Vols looked up from his list and started to jabber at the man in indignant Russian. The man kept his chair tilted back casually and replied to Vols in dismissive tones.

"Vols does not like me talking to you," the man told Abby, "but I think people should be being friendly, don't you?"

"Especially kidnappers," Connor said, watching the soldier suspiciously and becoming increasingly protective of Abby.

"I'm sorry?" the man asked.

Connor backtracked. The man had turned his attention to him.

"I said she's eating, actually," he muttered, slightly less defiantly.

"Leave it, Connor," Abby whispered.

"Yes, she is eating," the man agreed, tilting his chair back so far it seemed likely to topple. "The food it is not bad, yes?"

Vols said something else.

"Vols says I am interrupting him," the man said with a grin. "He is making a list. He has been told to look after you and get you the things — you know — from quartermaster. The things like bedrolls and gloves and toothbrush. He is trying to think of all the things you will need to have. I am Yuri. What is your name?"

"Abby," Abby said.

"Abby. Abby. Is nice name."

"And she's still very much eating," Connor said, putting his fork down.

"So what is your name?" Yuri asked him.

"Connor," he said.

"Hello, Connor. How are you doing?"

"I'm fine."

"Good," Yuri said. "I am Yuri Torosyan, and I am very happy to meet you. I —"

A command cut him off sharply, and he rocked his chair back onto four legs. A female officer had been dining alone in the corner of the mess tent and now, with her meal finished, she rose and approached the newcomers' table. She wore a smart field dress uniform, and she was young and extremely beautiful. She spoke quickly and quietly to Yuri Torosyan and his pals, and evidently had sufficient authority to make him return to his food and leave Abby alone.

She turned to look at them, and said a few words to Vols, who nodded obediently.

"I have told Vols that the men should not be allowed to bother you," she said in clear, slightly accented English.

"It was fine," Abby replied. "He was harmless."

"Harmless?" the woman echoed. "Yuri Torosyan is hardly harmless."

Abby stared up at her.

"He's quite good-looking, actually. Nice eyes."

The woman paused. She had slightly slavic features.

"Fraternisation is not recommended," she said.

"With him?"

"With anybody."

"Okay," Abby said, and she bobbed her head.

"Vols will bring you both to medical after your food, so I can make sure you are healthy," the woman said.

"You're the doctor?" Connor asked.

"Natacha Antila," she replied, "advance staff medical supervisor. I have been ordered to make sure you have clean bill of health."

"That's very kind," Connor said, and he smiled broadly.

Antila remained stern.

"When you are repatriated, we will not leave ourselves open

to accusations of mistreatment. The record will clearly show that you suffered no abuse before arriving at the camp."

"Charming," Abby said.

"And you are no use sick, either," Antila continued. "Mosquitos carry all sorts of filth in the oblast, and in early summer they are very busy." She reached out without warning, grabbed Connor's chin and turned his head to one side. "You've been bitten already. Here and here. You need cream for the bites, a shot, and repellant spray."

"What can I say?" Connor shrugged. "I'm just popular, I guess. Must taste good."

She let go of his face.

"I will expect you shortly," she said, and strode out of the tent.

Connor watched her go.

"Natacha," he murmured, "Natacha, eh?"

"What?" Abby asked.

"I should get rendited more often," he replied.

She kicked him under the table.

"Ow."

"Shall we walk?" Rina Suvova asked.

"You look well, Nicky," she said as they exited the tent, leaving Koshkin and Medyevin behind. "All grown up, not a boy any more. A professor, with students of your own."

"That's right," he agreed.

"It's good to see you. How long is it? Twenty years?"

"About that," Cutter replied with a nod. "I'm flattered that you remember me, Professor. It was a long time ago, and I was just an under-grad on a dig that lasted three months."

"You made an impression," Suvova said. "An earnest young man with ideas of his own. I knew then you would make a significant contribution to the field of palaeobiology."

She looked up at him. "Who knew how significant, eh?"

"I'm not sure it's really palaeobiology if the specimens are alive," he said.

She laughed and nodded.

"I've followed your career with admiration," Cutter said. "You've accomplished some amazing things, Professor Suvova. I was in the audience when you received the Drinker Cope Medal in Ottawa."

"You were there? For goodness' sake, why didn't you say hello?"

"I didn't think you'd remember me."

They walked slowly along the camp perimeter towards the river under the gloom of grey conifers and black larches. Clouds of tiny flies milled and swarmed in the patches of thin sunlight. Cutter slapped a mosquito that tried to bite him.

"And how is the other young undergraduate from that dig so long ago?" Suvova asked. "I heard you married her."

"Helen and I are no longer together," Cutter said.

Suvova nodded thoughtfully. "Ah, Nicky, these things."

She paused and looked at him.

"I want to apologise, Nicky, for the manner in which you were brought here."

"You could have asked me, and I'd have come," he said.

"Sadly, such niceties are not always available when the military takes charge of an operation."

"So I gather."

"I'm leader of the scientific group, which gives me some authority, but the state security component means that the government has the last say in everything. Executive orders brought the army in to watch over our work, and it was hard enough working with Markov. Now we have the special advisors."

"Who's Markov?" Cutter asked.

"He's the commanding officer," she replied. "You'll meet him soon enough. He's regular army, a decent sort, but rather old-fashioned. When I took over the leadership of the scientific group ten months ago, he found it quite a challenge to accept a woman in such a role. Then, as the situation grew rapidly more serious, he lacked the political nuance to nursemaid the anxieties of government officials, so we wound up with the special advisors. Koshkin you've met. There are two others. They are FSB."

"What does that mean?" Cutter asked. "I understood that Koshkin was some kind of special forces soldier?"

"Yes, special purposes and operations. The agency he works for is the FSB, which translates as the Federal Security Service, an institution that used to be known by a rather more notorious acronym."

"KGB?"

"Exactly," she nodded. "They are men with ugly souls. Expeditors. At once, the best and worst kind of soldiers."

"They're in charge now?"

"If it came to it, they could overrule me or Markov. As is so often the case, science keeps its place, and threads a careful path around the wishes of the military and state security. Anyway, the decision was made to bring in outside help. I begged for scientific expertise and assistance. The government was dead set against anybody on the outside finding out what was happening here. Then there was an incident, on Oxford Street, I believe."

"That?" Cutter said. "Yes."

"There had been rumours that things had been happening in England. It turns out that Russia's foreign intelligence networks are a great deal more effective than I would have believed. We found out about the ARC, and discovered we weren't the only people in the world experiencing these phenomena. Then I saw your name on the list of key personnel at the British facility, and I suggested that you be invited to join us."

She brushed the flies away from her face with her hand. They could hear the rushing of the dark, secret river.

"Unfortunately, the FSB was not eager to reveal how much sensitive information it had about the British establishment simply by extending such an invitation openly. It was decided — way above my head — that a more direct approach would be made. It was left in Koshkin's hands. So again, I'm sorry. I imagine the experience was unsubtle."

"That's one word for it," Cutter said. "We were more or less kidnapped at gunpoint."

Suvova gripped his arm.

"If only it could have been otherwise. I only found out what Koshkin was up to when he was already underway. I have lodged a written complaint through Markov, for all the good that will do."

"Professor, you should know that I will not tolerate any harm coming to my companions," Cutter said firmly as they arrived at the river's edge. "None at all. But I'm here now, and it's quite plain that whatever's happening here is on a scale way beyond our experience in the UK. So I'll help you in any way I can."

"Thank you, Nicky," she said. She looked out across the river at the forest and hills that lurked in the banks of mist beyond.

"This is old and remote country," she said, "and a vast tract of it has become... how can I put it? It has become a part of the Cretaceous. It is a lost world, like the book. Every week that passes, there are more sightings of erratics, more encounters. The erratics are becoming harder to contain. There have been deaths — too many, I think. Sooner or later, some towns and perhaps even cities in this region will be affected. What then?" She shrugged. "Public evacuation? More deaths? We need to understand what is going on. We need to know where these things are coming from."

"They're coming from exactly where you think they're coming from, Professor Suvova," Cutter replied. "They're coming from sixty-five million years ago."

FOURTEEN

It had begun to rain again, harder than before, and a properly nocturnal gloom settled over the advance camp. More lamps were switched on. Soldiers hurried under cover.

It is hard to believe, Abby thought, *that the dank sky above the tree-tops is both summer and midday.*

She waited under the awning of a tent block, standing with Vols. The rain drummed off the fabric overhead, then spattered in loose cascades through the drain slots and onto the earth on either side of them. Thunder rumbled somewhere far away. *At least it sounded like thunder*, Abby thought. It could quite easily have been the deep, distant booming calls of a duck-bill herd.

Connor emerged from the medical tent, pulled his ancient greatcoat up over his head, and hobbled through the rain to join them.

"Why are you walking funny?" Abby asked.

Connor got in under the awning and shook out his coat.

"The woman stuck a needle in my bum!" he exclaimed indignantly.

"You don't mean *Natacha*, do you?"

"Oh, shut up. Didn't she give *you* a shot?"

Abby shook her head.

"She looked at my tongue, shone a light in my eyes, and told me to take my shirt off."

Connor's eyes lit up.

"Do go on," he invited.

Abby scowled.

"She checked me for bruises. For signs of abuse. Then she got me to sign something. A waiver, I think."

"Me too," Connor said. "No needle in the posterior, then?"

"She gave me some tablets," Abby said, rattling a brown plastic bottle of pills. "Anti-bug stuff. Not convinced I'm going to take them, though."

Connor shifted uncomfortably.

"Well, she stuck a needle right in my backside. No warning. Not so much as a how do you do."

"Oh, she must really like you, Connor," Abby said, grinning.

"Uh, shut up."

"Hey, what's that?" Before Connor could stop her, she'd fished a leaflet out of the side pocket of his greatcoat.

"Oi!"

Connor tried to grab it back, but Abby danced out of his reach and started to read it.

"Did she give you this?"

"Give it back! Abby!"

"Did *Natacha* give you this?"

"Ab-by!"

"Oh my God," she laughed, fending Connor off with one arm as she studied the leaflet. "It's a pamphlet. It's an army pamphlet. All about the benefits of correct diet and healthy exercise! Look at all these photographs of young men in shorts, weight-training and doing star-jumps!"

"Give it back!"

Abby pursed her lips and held out the leaflet to Connor.

"I think *Natacha* is trying to tell you something," she said. "I think *Natacha* likes big, strong men with beefy muscles."

Connor snatched the pamphlet out of her hand and stuffed it inside his coat.

"Yeah, ha ha. Very funny. She just gave it to me, all right? I didn't ask for it. This must be so hilarious for you."

"It's certainly breaking the tension," she said.

Vols hadn't understood much of what had passed between Abby and Connor, but he was watching the antics with amusement.

"What are you laughing at, comrade?" Connor asked him.

Vols shrugged. "Vols laugh not be."

"Exactly, it's not funny, is it, Vols?" Abby said solemnly. "A young man should take his health very seriously."

"Da. Especially out here in the forests."

Suddenly Vols straightened up smartly. Abby and Connor looked around. Cutter and the older woman who'd called him "Nicky" were standing behind them.

Cutter shot Abby and Connor a wry smile.

"You two okay?" he asked.

They nodded.

"Please introduce us, Nicky," Suvova said.

"Abby Maitland, Connor Temple, this is Professor Rina Suvova," Cutter said. "She's in charge here."

"Not as much as I'd like to be," Suvova said, shaking hands with Abby and Connor.

"When I was a lot younger, a student," Cutter explained, "I was lucky enough to get some practical field experience on one of the professor's digs."

"Yes, I'm afraid I'm the real reason you're here," Suvova admitted.

"She's got some stuff to show me," Cutter said. "I wanted you both to see it, too."

Professor Suvova led them to the north end of the advance camp. Vols tagged along at their heels. The tents at the camp's north end were large prefab shelters.

As they approached, despite the cold rain, they could smell the musky odours of livestock, and the sharper smells of disinfectant products and dry feed.

Suvova unlatched the outer door of one of the larger structures, and brought them in out of the rain. The prefab windows were meshed with chicken wire, and roof-lights ran off a portable generator that hummed out back. It smelled like a zoo. The room was lined with shelves stacked with metal cage traps, sacks of feed, and scientific equipment. Doctor Medyevin was there, working alongside two other scientists at a bank of powered microscopes. He'd changed into work overalls, but there was still a strong scent of his favourite cologne.

He looked up and greeted them as they came in. Cutter was still wary of the young doctor. However unwillingly, Medyevin had participated in Koshkin's operation to conscript them. He had been used as a lure to blindside Cutter. For all his wide-eyed eagerness, Medyevin had the steely glint of a ruthless careerist about him.

Suvova introduced Medyevin's colleagues. Yushenko was a tall, swarthy man with bony hands and a big nose. He was unshaven and his manners were intense, as though he was full of nervous energy. Suvova said he was a botanist. Bulov was the group's conservator. He was a slightly plump, fastidious man who seemed rather aloof.

Large metal cages stood on the central benches, alongside a row of glass tanks. There were live animals and birds inside them.

"My God, you've collected specimens," Cutter said.

"Look at them," Abby said, practically squealing with delight.

"Of course," Suvova replied, "though most of our work is tracking and observation."

Following Abby's lead, Cutter peered into one of the larger cages where a hairy, badger-like creature was crunching on some live locusts.

"Didelphodon?" he asked.

"Yes, or a closely related marsupial," Medyevin replied, stepping up beside him. "We have quite a range of small mammalian and avian erratics. Most are not known from the fossil record."

Cutter looked through the wire of another cage at a tiny, crested bird.

"Small, delicate bones rarely survive," he said. "We tend to find the big, robust stuff."

The bird squawked and ruffled its feathers. Cutter moved to another cage and peered at another, slightly larger bird.

"We have found or observed thirteen new avian species," Suvova told them, "and twenty-six new small mammals, along with four mammalian types we were previously familiar with. We have marsupials, placentals and one monotreme."

"Wow," Cutter said.

"We even have an ultra-small pterosaur the size of a sparrow that we were not expecting to find, given that the evolutionary era seems to fit the Late Cretaceous."

"You got it alive?" Cutter asked eagerly.

Suvova shook her head. "No. We found it dead. We have it preserved in the freezer."

"Regardless, I'd love to see it."

"Of course," she said, and she nodded. "There will be time for that."

"I know there were mammals back then," Connor said, crouching down to examine the Didelphodon in its cage, "but you just don't imagine there being so many different types."

"The diversity stands to reason," Cutter said. He was inspecting two small, shrew-like creatures that were darting around in one of the tanks. "Mammals had been around for a while, but the fossil records show them to be essentially niche groups of small animals. Right up to the end of the Cretaceous, they weren't very common. It was only after the K-T boundary event that things swung their way."

"The what?" Abby asked. She was only half listening as she moved between the tanks, examining each creature intently.

"You know, the event that wiped out the dinosaurs," Connor told her.

"An event these creatures were resilient enough to survive," Cutter said. He looked down at the shrew-things as they raced around. "These little guys were around when dinosaurs ruled the Earth. These were the meek that inherited the Earth."

"That presupposes a great deal," Bulov interjected.

Cutter looked up at him. "How so?"

The scientist cleared his throat. His mannerisms were very precise.

"From day one, the group's theoretical model for this situation has been a survival."

"Theories are there to be tested, Grisha," Yushenko pointed

out. Bulov looked at his colleague disdainfully.

"I am familiar with scientific methodology, thank you," he replied curtly, "but the survival concept is the only one that really holds water. Professor Iachmann supported the ___"

"Professor Iachmann isn't in charge any more!" Yushenko interrupted.

"Here we go again," Medyevin groaned.

"Iachmann was convinced by the notion of a survival," Bulov went on, talking over Yushenko's objections.

"Wait, wait!" Cutter called out. "Iachmann? Jan Iachmann? Are we talking about the same guy who did all the work in Mongolia?"

"Of course," Bulov said.

"You know his work, then?" Yushenko asked.

"Absolutely," Cutter said. "He's a remarkable man."

"Professor Iachmann was the original leader of the scientific group," Suvova explained. "I took over from him."

"Then Iachmann thought this situation was the result of a survival?" Cutter asked.

"It's the only theoretical model that makes any practical sense," Bulov insisted. "This geographical region — for reasons we have not yet identified — has allowed certain species to persist and flourish long after the extinction of their kind in other parts of the world. It is the classic 'lost world' syndrome. There are numerous examples of such freak survivals in Antarctic ice-pockets, Indian Ocean islands, cave systems, Amazonian plateaus —"

"Plenty of examples, yes, but nothing on this scale," Cutter pointed out. "You honestly believe these creatures have been living here for sixty-five million years?"

"It is the only rational answer," Bulov maintained. "Also, it would account for the preponderance of mammal specimens that appear not to match the fossil record. This region has nurtured its own unique evolutionary process."

"I'm sorry to disappoint you, but I can promise you that it hasn't," Cutter said. He gestured at the cages. "These are all Late Cretaceous creatures. They're coming directly from the Cretaceous Era."

"That's preposterous," Bulov scoffed.

"Indeed, it's even more preposterous than the government's theory — that they are genetically designed terror weapons, created by NATO to undermine the Russian Federation," Yushenko put in.

"There are people who think NATO *built* these dinosaurs?" Connor said, and he laughed.

Yushenko nodded.

"Yes. I've been led to understand that the Federal Government believes NATO might have had some assistance from Hollywood." The look on his face showed that he didn't give the theory much credence.

"This part of Siberia is remote," Cutter persisted, "but it's not geographically discrete enough to account for a survival. Not on this scale, and not of creatures this big. They haven't been living here, undisturbed. They're *coming* here."

Bulov snorted.

"This is about your holes in time, isn't it Professor?" Medyevin asked.

"What?" Yushenko looked dubious.

"Professor Cutter told me about them on the journey here," Medyevin continued. "'Holes in time', he said. Please tell us what you mean, Professor."

The scientists all looked at Cutter so intently that he chuckled.

"Nicky?" Suvova asked. "Please? We need your help."

"We call them anomalies," Cutter began. "Don't ask me to explain the physics. I just know them as a fact. They're what the ARC was created to handle. The ARC. The Anomaly Research Centre."

"When we read the intelligence reports, we thought 'anomaly' referred to the creatures," Suvova said. "What we call erratics."

"Holes in time is a laughable idea," Cutter admitted, "but it's the simplest description. You've got an anomaly here. At least one, maybe more. From what you've told me, the phenomenon here is operating very differently from the anomalies I've studied. It's quite possibly larger, and it seems to have been open for much longer than usual. Perhaps years. Either that, or you have them opening and closing more frequently.

"Put in the most basic terms, you've got a viable gateway to the Cretaceous period somewhere in these forests."

"Time travel?" Bulov murmured. "Time travel?"

"Uhm, more sort of time transfer," Connor offered.

"Time travel?" Bulov repeated. He turned to Suvova, scorn written across his face. "*This* is what we've waited for? *This* is the fantastic, ground-breaking scientific insight you promised us?"

"Calm down, Grisha," Suvova said.

"I will *not* calm down! I will not have my wits insulted! Time travel!" Bulov almost spat each word out. "We need help, you said! We need help from the clever and very well-funded scientists in Great Britain and the United States! They will know what to do! They will know so much more than us!"

"In your position, I'd be sceptical too," Cutter said calmly to Bulov. "Give me a chance to find this anomaly for you. See for yourself."

"This is a survival!" Bulov growled. "There is no 'anomaly'."

"A little while back, there were Entelodons loose on Oxford

115

Street," Cutter said. "It got covered up, but it made the news. It's the main reason we got dragged here against our will. Tell me, Doctor Bulov, in your opinion, were those Entelodons in Central London a survival, too?"

Bulov looked away.

"The man makes a decent point," Yushenko shrugged.

"How do we find the anomaly?" Medyevin asked.

"I think this discussion should continue under more appropriate circumstances." Koshkin's harsh voice interrupted them as he pushed in through the hut door. He was wearing black BDUs, heavy boots, and a webbing belt with a holstered pistol. He was followed by the older man with the wire-framed glasses. The older man was dressed in the same kit as Koshkin.

All the scientists straightened up, and Vols snapped to attention.

"We were bringing Professor Cutter and his colleagues up to speed, Koshkin," Suvova said firmly, speaking English.

"You were conducting a classified discussion in front of a grunt with no clearance," Koshkin replied, following her example and gesturing at Vols, "and a pair of idealogues who like to run off at the mouth when they've had a few." He directed the last remark at Yushenko and Bulov.

"With respect, Specialist Koshkin," Bulov began.

"I have none for you, so shut up," Koshkin told him. He turned and looked at Suvova and Cutter. "Markov wants to find out how Cutter can assist us. I think we'd all like to hear the professor's science fiction stories in more detail."

"You overheard?" Cutter asked.

"I heard enough," Koshkin said.

"Science fiction?"

Koshkin sneered.

"This situation is a grave matter of state security. The increase in these incidents jeopardises an entire region. I require simple, practical solutions. I need a thorough threat analysis. I have theories of my own about what's happening here."

"I suppose you think NATO got Hollywood to run up a few dinosaurs," Connor responded.

Koshkin just glared at him.

Connor shrugged.

"It sounded funny when they said it to me," he added.

Koshkin looked at the man in the wire-framed glasses, who was waiting patiently by the shelter door.

"Umarov, let's take them over to the CO's hut."

The older man nodded, and held the door open.

"Please to come," he said.

"One thing," Cutter said, holding up a hand. "You said Jan Iachmann used to be in charge of the scientific group. What happened to him?"

"Professor Suvova replaced him," Koshkin replied.

"Yes, but where did Iachmann go?" Cutter asked.

"Ten months ago, he went out surveying south of the river with two other members of the group," Bulov said. "They never came back."

"I guess Baba Yaga got them too," Koshkin said.

FIFTEEN

"I've just spent three hours with the minister," Lester said. "It's turning into a nightmare. The Foreign Office has got hold of it, and so has 5."

"What did the minister tell you?" Jenny asked.

"That I can tell you?" Lester replied. "Virtually nothing."

Jake Hemple appeared in the office doorway.

"You sent for me?"

"Come in, and shut the door," Lester instructed. He sat down at his desk and rubbed the bridge of his nose.

"Seats," he offered. "We could be here for some time."

Jenny and Hemple sat down. Lester opened his briefcase, and slid out a batch of ten by eight photographs.

"It's taken three days, but our friends in 5 have managed to identify this man," Lester said, tapping the uppermost shot. "Nikolai Medyevin, Russian, thirty-three, palaeontologist, moving around on a South African passport with a European visa."

"Palaeontologist?" Jenny asked.

Lester nodded.

"Would you believe it? Not a spy at all. Just a scientist."

"What about the other man on the footage?" Hemple asked.

"Nothing," Lester said. "5 thinks he might be some kind of contractor or specialist. He's certainly in the country illegally."

"Why would these men kidnap Cutter and the others?" Jenny asked. "Why would a palaeontologist come to this country and kidnap a —"

She paused.

"Oh God," she said.

"Let's not jump the gun," Lester said. "Thus far 5 thinks it's all a mistake. This Medyevin fellow, he may know of Cutter, and he may think that Cutter is a viable target for extortion, if he believes, for instance, that Cutter is doing lucrative Government work under contract. Apparently, kidnap and extortion is a growth industry in Russia. This sort of thing happens all the time, I'm told — though seldom on UK soil."

"If that was the case, there'd have been some sort of demand," Hemple pointed out.

"Yes," Lester admitted. "That's where the whole argument starts to go soggy. And, of course, most people in 5 and the Home Office aren't aware of the precise *type* of work Cutter does for us. It's possible this is exactly what we think it is."

"The Russians have got the same problem we have," Hemple stated, "and they've taken the professor to find out what we know about it."

"It's so horribly ironic," Jenny mused. "Cutter was saying how desperately he wanted to make contact with any other people who'd had experience of this problem. He wanted to share information and ideas. But this probably isn't what he had in mind."

Lester began to knead his temples with the tips of his fingers.

"Well, if that's true, the implications for national security are mind-boggling."

"What about the implications for Nick, Abby and Connor?" Jenny asked.

"Well," Lester replied tetchily, "if it were up to me, we'd find out where they are, and we'd damn well go and get them back. I mean, what's the point of having a dedicated special-forces unit if you can't deploy it against a foreign power once in a while?"

"Say the word," Hemple said.

"Oh, put it away," Lester sighed. He sat back in his chair and looked at the ceiling. "There are two problems. One is, the Home Office and the Foreign Office would go berserk if we broke the rules."

"So we bend them," Hemple said. "I've learned to walk some very fine lines."

"Two," Lester carried on, "we haven't the faintest idea where they are. The van the Russians were using hasn't turned up. We've had no sightings, port watch hasn't seen anything, and Medyevin's passport hasn't been flagged by Customs."

"They will have left the country," Hemple said. "A ship, a private air-field, something like that."

"Yes," Lester agreed, "but we don't know where they've gone. We are so pathetically lacking in specifics, we're helpless. We're just going to have to wait."

Jenny looked at Hemple.

"Prep the alpha team anyway," she said.

SIXTEEN

General Grigoriy Markov was something of a survival himself. He was old-school, a dinosaur relic from the era of the Soviet Military who had managed to survive the cultural K-T boundary event in 1991 that had marked the start of the Russian Federation.

Rina Suvova told Cutter that the general had accumulated enough political capital to retain a senior post in the modern army, but it seemed his superiors weren't quite sure what to do with him. The Siberian mission was important because of the serious state security issues attached to it, and that befitted his status. At the same time, it was a wet-nurse posting to the middle of nowhere. Not even that, perhaps: the advance camp was so remote, it wasn't near the middle of *anything*.

He was waiting for them in his hut, standing beside a portable desk laden with report files. He had no English, and relied on his adjutant, a dapper man called Zvegin, for translations.

Cutter's first impression of Markov was of a big man, tall and overweight. With his bulk and his thick beard, Markov comically seemed to fit the Russian 'bear' stereotype. But he was getting old.

His hair was shaggy grey, his eyes heavy, his ears big and fleshy, and his bulk was weighed down by the law of gravity. Cutter thought he wasn't so much a bear as a giant sloth, or even an old bull elephant.

Markov had put on a dress uniform and his medals. There were so many of them, it looked as if the army had handed them out as freely as boy-scout initiative badges. Without words to establish his authority directly, most likely Markov was trying to show Cutter that he was indisputably in charge.

Koshkin, in his simple black BDUs, had infinitely more authority, however. He was the young bull who had usurped Markov's place in the herd. The old bull just hadn't fully realised it yet.

When Koshkin and Umarov, followed by the members of the science group, brought Cutter, Abby and Connor into the hut, Markov's manner was stilted. They were guests, whose help he was keen to secure, and it seemed part of him wanted to greet them with handshakes. But they were also prisoners, foreign nationals whose illegal arrest and deportation he had authorised.

He settled for an awkward nod of the head. Then he spoke, and Zvegin translated.

"General Markov is anxious that you provide technical scientific support for this mission," Zvegin said. "He is especially interested in your theories as to the origins of the erratics."

"I'm sure he is," Cutter replied.

Zvegin waited to see if anything else was forthcoming, and when it wasn't, seemed reluctant to translate Cutter's terse response. The general looked at his adjutant expectantly.

"Okay," Cutter said, "I'll repeat this for the general's benefit." Zvegin started to translate.

"I think we can help one another," Cutter continued. "I think we have a mutual problem that has consequences for the

122

entire human race, and has nothing at all to do with national boundaries. I will assist Professor Suvova in any way I can. But I condemn your seizure of me and my friends. It is totally unacceptable. If any further threats are made against us, my cooperation will vanish in a flash. Are we clear?"

Cutter waited until Zvegin had caught up with the translation. Koshkin scowled at him.

The general listened to the translation, cleared his throat and looked directly at Cutter. Before he could say anything, however, Cutter headed him off.

"Additionally," he continued, "I wish to be allowed contact with the British Government, to inform them of our condition and location."

"There is no way —" Koshkin snapped.

Markov began to speak, and Zvegin translated back to Cutter.

"The general assures you no further threats will be made, and that your cooperation is appreciated. However, on the second point, contact with your government is not possible at this time, due to state security measures."

"I'd like him to reconsider that," Cutter said.

"I'm sure the decision could be reviewed," the adjutant replied without reference to the general. "Perhaps a show of good faith? Can you offer us something of substance?"

Cutter glanced at Connor and Abby beside him.

"What do you think? In for a penny?"

"Go for it," Abby said.

"I just want to see some more dinos," Connor added.

Cutter turned back to Markov and his translator.

"The root cause of this situation is a phenomenon known to us as an anomaly. There may be more than one, in fact. If you supply us with the appropriate equipment and resources, we will do our very best to locate the anomaly."

Zvegin translated this for the general's benefit and then asked Cutter, "What is this anomaly?"

"It's a puncture in the fourth dimension," Cutter explained. "It's an interface between one discrete temporal era and another."

"It's a hole in time," Connor clarified.

Zvegin hesitated, and then translated. Markov listened. Then he laughed, assuming a translation mistake, and asked for clarification. Zvegin repeated what he'd said.

A certain amount of uproar followed. Markov began to make baffled demands, and Koshkin, Suvova, and the other scientists started arguing back and forth. It became heated.

Cutter looked at Connor and Abby.

"We'll just let them get on with it, shall we?" he asked.

They waited for another minute or so, but rather than calming down, the argument became even more fierce. Markov, Suvova and Koshkin were engaged in a three-way shouting match that Medyevin and the adjutant, Zvegin, were trying to referee, while Bulov and Yushenko sniped from the wings.

"So, World War Three," Abby observed.

"This is getting us nowhere," Cutter said. He made a move to intervene, but Connor stopped him.

"Allow me." Connor hooked his fingers in his mouth and blew a whistle so shrill it cut through the bellowing and yelling. All the Russians glared at him. He gave them a cheery wave.

"Look, hi. Hello. Not entirely clear what you're all arguing about, because I don't speak Russian," Connor said, "but now that I've got your attention, can I just say, I'm guessing it's about the whole idea of anomalies, right?"

Zvegin was translating rapidly for the general.

"So, some of you, like, believe my boss here might have

something," Connor went on, "and the rest of you think he's bonkers. That's all right. I think he's bonkers a lot of the time, too. But it occurs to me, you can stand around all day shouting at one another, or you can let us find the anomaly. Right, we find it for you, you can see it, it proves anomalies are real, and you won't have to argue about it any more."

Markov pointed a finger at Connor and said something.

"Ooh, am I going to get shot now?" Connor asked, suddenly nervous.

"The general says this is a simple and reasonable solution to the issue," Zvegin said.

"Absolutely," Connor said, relieved. "Save all the arguing for later. When we've found the anomaly for you, you can all have a brilliant row about what to do with it."

"You can do this, Nicky?" Rina Suvova asked Cutter.

"Connor's the real whiz at it," Cutter replied, "but, yeah. We can find it, I'm certain."

"What will you need?" Medyevin asked.

Connor shrugged.

"Whatever kit you've got, actually, but most of all a radio."

"Absolutely not!" Koshkin barked. "This is all just a trick so they can get their hands on a communications device!"

"Listen, Koshkin," Cutter said. "You brought us halfway round the planet to help you. Well, this is what we do. If you won't let us build an anomaly detector, then you might as well send us home, because that's all we've got to offer."

"Our understanding of this event has not advanced in months," Suvova appealed. "Let Professor Cutter at least try."

Koshkin exchanged a few more words with the general.

"Very well," he said at length. "But Umarov will supervise you at all times."

The older man in the wire-framed glasses nodded.

"You'll need a translator then," Medyevin said. "May I?"

"Get to work," Koshkin said. "Let us see where it takes us."

Night was not so much falling as flooding out of the forests to submerge them. In the main longhouse of the advance camp, Connor and Cutter worked with the tools and equipment Umarov had supplied. Connor had the back off a powerful, bulky field set from the radio room. He'd also scored one of the camp's heavy-grade military laptops.

"What do you think?" Cutter asked him.

Connor shrugged and put down a screwdriver. "It's not going to be the most portable thing in the world, but we'll just have to manage."

"The radio set is the key component?" Medyevin asked, watching them intently.

"Yeah," Cutter said. "Radio is the basis of the ADD units we use at the ARC."

"ADD — by which you mean anomaly detection devices?" Medyevin queried.

"That's right. Our experience is that anomalies cause radio interference on the 87.6FM frequency. We use the interference patterns to identify them, and then triangulate their location."

"That'll be the hard part," Connor said. "I'm not going to be able to rig up much more than a basic warmer/colder directional indicator. There's going to be some legwork involved."

He started playing around with the laptop.

"This is a pretty good piece of kit," he observed.

"You sound surprised," Medyevin said.

"Oh, you know, it's all those stories about cosmonaut's taking pencils into space," Connor said. "I thought Russian tech would be solid and very basic."

"Some of it still is," Medyevin responded, "but we source decent hardware these days. Russia really wouldn't be able to compete if it didn't."

"Well, respect," Connor said. "This is full on. That said, it's loaded with all sorts of applications I can't use because I don't have the military clearance code."

He looked at Umarov. The man in the wire-framed glasses simply smiled back.

"Yep, that's what I thought," Connor said. "No keys to the missile silo for me. But I can use the GPS system and a few other bits. I can't believe they've got coverage out here." He looked at Cutter. "Wireless broadband in the middle of darkest Siberia? How amazing is that?"

"Special services have been arranged," Medyevin said, "due to the sensitive nature of this operation. Communication was considered to be key."

"So, how long?" Cutter asked.

"If I work late, I can probably get the basic set rigged up for tomorrow morning," Connor replied. "That's not the issue. The fine tuning is the issue."

"Go on," Cutter said.

Connor turned a dial, and briefly filled the air with a hiss of white noise.

"The interference is there, right where we said it would be. There's absolutely no doubt at all that there's an anomaly here. But how close and where is another thing. I'm getting all sorts of weird readings."

"Back home, before we left, we were getting weird readings too," Cutter reminded him.

"It feels like the same sort of thing," Connor said. "I'll know a bit more when I've finished lashing this together, but right now it's really hard to finesse the readings in any way."

Cutter left Connor at work and went outside for a breath of air. He was tired, and Medyevin was asking too many questions that he couldn't answer.

The doctor had evidently bought the 'holes in time' theory, which made him a useful ally, but Cutter couldn't get past his blatant ambition. Given the situation, Medyevin was bound to be interested in their ideas and theories, but he seemed excessively keen.

He wants to learn, thought Cutter. He wants to know more about this than any of his colleagues, so that he can become Russia's foremost expert. This is about Nikolai Medyevin's career. This is his break into the big leagues, his opportunity to secure a reputation.

Abby was outside already, watching the stars come out. The sky above the black trees was a huge and luminous dark blue, almost lighter and clearer than the murky day had been. The air seemed fresh. The lamps of the advance camp burned yellow and white in the darkness of the forest clearing, but overhead the sky was full of glittering silver lights and fields of stars that looked like diamond dust.

"How's Connor doing?" she asked, seeing Cutter approach.

"Not bad," he replied as he joined her. "Let's hope we can get this situation sorted out, and then get on our way as soon as possible."

"You don't really want to do that though, do you?"

"What?"

"You didn't like getting kidnapped any more than we did,"

Abby said, and she grinned. "But now that you know what's here, you want to stay and see it, don't you?"

Cutter laughed and shook his head.

"It's the creatures they're talking about, and the numbers. That herd was one of the most amazing things I've ever seen. Of *course* I want to see more."

"I know what you mean," she replied. "But as much as I want to get in there and study all of those wonderful creatures, there may be something else we need to deal with."

"What are you talking about?"

"I was wondering what that was," Abby said. She pointed up at the sky just above the treeline. "I've been watching it for a while."

Cutter looked up. There was a shimmer in the night sky, a ghostly flicker of something.

"Is that the northern lights?" he asked.

"I don't know. Does that happen here?"

Cutter shrugged.

"I don't even know where *here* is," he said. "I mean, not exactly. Siberia, boom. It's a big place. But if that isn't the aurora borealis, then I have a feeling I know what it is…"

They went back inside the longhouse.

"I'd like to see a map," Cutter said.

When Medyevin had translated the request, Umarov seemed uncertain.

"You've got to show me a map sooner or later," Cutter pointed out with exaggerated patience. "I'm going to need one tomorrow when we start hunting for this anomaly. So you might as well do it now."

Umarov shrugged his shoulders. He rummaged through some papers on the bench beside him and produced a large-scale military survey map. He handed it to Cutter, who unfolded it.

"So this is the region?" he asked. "Wow, this is wilderness. There's a whole lot of nothing out here."

"It is a particularly remote and empty quarter of the Krasnoyarsk Krai," Medyevin agreed.

"Okay, this is the river that runs outside the camp. That's got to be at least a thousand kilometres long all by itself, and it's part of a much bigger river system." Cutter laughed to himself, tracing his finger across the map. "We're going to have to get used to a completely different notion of scale," he said. "This is a huge country. We —"

He fell silent.

"Is that the name of this river?" he asked Medyevin.

"Yes, it is," Medyevin replied.

"The river right outside?" Cutter pressed.

Medyevin nodded, puzzled.

"What is it?" Abby asked. "What's the matter?"

"That's got to be more than a coincidence," Cutter murmured, staring at the map.

"What has?" Connor asked.

"This place, that river," Cutter said, looking at them both. "It's Tunguska."

SEVENTEEN

Cutter and Umarov helped Connor to load the makeshift ADD into the back of a 4x4.

"Careful, careful," Connor said. "It's a bit delicate."

The heavy field radio had been stripped out and extensively altered, and several additional components had been wired into it. The result looked like a science project gone enthusiastically wrong. Once it was bedded down in the back of the 4x4, Connor flipped down the set's front cover and threw the power toggles.

The set hummed as it came up to power. Indicators lit up. It emitted a soft, crackling hiss that stopped when Connor plugged in and put on a pair of headphones. He picked up a wand made of bare wire with a handle of duct tape and played out the long flex that connected the wand to the side of the radio set. Then he stood up in the back of the 4x4 and began to sweep the wand around like a conductor with a baton.

It was early morning, and the mist was still heavy and cold, so thick they could barely see across the yard of the advance camp. A group had assembled in the dawn gloom to watch Connor's first test. The scientists Suvova, Bulov, Medyevin and Yushenko stood with Abby, all huddled down in winter coats. Yushenko had brought a digital video camera, and was keeping a record of the proceedings.

A grim-faced Koshkin and Umarov had been joined by the general's adjutant Zvegin and a trio of soldiers.

Abby had grabbed a cup of coffee from the mess tent. She was cold and tired. The bunk and bedroll she'd been given had been damp and uncomfortable, and she'd found it very difficult to sleep. She kept thinking about what Cutter had told her the night before. He'd seemed particularly fascinated that the place was called Tunguska. According to him, there'd been a natural disaster here in the early part of the twentieth century. A meteor or a comet had hit the remote region, devastating the forests. The incident was still shrouded in mystery.

"It struck this area," Cutter said, "which was so far from anywhere, very few people realised what had happened. But the blast was heard thousands of miles away, and it changed the world's weather for a year or more. If it had hit a population centre, a city, it would have been a very different story."

"It's just a coincidence, isn't it?" she'd asked him. "I mean, it can't have anything to do with the anomalies, can it?"

"I'm not sure we can rule out anything any more," he had replied.

As she stood with the scientific group, watching Connor get ready, she saw Vols hurrying to join them, buttoning his tunic. She had to smile. He was there to protect her again, like a loyal guard dog.

"Getting anything?" Cutter called up to Connor.

Connor played the wand around a bit more, and then began to point it in a rather more specific direction.

"I'm getting something!" he announced in an overloud voice.

Cutter tapped his ears.

Connor pulled the headphones off.

"Sorry. I said, I think I'm getting something. Hang on, I'll put it on the speaker."

He flipped a switch. The background noise crackled out of the set again, but when Connor aimed the wand in a particular direction, the noise began to wail and sing with distortion.

"There's your anomaly," Cutter said to Koshkin.

"That proves nothing," Bulov said, and he stalked off back to his bunk.

"Shall we check it out?" Connor asked.

"No time like the present." Cutter looked at Koshkin. "Let's take it out for a little field test," he suggested, and he held out his hand.

"What?" Koshkin asked, eyeing the hand suspiciously.

"Give me the keys. I'm driving. You can follow me."

The Russian narrowed his eyes.

"Oh, come on," Cutter said. "I'm going to escape by driving across Siberia in a jeep?"

Reluctantly, Koshkin handed over the keys.

Cutter and Abby climbed aboard with Connor, and Cutter let Vols take the other seat. Koshkin, Suvova and Zvegin climbed into a second 4x4 driven by Umarov, and Yushenko and Medyevin boarded a third that was manned by another pair of soldiers. Yushenko was still clutching his video camera. There was a rattle of starter motors, and the three vehicles switched on their headlamps and rolled forward in convoy.

Standing up in the rear if the leading 4x4 with the wand in his hand and the headphones back on, Connor held onto the roll bar and peered at the dashboard compass.

"Roughly north," he said.

They led the convoy out through the camp. Near the river, in the chilly dawn, they saw Natacha Antila leading a squad of troopers in early morning calisthenics.

"That's just trying way too hard," Abby said. She looked up at Connor and laughed as he threw medic Antila a joke-serious salute from the back of the 4x4 as they drove past.

The doctor did not acknowledge him.

They followed the trail away from the camp and into the woods. Wherever the mist cleared in patches, Cutter put his foot down and raced ahead of Umarov. Looking back, he saw Koshkin berating the other FSB specialist for not driving fast enough. That caused him to grin, and when Vols followed his gaze, even he seemed to find it amusing.

The woods were wild and dense, but Cutter saw evidence of both motorised and foot patrols from the advance camp. Markov's garrison had established a significant perimeter around the site. There was a radiating series of guard posts and observation nests. Bleary-eyed soldiers watched the trio of 4x4s as they dashed past through the mist.

After half an hour, Umarov sounded his horn, signalling for Cutter to pull over. They halted in a glade of immense spruce trees where the backlit mist was coiling like luminous yellow smoke. Koshkin dismounted and ran forward to Cutter's vehicle.

"What's the matter?" Cutter asked.

"We stay put here for five minutes," Koshkin told him.

"Why?"

"I just got a radio call from obs post eighteen, which is about a kilometre west of here. Something came through the perimeter about ten minutes ago. Whatever it was, it was big. Post eighteen is going to send a sweep team in to find it, but we're going to sit here engines off for a moment."

"It's likely to be more scared of three noisy trucks than we are of it," Cutter said.

"Let's just sit," Koshkin insisted. "Please, turn off your engine."

Cutter obeyed. The Russian walked back to his vehicle. Medyevin and Yushenko got out of their 4x4 and stretched their legs. Yushenko hoisted his camera again and took some idle footage of the scene. It was oppressively quiet without the sound of the engines. Cutter heard a few bird calls, and the occasional twig crack from the undergrowth.

He looked at Connor, who still had the headphones on and was making adjustments to the radio set dials.

"Okay?" Cutter asked.

Connor shook his head.

"I'm worried about it overheating!" he shouted.

Cutter tapped his ears.

Connor took off the cans.

"Sorry. I said, I'm worried about it overheating."

"Shut it down for a bit. Give it a rest," Cutter suggested.

"No, it's all right for now." Connor put the headphones back on. He began to fiddle obsessively with the controls.

Cutter looked at Abby, who smiled and shrugged.

A minute or two went by. Cutter sat back and waited. He heard what sounded like a hornbill, and something else that was either a bullfrog or some kind of thrush. Then he heard something else.

It was a deep, rumbling cry, part growl, part snort.

He sat up.

"Before you ask, yes, I did hear that," Abby said.

The others had heard it, too. Cutter looked back and saw the occupants of the other 4x4s, alert and wary. Vols got out of the vehicle and stood ready with his AK.

They heard the guttural cry again, closer this time.

"Came from that way," Cutter said, pointing out across the glade.

"Absolutely," Abby agreed. They jumped down together and began to head off across the leaf litter, heads low. Vols gave a little gasp of alarm and hurried after them. Connor was so busy with his jury-rigged ADD he didn't seem to notice that they had left the 4x4.

Cutter heard the cry a third time, and they adjusted their direction. Vols caught up with them.

"Please to be back," he requested, keeping his voice low. Despite the matt-black assault weapon in his hands, he looked scared.

"It's fine," Abby said in a reassuring voice.

"Be back!" Vols insisted.

Something moved up ahead of them, stirring the undergrowth. It came into view out of the mist.

"Oh, look at that," Cutter whispered.

It was a horned dinosaur.

EIGHTEEN

The Ceratopsian was about four metres long from its beaked snout to the tip of its raised and surprisingly thin tail. Its quadrupedal body was large, stable and low to the ground. Cutter estimated its weight at around three tons. It was a sub-adult, a calf. The horns on its nose and brows were not far off the huge size they would reach in maturity, and its large, crested skull was very distinctive.

"Triceratops?" Abby whispered at Cutter's side.

"No, no," he hissed back softly. "Torosaurus. Look at the size of the frill."

With Vols hovering anxiously behind them, they took another step or two towards it.

The bass, lowing noise, a combination of growl and snort, was coming from the creature. It was welling up from deep inside its enormous torso, and then grumbling out of its throat.

The Torosaurus had emerged from the undergrowth and mist with its left side to Cutter and Abby, a profile view that allowed them to see the full projection of its awesome crest and the muted slate-and-ash stripes that ran horizontally along its flanks. Its head was tipped forward, beak down, eyes half closed. Discharge, like tree sap, had gathered around the eye they could see, and when it groaned, steam puffed from its nostrils.

"Look at the crest," Cutter whispered.

The creature's spectacular frill was pulsing with colour. Aposematic patterns of amber and black rippled through the surface scales of the bicorn crest, and two dramatic, encircled dots had appeared like giant staring eyes in the centre of each lobe of the frill.

"It can change colour," Abby murmured in delight.

"The crest is full of blood vessels," Cutter explained quietly. "The theory's always been that they use their crests for display and signalling. I think this one's in distress."

"How do you get that?" she asked.

"I don't know. Lost, maybe. It's just a juvenile. It's got separated from its herd. This is amazing, Abby. There was another theory that Torosaurus was simply an adult form of Triceratops. We'd never found a juvenile, you see, so the suggestion was that the huge crest was a sexual dimorphic feature of mature specimens. This sub-adult proves that theory wrong. Torosaurus are a completely separate Ceratopsid genus."

"You really think it's in distress?" Abby pressed.

Cutter nodded.

"What's that smell?" Abby asked.

"I don't know," Cutter replied.

He was used to the fact that almost every creature they encountered had a distinctive odour, and most of them weren't especially pleasant, but a particularly nasty smell hung in the cold morning air. It was warm and bovine, ripe and rotten. It smelled of dung and gas and raw meat.

He was reasonably certain it didn't bode well.

The creature rasped and snorted again.

"I think it's having respiratory difficulties," Cutter said, stepping still closer. "And is it me, or is it limping a little?"

The Torosaurus took another few steps, its head still down.

"I think it is limping." Abby edged towards the creature with Cutter. "It's favouring its left foreleg."

"Please to be back!" Vols hissed strenuously.

Someone shouted. Cutter looked over his shoulder, and saw Koshkin and Umarov moving forward with the two armed troopers. Koshkin was clutching an AK of his own. Suvova and the others were following them, though Connor was still working on the ADD in the lead 4x4, oblivious to it all.

Yushenko was filming eagerly.

Koshkin shouted again. Cutter signalled for him to stay back and shut up. At the sound of the Russian's voice, however, the calf lifted its nose a little, exhaled with a rough, barking cough, and began to swing its head from side to side, threatening with its horns and coloured crest.

It started to turn towards them.

Abby edged to the left to look at its right flank.

"Oh God," she breathed, and gestured to Cutter to move sidelong with her.

With Vols following, they circled to the right of the calf, where they were able to see its other profile for the first time. Part of its torso, a section just behind its right foreleg, was missing. A considerable chunk of meat had been removed, leaving a ghastly open wound that was so deep they could see layers of yellow fat and the sugar-pink of several ribs. The wound was glistening red and crawling with shiny black flies.

The young Torosaurus was dying. It was bewildered by pain, shock and blood loss.

Something had taken a devastatingly large bite out of it.

"Oh the poor thing," Abby murmured softly.

Cutter started to study their surroundings intently.

"Okay, now we've got another problem," he said quietly. "That bite looks pretty fresh. Whatever did it could be close by. We may have walked right into the middle of a hunt. The predator's driven the calf away from its family group so it can pick it off. It might be waiting for it to die from the injury. It might be watching us right now."

Abby halted and slowly began to scan the trees, the undergrowth and the sheets of mist nearby.

"Okay," she said stiffly, "that's not a happy thought."

"Let's back off," Cutter whispered. He looked at Vols. "Be back, eh? We go back?"

Vols nodded eagerly.

They began to back away. The calf uttered another painful, lowing groan.

This time it was answered. But the reply was a booming roar that started as a bestial bellow and ended as a shriek, like tortured metal. The sound echoed around the misty glade.

Six tons of adult Torosaurus, nearly nine metres long, entered the glade on the far side. It paced forward through the bracken and ground cover, chuffing and snorting like a steam engine. Its horns were huge, and it lowered them in a bowing display that made the vast frill of its crest rise up like the banner of a medieval warlord. The adult's crest was streaked with red, black and yellow bands that trickled like slow moving water, and the eye-like dots on the lobes of its frill were almost white with fury.

Cutter reached out gently and touched Abby's sleeve.

"Don't make any sudden movements," he whispered.

"Wasn't going to," she whispered back.

Koshkin and Umarov ran up with the soldiers. All of them were brandishing weapons. They faced the massive adult and began to shout at it to drive it off. Koshkin and one of the troopers rattled a few rounds of gunfire into the air. It bellowed back at them, swinging its titanic skull from side to side.

"Don't get in front of it!" Cutter cried, moving forwards. "Koshkin! For God's sake, don't get between it and the calf! Don't get between the adult and its young!"

But the damage had been done.

The adult Torosaurus found itself cut off from its offspring by small but noisy and aggressive creatures. It was already excessively agitated. It could hear the calf lowing. Its instinct for parental protection snapped in, reinforced by panic.

All six tons of it came for them.

"Move!" Cutter yelled.

A fully mature Torosaurus was never likely to break any speed records, but it bore down — huge and inexorable — like an eighteen-wheeler that had lost control and gone into a skid. The horns were thrust forward like the tines of a container-port forklift. The florid crest rose above them like a cliff. The earth wobbled as each cantering footfall landed.

It bellowed again, mingling roar with shriek.

Cutter grabbed Abby's hand and began to run, pulling her out of the line of the charge. She didn't hesitate. Light on her feet, she accelerated and began to pull him instead. His boots slithered among the ferns and loose stones. Vols followed them.

The other two troopers ran as well. One slipped over and got back on his feet with almost comical speed.

Koshkin and Umarov faced the Torosaurus down. Cutter really wasn't sure if the FSB specialists were very brave or exceptionally stupid. It was possible that they were displaying selfless courage by attempting to protect the group. It was equally possible that they had been trained to such a pitch of fearless self-confidence that it simply didn't occur to them that some risks might be immune to uncompromising nerve and Izhmash-built firepower.

Koshkin blatted away with his AK. Umarov pumped rounds out of his double-action 'Viking' combat pistol. Sprays of blood misted the air around the head and crest of the onrushing creature. The membrane of the spectacular display popped and tore on the right-hand lobe like the skin of a burst drum.

The Torosaurus did not halt. An awful, slo-mo moment of recognition arrived as the two men understood they had lost the game of Mesozoic chicken. Koshkin threw himself over in a headlong dive, like a goalkeeper going for a loose ball. Umarov hurled himself the other way, but he wasn't fast enough. The Torosaurus's right-hand brow horn, a spear two metres long, caught him and, a second later, so did the thick point of its cheek frill. Umarov flew into the air, slack-limbed and spinning, as if he'd been mown down by a car.

Cutter winced as he heard the unmistakable crack of bone behind him. He looked back in time to see Umarov landing on the leaf-litter of the forest floor.

He and Abby had run away from the parked vehicles and into the treeline, but the soldiers had run for the questionable safety of the convoy, and the Torosaurus was wheeling across the glade after them to press its attack on any creatures that might be threatening its calf. Suvova, Medyevin, Yushenko and the adjutant Zvegin scattered.

With his headphones, and his concentration focused on the ADD, Connor remained oblivious.

"Connor! Connor!" Abby yelled. She and Cutter began to

run back towards the 4x4s, following in the trampled wake of the giant Torosaurus.

Vols came after them, shouting, "Be stop! Be stop!"

The Torosaurus was almost galloping. Its head went down like a bull's. Its frill had coloured to fury-white, pink and patches of loam brown, like the spread wings of a gigantic moth. The seismic impact of its approach shook the ground, and the vibration was transmitted up through the tyres and shocks of the stationary 4x4s.

His ears were full of warbling white noise and static, but Connor felt the vehicle quiver. He looked up, slipped the headphones down around his neck and flinched as he suddenly heard the thunder of hooves, the bellowing, and the desperate warning shouts.

He saw the nightmare horns and crest of the Torosaurus coming straight for him.

His eyes grew very wide.

NINETEEN

Abby screamed Connor's name.

Connor half-rose in the back of the 4x4 as if trying to decide what to do for the best. The look on his face made it clear how limited the options were. It also protested how astonishingly unfair it was to suddenly find oneself about to be ploughed down by a locomotive in animal form.

He seemed to tense, as if preparing to jump clear, but hesitated too long.

The Torosaurus rammed the lead 4x4 side-on. There was a sound like an anvil being dropped into a skip. The side of the vehicle folded up. Connor disappeared. One of the Torosaurus's brow horns punched through the passenger side seat like a lance. The other ripped through, collapsing the windscreen assembly, and hooked through the spokes of the plastic steering wheel, which shattered with a bang as the Torosaurus began to worry its head and apply shearing forces.

Abby screamed again, and Cutter grabbed hold of her to stop her from running to the abused vehicle. He held her tightly until she turned away, sobbing into his chest.

The creature drove against the 4x4, shoving it sideways across the soil and undergrowth. The vehicle shuddered. Metal groaned as it deformed. One of the front wheels buckled on its axle head as it was driven sidelong into the ground. It folded up under the vehicle, and the tyre blew with a sound like a gunshot. Earth and scrub began to build up ahead of the 4x4 as it was shovelled sideways.

Then the Torosaurus finally engaged its nose horn under the rim of the bodywork. It snapped its gigantic head up, using its immensely powerful neck muscles, and the vehicle flipped.

It flipped with such force that it went over and over four times, crunching and disintegrating as it rolled. Bodywork splintered. A wheel, part of the exhaust, a jerry can and the shattered windscreen assembly all flew off, along with pieces of broken glass and debris fragments. The Torosaurus came away with the shredded passenger seat still skewered onto the horn that had impaled it.

The 4x4 landed upside down in some bracken. The Torosaurus gored it again, scraping it even further across the soil before flipping it for a second time. Pieces of it flew off. Cutter could smell petrol gushing out of the ruptured tank and fuel line. The creature shook its head fiercely, and the stabbed seat sailed off its horn and into the trees.

Cutter released the weeping Abby and began shouting at the creature and clapping his hands, trying to attract its attention and get it to leave the 4x4 alone.

Shaking her head as though to pull herself together, Abby joined in. Vols ran up beside them and fired a burst from his AK-74 at the Torosaurus. The shots whacked ugly, red dents and punctures into its back and tail. Koshkin, back on his feet, opened fire too.

"Stop — don't kill it!" Cutter shouted, but if they could hear him over the din, the soldiers were ignoring him.

The Torosaurus bellowed and swung around. Blood streamed from the body wounds the Russian guns had inflicted upon it.

It dropped its horns and began to canter back towards the men who were hurting it. Vols and Koshkin kept firing. The Torosaurus let out a dreadful warbling roar and ran wide, head back, driven off by the pain. It crashed into the treeline, uprooting several small trees, and plunged away into the mist. They could hear its enraged and injured bellowing long after it had vanished.

Zvegin and Suvova ran to Umarov's side.

He's not going to get back up, Cutter thought, but the old soldier was sturdier than he suspected.

"Leg and arm broken, I think," Suvova shouted, "but he's alive!"

Cutter and Abby were too busy looking for Connor to pay much attention. The lead 4x4 was a chillingly comprehensive wreck. Cutter realised that many of the bits of debris littering the area around the upturned chassis had been part of Connor's ADD.

"Here! Here!" Abby yelled. Cutter ran over to her, followed by Vols and Medyevin.

Connor was lying on his back in a patch of ferns. He was pale, and perfectly still, and his eyes were closed, but there didn't appear to be any messy, horn-shaped holes in him.

"Connor? Connor!"

His eyes fluttered open and he looked up into Abby's desperately anxious, tear-stained face.

"Morning," he gasped.

"Are you all right?"

"What happened?"

"A dirty great Triceratops ran you over!" Abby exclaimed.

"Torosaurus," Cutter corrected automatically, kneeling at her side. He caught himself. "Not that that matters at all just now."

"Did it miss me?" Connor asked weakly.

"I think you must have been thrown clear," Cutter said, "but the jeep's a write-off."

"Is be good?" Vols asked in concern.

Abby looked up at him.

"He's okay. I think he's okay."

"Can you sit up?" Cutter asked.

Very slowly, with help from Abby and Cutter, Connor sat up. He was still ashen and drawn.

"Little bit of shock, maybe," Cutter said. "He'll be okay. Let's keep him warm and get him back."

"Ow," Connor murmured.

"What?" asked Abby.

"My hand hurts," he said, his voice very small. "I think I was lying on it funny."

He held his hand up. His wrist was quite clearly broken.

Connor stared at his bent limb and fainted.

"Let's get him onto a vehicle," Cutter said. "Mind his arm."

Yushenko and Zvegin were already trying to make Umarov comfortable in one of the surviving 4x4s. As he helped carry Connor towards the other one, Cutter took a last look around the glade. In all the drama, the wounded calf had disappeared.

After he had deposited Connor gently inside the car, Cutter jogged over to where the calf had been standing. Koshkin followed him.

"What are you looking for?" he asked.

"It can't have gone far," Cutter said. "Maybe it followed its parent's cries."

There was blood on the ground where the calf had been standing, and spots of blood on some nearby ferns and grass. Cutter followed the trail a little way into the mist. He saw a smear of blood on a tree bole, and some more spots on a stone.

He halted.

A few metres further on, under some birch trees, the ground looked as if someone had emptied a bath tub full of blood onto it. The ground was soaked, and a vast quantity of it had pooled in a deep, muddy slick. The smell was intense, like an abattoir. Blood had splashed up nearby trees and drenched surrounding foliage. The spatter radius was considerable.

"I don't understand," Koshkin said.

"While we were occupied with the adult," Cutter explained, "something else was busy with the calf. It was right here, Koshkin, and we didn't notice."

He pointed. Whatever had taken the calf had left a single, clear footprint in the mire created by the excess blood. The track had three main toes and there were the impressions of significant claws on each of the toes. It looked a little bit like the imprint of a chicken's foot.

But it was well over a metre long.

TWENTY

"Nicky, how is the boy?" Professor Suvova asked.

"He'll live," Cutter replied. "Broken wrist, bruised ribs, bumps and knocks. And a little shock, of course."

"It was unfortunate," Medyevin said.

"It was a dinosaur," Cutter snapped back. "This is a high risk environment."

They were eating supper in the mess tent. It was already dark, and lamps had been hung from the rafters, casting an almost homely yellow glow. Moths were busily assaulting the mesh screens covering the windows. Some of them were breathtakingly large.

It was hot and busy in the mess tent. The air smelled of cabbage and steam and oxtail, and there was a noisy chatter of voices. Abby picked at her food, she still looked shaken up by the events of the day, but Cutter was famished. He hadn't eaten properly in what felt like days.

"The detector was destroyed," Medyevin noted, stabbing a chunk of potato with a battered, army-issue fork.

"That was a fool's errand anyway," Bulov, his fellow scientist, muttered.

"Oh, shut up, Grisha," Medyevin retorted.

"We'll build a new one tomorrow," Cutter told Koshkin.

"The boy won't be much use," Koshkin said, "not with a broken wrist."

"I'll build it," Cutter replied. "Just make sure I've got access to the basic components."

"I could help you," Medyevin offered, sipping coffee from a tin cup. "I watched Connor build the first one."

I bet you did, Cutter thought.

"How's your friend?" Abby asked Koshkin.

Koshkin looked at her across the table and frowned. "Who?"

"What's his name?" Abby said. "Umarov?"

Koshkin nodded, understanding, as if it had never occurred to him to consider the other FSB specialist a friend. There was clearly no sentiment amongst them at all.

"Smashed up," he said. "He'll get a good disability pension, I guess."

"Shouldn't you medivac him to a proper hospital?" Cutter asked.

"Umarov can wait," Koshkin said, and he shrugged dismissively. "He can go out on the next scheduled flight. I'm not laying on an extraction especially for him."

Suvova glanced at Cutter.

"Markov wouldn't sign the consent form for it. Unnecessary expenditure of the operational budget."

Cutter shook his head. He dropped his fork into his empty tin bowl and got up.

"Where are you going?" Koshkin asked.

"To see how Connor's doing," Cutter said.

"I'll go with you," Abby piped in.

They exited the tent and walked across the yard in the dark. Cutter could hear laughter and conversation from some of the dorm tents. It was crisply cold, and the sky was coruscating with stars.

"The northern lights are back." Abby pointed towards the sky.

"Yeah, I never did ask about that," Cutter said. The odd, distorting shimmer of light seemed brighter that night. It shifted above the dense blackness of the treeline like lights moving behind frosted glass.

"You can't tell me what to do," Connor protested.

"I believe that's *precisely* my role here," Natacha Antila replied. "Get back into bed."

"You have no idea," Connor responded, attempting to button his shirt, "how many scenarios there are in which I'd be keen to hear you say those words, but right now, I'm getting dressed."

"Do not disobey!" Antila exclaimed.

"Is there some kind of problem?" Cutter asked as he and Abby stepped into the medical tent. Connor was sitting on the edge of one of the ward bunks, half-dressed, with Natacha Antila standing in front of him, her arms folded defiantly. With her pose and her crisp uniform, she looked like a propaganda figure from some Soviet-era poster.

Medical was otherwise empty, except for a male orderly who was cleaning instruments at a scrub sink and Umarov, bandaged and unconscious in another cot. Connor's right hand and forearm was heavily splinted and wrapped in a field cast.

"I'm getting up," Connor said.

"He's not getting up," Antila contradicted.

"I am," Connor insisted. He looked at Cutter. "You need my help."

"He can't even do his own shirt up," Antila said.

"It's this thing." Connor waved his cast. "I feel like Hellboy. Just give me a hand with my buttons and I'll be good to go."

"You should stay in bed," Abby said.

"Don't *you* start," Connor warned her.

"The bimbo is correct," Antila said.

"Oi! Who are you calling a bimbo?" Abby demanded.

"It is word meaning 'fake blonde', yes?" Antila asked.

"No, it isn't!" Abby snapped.

"It really isn't," Connor said.

Antila shrugged.

"Then my apologies, but you are right. He should be in bed."

"Yeah," Abby told Connor. "You're suffering from shock."

"I'm not having you two ganging up on me," Connor said.

"Oh, be quiet, everyone." Cutter interrupted the bickering impatiently.

"We need to rebuild the detector," Connor said.

"We do," Cutter admitted.

"Then you need me. You can't do it. You need me to build it."

"I can't pretend I couldn't use your help," Cutter said, "but you should get some rest. We can do it in the morning."

"Come on!" Connor's voice rose in frustration. "I feel fine. It'd be therapeutic doing a bit of work. And it's hardly, like, strenuous, sitting at a bench."

"I insist he stays in medical," Antila said, "and I insist on being able to keep him under observation, at least for a day or so."

"What if…" Connor began, "what if the bench was in here?" He looked at Cutter and Antila hopefully.

"How about that?" Cutter asked the doctor. "We set him up in here. He can work, you can watch him. How about it?"

Natacha Antila pursed her lips and considered the proposal.

"Very well."

With help from Vols and some of the soldiers, Cutter and Abby spent about an hour lugging tools and components over to the medical tent and setting them up for Connor. A second field radio set was the heaviest item. Medyevin also brought Umarov's laptop over from the longhouse.

Antila looked on dubiously as her infirmary was invaded.

"He will need to rest regularly," she warned.

"Yeah, yeah," Connor told her with a brush of his left hand.

Once they were done setting up, Cutter, Abby and Medyevin sat in medical and drank coffee while Connor got down to work.

Just before midnight, the sun came out.

TWENTY-ONE

Connor had been chattering away, probing the innards of the replacement radio set with a screwdriver. Abby had been wondering when the manic energy would finally run out of him and allow him to sleep.

There was a flash of painfully bright light. For what seemed like a few seconds, it was as light as day outside.

Connor interrupted himself.

"What —" he began.

As the flash died, they felt it. The ground shook wildly. Beakers and tools tumbled off the infirmary shelves. Abby's mug bounced off the bench, spraying coffee. Medyevin almost fell off the edge of the cot where he was perched. There was a thunderclap, a sonic detonation so profound that it hurt.

Cutter was already on his feet. The roof lamps were swinging crazily from the overheads. Outside, voices rose in agitation. They could hear people shouting and whistles blowing.

"What the hell was that?" Connor asked.

Cutter rushed outside, followed by Abby, Medyevin and

Antila. Chaos had gripped the advance camp. Personnel, some of them in their long underwear, bedrolls clamped around their shoulders, were milling in the yard. Cutter heard the general's adjunct Zvegin shouting orders.

The wind hit them. It was coming out of the northwest, hard on the heels of the shockwave. It went from zero to force ten in a split second. The forest around the camp swirled and thrashed, and the tent structures buffeted and cracked like sails in a gale. Everyone covered their faces, staggered by the fury. Several guy wires snapped, cracking like whips. One of them struck a soldier and sent his body flying. Part of a tent section ripped away and took off into the sky like a camouflage magic carpet.

The riptide of wind lasted about fifteen seconds and then it dropped. The vast Siberian midnight returned to the way it had been minutes before, except that now, to the northwest, a patch of sky on the horizon was lit up.

It was the underglow of a huge fire.

Cutter headed for the longhouse. Inside, officers were shouting and arguing with one another, or demanding information and responses from radio sets that whined and wailed with electrostatic lament. Cutter saw General Markov talking agitatedly with several aides, and Koshkin trying to get a heavy-duty military walkie-talkie to work.

Cutter shouldered his way through the press, with Abby right behind.

"What just happened?" he demanded of Koshkin.

"Go back to your billet," Koshkin said, struggling with the device.

"Tell me what just happened."

Koshkin looked at them.

"There has been an incident. An explosion. You know as much as I do."

"Not really."

Koshkin shrugged.

"Something has detonated to the northwest of this position. It may have been a munitions accident."

"A munitions accident?" Cutter echoed. "Out here?"

"There are a number of armour and artillery units deployed in this region under the general's command."

"You mean tanks?" Cutter asked.

"Amongst other things," Koshkin replied. He gave up on the walkie-talkie and tossed the handset back onto a desk, grunting in frustration. "Radios are down."

"You've got tanks out here?" Cutter pressed.

"We have armour. We have air cover," Koshkin said. "How else do you think we can keep the herds contained?"

"And you think... what?" Cutter raised his hands. "That a tank just exploded?"

"It happens sometimes. A misfire can cause a catastrophic ignition of the magazine."

"That wasn't a tank exploding," Cutter stated. "God, not even a full magazine could do that."

"If it wasn't a military accident," Koshkin said, "do you really want to consider the alternative? That it was a bomb? A warhead? A strike by some enemy?"

"This is the backend of Siberia, you fool," Cutter snapped. "It's hardly a key target for any hostile power. What we just heard and felt was something else entirely."

Koshkin stared at him, eyes flashing at the insult.

"Go back to your billet, or I will have you *taken* back to your billet."

Cutter met his gaze.

"I thought I was here to help you."

"Exactly how can you help with this, Professor Cutter?"

"I'm not sure, but I know this has happened here before," Cutter said. Koshkin's face went dark.

"That is strictly classified inf —"

"It's in all the history books," Cutter interrupted irritably. "Hell, you can Google it. Tunguska. 1908. An asteroid strike flattened over 2,000 square kilometres of forest. Wait... What did you think I meant?"

"Nothing."

"Just stop it! Talk to me! Something like this has happened here *since* 1908, hasn't it? That wasn't an isolated incident!"

Abby glanced from one to the other of them in alarm. Cutter looked so fierce, and Koshkin so murderous, she wasn't sure which one of them was in more danger.

"Please just tell us," she said to Koshkin.

The Russian looked at her, and then back at Cutter.

"If what has just happened is what you say, it may be the fourth time such a thing has occurred in this region."

"Fourth?" Cutter asked, amazed. "That includes 1908?"

"Yes. Local tribesmen reported another incident in the early sixties. Much smaller. The third was just over two years ago. It's what brought us to this region in the first place. The government thought there had been some kind of nuclear accident. The blast site found was, again, much smaller than the 1908 incident. In locating it, we encountered our first erratics."

"So there could have been four?"

"The number could be higher than that," Koshkin said. "We have circumstantial evidence suggesting there may have been almost a dozen strikes in this region in the last hundred years.

The 1908 strike was by far the most destructive."

"How does that happen?" Abby asked. "How do so many meteorites all end up hitting the same place? That doesn't make any sense."

"It's a big place," Koshkin said. But he looked skeptical.

"Even so," she replied, "the statistical chances have got to be..."

"Astronomical?" Cutter suggested.

"You've got a theory, haven't you?" Abby asked him.

"Maybe," Cutter replied. He looked at Koshkin.

"We're going to look at the impact site," he said.

It wasn't a request.

TWENTY-TWO

They left the advance camp long before dawn, travelling into the north-west aboard a pair of grumbling all-terrain vehicles that lit the forest trail with their high-beam headlamps and running spots.

Before they left they packed everything they thought they might need. Used to having the resources of the ARC at his disposal, Cutter found little that would be helpful. Yushenko brought his ubiquitous video camera. Suvova was the best-equipped, he noticed with a touch of admiration. He was curious, though, when she packed what seemed to be a can of spray paint.

Cutter and Abby rode in the lead vehicle with all the members of the scientific group except Medyevin, who had stayed at the camp to help Connor. Cutter had insisted that Koshkin should allow the scientific group to accompany the expedition.

They sat together in the crew space of the lumbering ATV, lit by little green roof lights, rocking and lurching as it bounced along. Bulov sat in a corner, folded his arms, and made a show of sleeping. Koshkin travelled up front with the driver. Every ten minutes, he tried the radio. They were still getting nothing.

"So what will we find?" Abby asked. "A crater, right?"

"A big one, I should think," Yushenko said, and he nodded.

"Actually, not if it's anything like the 1908 event," Cutter countered. "This area is so remote, back then it took twenty-five years for an expedition to arrive and investigate. It was a team led by... ah, the name escapes me."

"Kulik," Bulov said without opening his eyes. "Leonid Kulik."

"That's right," Cutter said, "Leonid Kulik. He expected to find a huge crater, but there wasn't one. Just a circular patch of charred trees about fifty, sixty kilometres across."

"That's huge," Abby said.

"Yeah," Cutter agreed. "It's estimated the blast was the equivalent of 800 atomic bombs."

Abby whistled. "But no crater?"

"It was an airburst," Cutter explained. "The asteroid punched into the atmosphere and burnt up before it hit the ground."

"Why?" Abby asked.

"The object disintegrated due to the extreme stresses of atmospheric entry," Bulov said.

"You seem to know the details," Cutter observed.

"When I heard I was being posted here, I read up on the subject." Bulov opened his eyes for the first time. He looked across the crew space at them. "Tunguska is clearly a remarkable place; it always has been. Stars fall from the sky; monstrous beasts roam the dark forests. Folklore has always told these tales."

"Folklore is often a surprising indicator of hidden truths," Suvova remarked.

"Indeed it is," Cutter said, with a nod to his former professor. "That's kind of what I've been trying to say all along. There's something here that explains it all. You scoffed at the notion of a temporal anomaly, Bulov, and that's fair enough. Believe what you want. I certainly haven't ever observed an anomaly that's remained active for any longer than a few days. But maybe there *is* something here, a focus — something that's been going on for decades, or even centuries."

No one responded. Everyone was lost in their own thoughts for a moment as the ATV rumbled along.

"So how big was it?" Yushenko asked eventually.

"What?" Cutter responded.

"The asteroid. You say it destroyed... What was it?"

"It flattened 2,000 square kilometres of forest," Cutter replied. "The impact was picked up on seismometers on the other side of the planet."

"And the pressure shock," Bulov said, "travelled around the planet at least three times. There are barograph records to prove it. So much dust and gas was thrown into the atmosphere it resulted in unusually brilliant night skies across the northern hemisphere for almost a year. I seem to remember that they were famously able to play after midnight at your Lord's cricket ground in London."

Cutter nodded. "Apparently."

"So it was huge?" Yushenko said. "A huge explosion, a huge asteroid?"

"The Tunguska impactor was probably about fifty metres across," Bulov said.

"That doesn't sound so big." Yushenko sounded disappointed.

"Velocity can be as important as mass," Cutter explained. "If it was a long-period comet, it would have been travelling a great deal faster than a near-Earth asteroid. It's the difference between throwing a rock at a target or shooting a bullet at it."

"Was it like the meteor that killed off the dinosaurs?" Abby inquired. "The boundary event thing?"

"The K-T boundary event was an object that hit the planet off the Mexican coast," Bulov said. "It's known as the Chicxulub impactor. We don't know if it was a comet or a meteor, but it was similar to the Tunguska event. However, it did leave a crater."

"The principle differences," Cutter put in, "are that the Chicxulub impactor hit the sea, and was somewhat larger."

"How much larger?" Abby asked. "Seventy-five metres? A hundred?"

"Ten thousand," Bulov replied.

TWENTY-THREE

Connor woke to the sound of drumming. It took him a moment to remember where he was, and a little longer to realise the sound was being caused by rain pattering off the roof of the medical tent.

His arm throbbed, and he was far more aware of his aches and bruises than he had been the night before. Sleep had rested his mind a little, but it had allowed his body to stiffen and become sore. He sat up on his bunk, trying to get his arm to loosen.

Apart from the rain, it was quiet. One lamp was still burning. Pale daylight threaded in through the window sections. Connor got up and hobbled over to the workbench with a blanket around his shoulders. The bench surface was littered with tools and component parts.

There was still so much to do. Despite his enthusiasm the previous evening, he'd already begun to realise the scale of the task he'd set himself. Building the first ADD had been hard enough. Doing it again, with a hand that didn't work and couldn't give him anything like the degree of precise control he needed, wasn't going to be a picnic.

He sighed, and picked through some of the bits and pieces on the bench. He wondered how Abby and Cutter were doing. He wondered *what* they were doing.

Umarov's laptop lay at one end of the bench. It was plugged into one of the generator sockets to recharge. Connor stared at it for a moment, and then opened it and woke it up.

He glanced across the infirmary. Umarov, the only other person in the place, was still unconscious in his cot, sleeping a deep, dreamless sleep induced by pain-control drugs.

One-handed, Connor typed in a few commands on the keyboard to bring up the GPS programs he'd been using the night before. He stared at the screen a little more, and wondered about some of the other application logos.

"You're awake."

Connor jumped at the voice and turned. Medyevin was coming in through the tent door, rain dripping off the slicker he was wearing. Connor quickly closed the lid of the laptop.

"How are you?" Medyevin asked, wiping the rainwater off his face. He smiled cheerily. "I wanted to get started again, but I didn't want to wake you too early."

"I'm fine," he replied. "Little stiff in the old joints."

"I'm not surprised," Medyevin laughed. "I thought you were finished yesterday for sure."

"Yeah, close call, huh?"

Medyevin peered up through the tent window at the sky.

"Terrible weather, isn't it? Terrible rain."

"What?" He really didn't want to make small talk.

"The weather, it is bad." Medyevin smiled again. "I thought it was the British pastime — to talk about the weather?"

"Now that you mention it," Connor said, nodding, "it is."

"Well, this is Sibir," Medyevin chuckled. "Even in summer, which is now, can you believe it? Even in summer, the weather is not so good."

"Just glad I don't have to go out in it," Connor said. "Speaking of which, have we heard anything from the professor and Abby?"

"I don't know," Medyevin replied. "I could check."

"That'd be good," Connor said. "I'd like to know that they're both okay. And it would be useful to find out if the radio is back up and working this morning, too. We're going to need it."

Medyevin pulled up the hood of his slicker again.

"I'll go over to the longhouse and check with the radio room. I'll only be a couple of minutes. Can I get anything for you while I'm there? Some coffee?"

"Now you're talking," Connor said eagerly.

Medyevin hurried back out into the rain, head down. Connor heard his footsteps splash away across the yard.

He flipped the laptop back open, and began to work as quickly as his one hand allowed. He launched an application and then pulled down a sub-menu. He began to fiddle. Medyevin had told him, rather proudly, that Russia was outsourcing its hardware to ensure high-end quality. As a result, most of the aps were universally used standards that he was more than a little familiar with, even if some of them had been modified for military use.

"Come on," he murmured to the machine. "I don't want Cyrillic. Thank you. Okay, what are you? Oh, I know you. Yeah, you'll do."

"What do you think you're doing?" Natacha Antila asked.

Connor spun round, trying not to look guilty.

"Nothing!" he said.

"You are out of your bed," she said. "You should be in your bed. You are a most disobedient patient."

"Sorry," he said, reaching behind his back to lower the laptop's screen. Antila was wearing a tracksuit. She had come in through the medical tent's main doorway, and was busy toweling dry. She was soaked through.

"Have you been out running?" Connor asked.

"I like to start my day with a run, before calisthenics."

"Wow, that's healthy," he said.

"Were you working?" she asked.

"When?"

"Just as I came in."

"Oh, yeah, yeah, just playing around. There's so much to do."

Antila looked him up and down and her eyes narrowed.

"You look like there's something wrong," she observed.

"No, nothing." That time he was *sure* he sounded guilty.

"You're hiding something."

"Really, I'm not," he said.

"Did you get up too fast? Are you feeling any pain? You look pale."

"I guess," Connor began. "I guess maybe I am a little woozy. My arm's sore."

"That's understandable," she said. "You're trying to do too much. I'll get you some painkillers."

"That'd be great," Connor said, and he smiled.

Antila took a last look at him, and then walked into the part of the tent that served as the dispensary. Connor heard her unlock the pharms cabinet.

He flipped the laptop back open, and finished what he'd been doing as fast as he could, then he waited while the completion bar slowly loaded.

"Come on, come on…" he whispered.

"Did you speak?" Antila called from the dispensary.

"No, nothing," he replied. "Just talking to myself."

Done.

Connor quit the aps he'd been using, and closed the lid of the laptop just as Medyevin hurried back in.

"It's raining even harder now!" the scientist complained. He handed Connor a mug of coffee. "I had to hold it under my slicker to stop the rain falling in it."

"Thanks," Connor said. "Anything from the professor?"

Medyevin shook his head. "No contact. Radios have been working again since dawn, but it's patchy. Nothing reliable. We'll just have to wait."

Connor nodded. Antila came back in, greeted Medyevin, and handed Connor a paper cone with some tablets in it.

On the far side of the tent, silent and still, Umarov stared at Connor, and then closed his eyes again.

TWENTY-FOUR

As dawn came up, the pair of ATVs toiled along the forest track in the heavy rain. Thunder grumbled out across the mist-veiled forest. The cab radio began to offer snatches of voices and half-heard words.

As they approached another branch of the river, they saw monsters waiting for them. These monsters were manmade.

"He wasn't kidding about the tanks," Cutter said to Abby.

Two massive T-90 main battle tanks were halted on the scarp above the river. They were painted a forest-drab camouflage.

When the ATVs pulled over, Koshkin dismounted and ran across to the tanks to talk to the commanders. Despite the rain, everyone else got out to stretch their legs.

It was cold. Abby shivered. A breeze was stirring the stands of black trees and chasing the mist so that it billowed through the white air overhead like smoke. Every time it shook the rain-heavy branches, extra heavy loads of water showered down out of the canopy.

"Rain this heavy is unusual for the time of year," Yushenko

remarked, turning his collar up.

"I think it's an aftermath symptom," Cutter said. "The impact will have thrown a lot of ash and gas up, and also punched the local climate hard. This rainstorm could simply be a consequence of overpressure."

"The rain tastes of pumice," Professor Suvova observed, licking her fingertips.

"Rigorous method, Professor," Bulov snorted, coming up beside her. "Let's hope the rain doesn't also taste of extraterrestrial contamination."

"Contamination?" Abby asked. She shot Cutter a worried look.

"You've seen too many Hollywood movies, Grisha," Suvova said.

"Not at all," Bulov insisted.

"Come on," Yushenko said. "One of the government's other pet theories is that the erratics in this zone hatched out of eggs brought to Earth by the 1908 meteorite."

"That these are alien dinosaurs?" Abby asked sarcastically.

"Could be!" Yushenko acknowledged with a mocking shrug of his long, thin arms. "No more unlikely than the idea that they were made for NATO by Steven Spielberg. If it isn't the damned capitalists, it's aliens."

"I'm serious," Bulov objected, looking wounded. "Radiation. Viruses. Xenobacteria. These are all legitimate concerns."

"Are they?" Abby asked Cutter.

"No," he replied firmly. He was lying. Radiation hadn't even occurred to him. "We could run some checks though, to keep Doctor Bulov happy. Do you have a geiger counter among your equipment?"

"Yes," Yushenko said. "I'll get it." He hauled his gangly body back inside the ATV.

The soldiers riding aboard the other vehicle had also dismounted for a break. A couple of them were smoking. The smell was especially pungent in the cold, pure forest air. Abby saw that one of the troopers was Yuri Torosyan, the good-looking rogue she'd met on the first day.

"Hey, no smoking!" Suvova called across at the soldiers genially.

"Oh, but Professor," Torosyan answered, speaking English because he knew he had an audience, "the general's edict doesn't extend all the way out here, surely?"

"It's bad for your health," Cutter called back.

"Oh, but just one cigarette," Torosyan replied.

"It depends what smells it," Cutter told him.

Torosyan laughed and carried on smoking. He smiled and waved.

"Hello, Abby!" he called. "Remember me? I am Yuri. Such a nasty day, eh? Be better to be indoors, somewhere warm, eh? What do you say?"

She smiled and waved back.

"In your dreams," she called cheerily.

"You okay?" Cutter asked her quietly.

"Yeah," she said. She could handle the wolfish come-ons of Yuri Torosyan, but she was beginning to wish Vols had been assigned to the expedition. Having him around had started to feel reassuring.

"What did you mean when you said it depends what smells it?" she asked, warily.

Cutter shrugged.

"I think Baba Yaga is a big predator, a Carnosaur. The Carnosaurs of this era developed an amazingly acute sense of smell. They hunted by it, more than they used sight or sound.

Something that smells as strong as those cigarettes will carry a mighty long way in this environment."

"We haven't seen it, though," Abby said. "I mean, we both know what you're talking about. You won't even say the name."

Cutter grinned self-consciously. He wiped raindrops off the end of his nose.

"Tyrannosaurus. There I said it," he countered. "But you're right, it feels like tempting fate just uttering the word."

"We haven't even seen a glimpse," Abby pointed out. "I thought they were supposed to be big and heavy and stompy?"

"Hollywood movies again," he said. "We're learning here. Baba Yaga seems to be a real ambush predator. Quiet, methodical, patient. It stays hidden; it stalks. It makes perfect sense. You think about other apex predators — the tiger, for example, or the polar bear, or the Great White. Their greatest weapons, ultimately, are cunning and surprise. Baba Yaga could be looking right at us as we speak, choosing her moment."

Abby looked apprehensively at the black, dank forest.

"Thanks for that," she said.

Yushenko had re-emerged from the ATV, and was testing the geiger counter he'd located. Once he was sure it was in working order, he handed it to Bulov.

"Here you go," he said. "If it puts your mind at rest."

Abby watched the two men.

"Is radiation really an issue?" she asked Cutter. He shook his head.

"Not here, yet, but we should keep checking as we approach the impact site. It could become a problem."

Yushenko had also fetched the video camera, and he began filming again.

"Get that thing out of my face," Bulov snapped at him.

There was a sudden, loud, sputtering roar. It made Abby jump and even took Cutter off-guard. The tanks had started their engines. Their exhausts throbbed and rattled. Koshkin hurried back over to the ATVs.

"The impact site has been located," he said. "It's about eight kilometres north of here."

"You've got people on the ground?" Cutter asked.

"No," Koshkin said. As if on cue, there was another new, loud noise. The threatening shape of a helicopter gunship chattered overhead, heading south. It was low enough for them to see the gleam of daylight off its canopy and the sinister bulk of its chin turret.

"Air cover spotted it," Koshkin continued. "There's quite a large area of disruption, and the impact seems to have spooked some panic movement in the herds of erratics. So we will advance from here with an escort."

"The tanks?" Cutter asked.

The Russian nodded.

"Let's hope we don't need them," he said.

TWENTY-FIVE

Nick Cutter was saying something to her, but Jenny couldn't quite hear him. Then she realised that she couldn't hear him because he wasn't actually there.

She sat up and looked around. It was true. He really wasn't there.

No one was.

Her office was empty, and she could see through the half-open door into the empty hallway outside. Apart from the sigh of air-con and the soft murmur of electronics, the ARC was entirely quiet.

Jenny got up. It was the second time since Cutter and the others had vanished that she'd slept on the couch in her office instead of going home, and she knew it was a bad idea. Anyone responsible for public relations knew better than to sleep in their clothes. She didn't have anything fresh to wear, and she needed to wake herself up with a shower, and a proper cup of coffee from her expensive espresso maker, instead of a cup of instant-caffeine-headache from the vending machine in the mess.

She looked at her watch. It was just before five in the morning.

She could go home, spend an hour or two getting her head together, and then come back in for the start of the day.

She picked up her handbag and shoes and walked out into the hall, wandered in her stocking feet down the midline of the ARC complex. Most of the offices and labs were dark, or lurked in gloom with their lights dimmed. Little coloured LEDs twinkled out of the twilight. The main hallway lighting was on, stark and white and hard, like a hospital. She heard trays and boxes thumping around in the mess as the first-shift staff unloaded produce from the delivery truck and got ready for breakfast.

The air-con hissed like a distant sea. Apart from her, walking along with her shoes in her hand, the only movement was the gentle twitch of the paper strips that dangled in front of the ventilation ducts.

She headed towards the main control chamber, intending to check with the night-shift staff who were manning the ADD watch stations, but as she passed Cutter's laboratory, she hesitated.

The door was open. Jenny stepped inside and switched on the lights. It seemed no one had disturbed anything. It was as if Cutter had just stepped out for a moment. The benches were cluttered with papers covered in sketches of his theoretical models, graphs and notes.

Cutter had tried to explain the purpose of the graphs several times. It wasn't that she couldn't follow what he was saying — it was more like he wasn't sure of the theories he was pioneering.

His most recent idea dominated one wall. Various pieces of graph paper were stuck together haphazardly. It showed — with the help of little annotated labels made out of scraps of paper and pieces of Post-it notes — the pathway of the anomalies they had tracked and recorded so far. It was a map of creation, a map of time as much as of space. It was a map of a secret universe that brushed against the one she lived in, and hid in the shadows cast by her daylight. She ran a fingertip along one curved, annotated line. According to the labels at either end, its twisted path linked the Middle Permian to a July afternoon in 2007.

She wondered where on the map Cutter was.

"Jenny?"

She jumped.

"You scared me!"

"I'm sorry," Hemple said. He was standing in the lab doorway. "I was up at the security station, and I saw the lights come on down here. I didn't know you were still in the building."

Jenny breathed deeply.

"No harm done," she said with a smile. She looked at Hemple. "Nothing still, I take it?"

He shook his head.

She walked over to the door.

"I'm heading home for a few hours," she told him. He held the door open for her, and stood aside as she came out of the lab and paused to switch the lights off.

Then she switched them back on again.

"What's the matter?" he asked.

Jenny went back into the lab. As she'd turned off the lights, she'd seen something in the dark. Something that hadn't been there when she'd entered the lab five minutes before.

"Jenny?"

The monitor of Cutter's main PC had woken up. The drifting screen saver of William Stout drawings had gone, and the screen had become Cutter's desktop. A small, bright icon was rotating in the centre of the screen. Jenny bent down over the PC, and fished the mouse out from under a pile of notebooks and baled wire.

You've got mail.

She double-clicked the icon. Hemple was right beside her.

The message box opened on-screen. It contained a string of numerals and two words.

"That's a set of GPS coordinates," Hemple said immediately.

"Are you sure?" she asked. She looked at him and saw the expression on his face. "Sorry. Of course you're sure."

"Cutter sent this," Hemple said.

"You're saying that because…?"

"Because we change code names regularly and randomly," Hemple said, "but I know he knows this one."

She looked at the message box. The two words were *Bone Idol*.

TWENTY-SIX

"So he's communicated?" Lester asked. Despite the early hour, and the fact that he'd been rushed to the ARC by an urgent call, he seemed very alert.

"We think it's probably Connor, actually," Jenny said. "He's the e-whiz."

"Is that a real word?" Lester asked her. "Because if it is, I might have to write to *The Times* decrying the deterioration of the English language. Again."

They were striding side by side across the main chamber of the ARC. The morning staff had come on early, and there was a steady bustle of activity. Bright columns of data flickered across the huge main screens. Jenny led her boss down the bright access corridor into one of the briefing rooms that looked out onto the main chamber through a thick window plate.

"The message has come via a tortuous route," she explained. "We're still trying to unpick it. It was a very non-standard means of getting a message out. It was concealed, and then attached to something that wasn't meant to be used as a mail carrier." She shrugged. "Basically, it's quite ingenious."

Lester crossed his arms and looked at her.

"And you'd need to be somebody like Connor Temple to manage it?"

"Exactly," she acknowledged.

Technicians were clustered around a monitor in the briefing room. The message box was on display. Lester uncrossed his arms and peered at it.

"Bone Idol?"

Jenny smiled.

"It's alpha team's code name for Cutter."

Lester thought about that.

"Do we all have code names?" he asked.

"We do," Jenny confirmed.

"Do I have a code name?"

"Yes," Hemple said, striding into the briefing room and joining them at the monitor. He was dressed in full alpha team kit, and an automatic pistol was buckled at his hip. "We've locked up the GPS coordinates."

"Show me," Lester commanded. Hemple shooed the technicians aside and called up a new screen on the monitor.

"Oh my God," Jenny murmured. "If we know where they are, we can go and get them."

"Don't get too excited," Hemple said. The screen image was a satellite map, overlaid with indicator graphics.

Lester turned his head to one side, studying the map.

"I give up. Where is it?"

"It's a tributary of the Podkamennaya or Lower Stony Tunguska River in the Krasnoyarsk Krai," Hemple replied.

"Really?" Lester raised an eyebrow. "Isn't that near Leatherhead?"

"It's Siberia," Hemple informed him.

Lester looked at Jenny.

"Oh *that* Podkamennaya Tunguska."

"Siberia?" Jenny repeated, shock making her voice squeak slightly. Hemple nodded.

"Well, that's rather spoiled everything, hasn't it?" Lester said. "Inserting anybody into the Russian Federation is going to be pretty well impossible, let alone an armed retrieval team. The Russians are oddly sensitive about things like that."

"Rules can always be bent," Jenny said, struggling to recover herself. "The Foreign Office could —"

"Please try to live in the real world," Lester interrupted impatiently. "This is a whole new ball game. The Foreign Office is not going to authorise — even clandestinely — what would amount to a military invasion of Russian Federal territory, and the Russians would hardly tolerate it even if the FO did authorise it. And even if those two gigantic and insurmountable problems weren't enough," he continued, "this is one of the most remote and inhospitable locations on the planet."

"Then it should be done covertly," Jenny said. She wasn't going to let it go.

"I'm sorry," Hemple said. "It's just not doable. The only practical way to insert would be by air, and even if we found a friendly airfield to fly out of, we'd be up in Russian airspace for hours before we were on the fix."

"You can fly really low, under the radar," Jenny insisted. "I know. I've seen it in films."

"It doesn't quite work like that, not on this scale," Hemple responded gently, "and not over these kinds of distances. With this kind of operational range, there would be refuelling issues and —"

"Are you saying that after all this," Jenny said, "we know exactly where they are, and we can't go and get them?"

"I'm afraid," Lester said, "that's precisely what we're saying."

TWENTY-SEVEN

The rain grew heavier, as if it were coming down under pressure. They crossed the branch of the river, meltwater from the mountains frothing around the high-axled wheels of the vehicles, and rolled north.

The T-90 battle tanks led the way, rumbling seismically. The throaty judder of their exhausts echoed off the weird acoustics of the tree trunks around them.

The terrain climbed a little, and then flattened out. The heavy rain seemed to be thickening the mist. Once or twice they glimpsed the helicopter gunship passing overhead, chopping the air with its huge rotors, appearing and then disappearing through gaps in the tree canopy.

After about an hour, the tree cover began to thin rapidly, and they drove out of the forest and into a markedly different landscape. The ground was covered in loose stone, like a beach of grey pebbles. A shallow tributary of the Tunguska, just a babbling stream, ran through the stone bed, mostly invisible as it splashed between and beneath the stones. On one side, imposing stands of spruce and larch picketed the broad stone bank. On the other, promontories of rock rose in jagged, sharp cliffs to form the walls of a gorge above the tributary. This natural cleft looked to be about a quarter of a kilometre wide.

The ATVs followed the tanks out across the stone bed. The wheels and tracks began to rattle and clatter loudly, and loose pebbles spat up like bullets, ricocheting off mudguards and sponsons. In the lead ATV, Cutter and Abby could hear stones banging off the vehicle's underside and clattering into the wheel arches.

Overhead, the cloud cover blew like chalk dust, and the sky desperately tried to be pale blue.

Cutter heard Koshkin let out a curse, and the ATV came to a halt. He moved up to the driving position.

"What is it?" he asked, but he could immediately see.

A herd of Torosaurs was moving down the watercourse towards them. There were dozens of them, ranging in size from juvenile calves to colossal mature adults.

"You don't want them to stampede," Cutter advised Koshkin.

"I'm well aware of that," Koshkin snapped.

"I'm serious," Cutter persisted.

"We've got two main battle tanks to protect us," Koshkin pointed out.

"Leaving aside the fact that I don't want you killing any of these creatures," Cutter continued, "we really do not want them to break. The tank crews will be fine. They're riding inside armoured hulls. But we're in lightweight ATVs. You saw for yourself what one of those did to a 4x4."

The herd had sensed the vehicles ahead of them, and came to a stop about thirty metres away across the stone bed. They evidently didn't like the smell, or the engine noise, or simply the sight of the four heavy machines. Patterns of lowing and snorting started up, and they could hear them even through the ATV's plated hull.

The bull Torosaurs had formed a defiant line at the vanguard of the herd, and were beginning to display, swinging their huge crests and horns from side to side. Their frills flushed pink, and dark, and threatening dots appeared in the middle of their crest lobes.

"We're going to have to back up," Cutter said.

"I'm not backing up," Koshkin stated.

Yushenko moved to open the side door.

"I want to get some footage," he said.

"No!" Bulov, Suvova and Abby all chorused.

"Stay inside," Cutter said firmly. He looked at Koshkin. "Let's not all be idiots. Get us rolling back slowly."

Koshkin looked doubtful.

"Too late," Abby said. She pointed through the windscreen. The herd had started to move again. "Presumably, they've given us a sniff and they think we're safe enough," she added.

"Okay, don't move now," Cutter said. "Just let them go by."

Koshkin lifted the radio hand set to rap out an order. The first of the big bulls was drawing closer, head down, puffing throaty sounds out of its gullet. It passed to the right of the lead ATV, moving between it and one of the T-90s. Almost immediately, an even larger creature went by on their left. It blocked out the sun for a moment. They could hear stones crunching under the creatures' feet.

"Steady, steady..." Cutter murmured.

There was a bang. It was sudden, and very loud, and came as a complete surprise. For a moment, no one knew what had happened. Then the situation deteriorated very quickly indeed.

One of the tanks had fired its main gun into the herd. The

shell had killed two creatures instantly, but the main effect of the noise and flash was to spur the already tense creatures into a panic.

"*The idiots!*" Cutter spat, swearing.

The Torosaurs began moving as fast as they could to get past the machines and out of the gorge. The mature bulls bolted. Cows and calves began to squeal and grunt in distress. The ground began to shake.

"Hold on!" Cutter yelled.

The herd poured past them, a river of horns and plate. Crest frills and shoulders barged and thumped against the sides of the ATV, rocking it hard. Dents appeared in the skin of the hull. Suvova cried out as a slit window beside her shattered, but the horn withdrew without becoming lodged. Huge creatures sideswiped the vehicle as they went past, trying to get between the tanks and the ATVs.

The tip of a horn suddenly punched through the side of the hull, and cut a half-metre long tear in the metal before vanishing. The entire ATV jerked backwards as a bull adult butted the front fender with his nose horn in an effort to clear a path.

Another creature hit the left-hand side of the ATV so hard that Yushenko was thrown off his feet. He bounced off one of the body struts, and cried out as he cut the back of his hand trying to protect the camcorder.

"Stay down!" Abby hissed at him. "You can't fall off the floor!"

Another horn tip stabbed through the side door. It twisted as it tried to disengage, and buckled the sliding door off its runner mechanism. The rubber seam around the door socket ruptured, and thousands of small, lubed ball bearings showered out of the seal.

Ignoring Abby's advice, Yushenko tried to get up, but his feet shot out from under him as he stood on the scattered bearings.

"Stay down!" Bulov shouted. "Listen to the girl!"

Like Abby, Bulov and Suvova, Cutter was hanging on to a handrail strap. To his disbelief, he saw and heard the T-90 to their left fire into the herd again. The huge report rolled around the gorge like a thunderclap. Gunsmoke coiled off the massive tank like steam. Two more creatures barrelled into the ATV in terror.

"You've got to stop them from doing that!" Cutter yelled. "They're going to get us killed!"

Koshkin was already bellowing into his handset.

"Nicky!" Suvova screamed.

Cutter looked up. A big female was coming right for them. Her crest was up, white with panic, and she was running virtually blind, her horns lowered to clear the way. It was going to be a head-on collision.

Cutter grabbed Koshkin and tried to haul him out of his seat. Beside them, the ATV driver uttered a cry of terror and began to bail, too.

But there wasn't time.

The creature hit them.

TWENTY-EIGHT

The impact was square on. Despite their handholds, everybody was knocked off their feet. The ATV was thrown backwards three or four metres, and the front end buckled.

As the creature's massive nose horn crushed the vehicle's bull-bars and fender, the two huge brow horns plunged through the windscreen as neatly as if they'd been aimed, one each side of the central window pillar. The windscreen sections both perished in sprays of safety glass rubble, and the lethal horns kept going. One punched through the back of the driver's seat, the other through the co-driver's.

Koshkin was no longer sitting in the co-driver's seat. Cutter had removed him, bodily, dragging the bigger man out of the way milli-seconds before the spear of bone and keratin impaled the spot where he had just been sitting. Cutter hauled Koshkin so hard that the man ended up on his back on the floor of the ATV with the radio mic — its lead snapped — still in his hand.

The other horn missed the driver. In desperation, he had simply cowered wildly, and the tip had just missed his right shoulder before skewering the seat and snapping off the headrest.

The driver looked up, let out a nervous laugh of relief and then threw open his door and leapt out.

"Don't!" Cutter yelled.

They saw the driver land on the shingle outside, rise and then vanish as a sub-adult male ran him down and carried him away on his horns. The passing force slammed the driver's door shut, though it immediately swung open again, too deformed by the impact to fit in its frame any more.

The ATV shuddered as the female shook her head, and then the horns withdrew like blades out of a pair of stab wounds. There was another violent, glancing jolt, and then she was off on her way.

"Is that the last of them?" Yushenko asked.

It wasn't. Another impact jarred them as one last stray creature ploughed past. The ATV was turned through ninety degrees and left rocking on its springs.

The stampede had cleared them.

They clambered out into the open air. Both of the ATVs were badly battered and dented, but Koshkin's driver had been the only casualty. There was no sign of his body.

Abby tried to help Yushenko with the cut on the back of his hand.

"It's nothing, it's all right," he told her, though the wound had bled enough to soak the cuff of his jacket. He'd covered the gash with a piece of gaffer tape.

"It needs to be cleaned," she said.

"When we get back," Yushenko replied, "Antila can do it." He hoisted the camcorder and began to film the damage inflicted to both ATVs. A nose horn had burst one of the thick tyres on the second vehicle, and the troops had dismounted to switch in the spare that was carried on the tailgate.

"Look at this," Yushenko called. A metre-long section of Torosaurus brow-horn was sticking out of one of the T-90's track guards. It had wedged there in a passing impact and snapped off. Cutter didn't feel much like approaching the tank to examine it.

He could see up ahead on the stone bed the exploded carcasses of the creatures killed by the tank rounds.

They started moving again once the troops had changed the second ATV's wheel. They advanced up the river gorge for about four kilometres. Despite being badly pummeled, both ATVs were serviceable, though Cutter had misgivings about the one they were riding in. Since the clash with the herd, its engine sound included a bad, persistent rattle, and it had become prone to misfires.

From the long stone bed of the tributary, they advanced into sparse forest glades where the fog still clung on despite the hour. Grey lichens caked the bark of the silent trees like mould, and skeletal spider ferns seemed to claw at the sheen of airborne moisture. Thin sunlight stabbed down through the canopy in rungs of yellow that appeared just a little brighter than the white mist, as if the light were watered down.

It didn't last long, and soon the rain began to fall again.

"Over there," Abby called out.

Through the smashed screen of the ATV, they could see a pair of duck-billed Hadrosaurs about half a kilometre away through the forest. They were smaller than the mature Hadrosaurs they had seen previously, though it was possible they were juveniles.

It was too far away for a clear identification. The Hadrosaurs seemed agitated, circling oddly through the stand of trees before finally breaking and bounding away through the trees as the vehicles drew near.

Koshkin was driving the lead ATV, and all the passengers had huddled up in slickers and coats. With the windscreen smashed, the cold air and the rain blitzed in, and the vehicle's heaters were useless.

A few minutes after Abby had spotted the first duck-bills, they saw more of them. Another pair crossed their path, running fast, and then a trio went by through the trees, two mature adults curiously following a sub-adult. Every few minutes, a brass-band honk or snort echoed through the glades.

"The needle just rose," Bulov said suddenly from the back.

"What?" Koshkin demanded.

Bulov was studying the geiger counter. It was clicking quietly, like a wood-boring beetle.

"It's just a trace, nothing close to a concerning level, but the needle is lifting now," he said.

"I'm not turning back," Koshkin announced.

"No one's asking you to," Suvova said.

"We're going to have to think about what we do soon," Cutter put in. "It's going to be dark in a few hours."

"I'm not spending the night out here," Bulov said flatly.

Then they came upon the dead.

TWENTY-NINE

Cutter jumped down out of the ATV and walked ahead through the glade. Apart from the occasional and now quite distant honk of the Hadrosaurs, it was very quiet. He could hear insects in the leaf mould, flies buzzing, the knock and pop of woodpeckers, and the patter of rain through the leaves.

He could smell death.

"How did this happen?" Abby whispered at his side.

From where they were standing, in front of the halted vehicles, they could count almost forty corpses, all Hadrosaurs. The bodies were scattered over a wide area through the forest, some half hidden in tangles of undergrowth. Cutter and Abby walked towards the nearest one, a sub-adult curled on its side with one hind limb raised and crooked, eyes staring, and a pallid blue tongue bulging from its bill.

Beards of black flies were busy around it, seething in the pale light.

"There's not a mark on it," Abby said.

Yushenko had come after them, the camcorder whirring.

Behind them, Koshkin, Bulov and Suvova had spread out to look, along with soldiers from the second ATV. The tanks killed their engines and waited under the trees.

"I thought it was another display of Russian firepower at first," Cutter said, "but you're right. There are no wounds, no signs of damage."

They moved to look at the next creature, and then another. There was a sour smell of ferment from their barrel stomachs. Flies covered their snouts and bellies like anthracite dust.

"I think it was the impact," Cutter said at last. "I've seen this sort of thing before. Flocks of sheep, herds of cattle, all found dead. A close lightning strike will do it. It's shock."

Abby looked surprised.

"So the impact did this?" she asked.

Cutter nodded.

"The noise. The light-flash. The whole force of it. Herbivores are often quite timid creatures, and it doesn't take much to upset them."

"The meteor really accomplished this?" Yushenko asked, aiming the camcorder at Cutter.

"I can't be certain, but I think so." Cutter reached forward impatiently to push away the camcorder. "Point that thing somewhere else," he snapped. Then he added. "It would also explain the bewildered behaviour exhibited by the other Hadrosaurs we've seen in the forest."

"Couldn't there be other explanations for the deaths?" Bulov asked.

"Like what?" Cutter turned to look at his fellow scientist.

Bulov paused, as though reluctant to say his next words.

"Radiation poisoning?"

Cutter shook his head.

"Is your counter picking up anything more than it was just now?"

"No," Bulov admitted.

"Trace levels wouldn't do this. Even if the levels were moderately harmful, radiation would take weeks or months to kill creatures this big. Look at the attitude of the bodies. These creatures died suddenly. They fell where they were standing. There was no staggering or limping, no sign of a progressive ailment before collapse. It was like the flick of a switch. Alive, then dead."

Bulov didn't seem convinced.

"What if it's something else?" he persisted. He gestured with the geiger counter. "Something we can't measure?"

"Your xenobacteria, eh, Grisha?" Yushenko asked.

"Shut up," Bulov replied.

"I really don't think so," Cutter said. "Again, it would take time. It wouldn't leave a mortality site like this."

Koshkin suddenly raised the AK he was carrying to his shoulder.

"What is it?" Suvova asked.

He tilted his head to indicate.

"Something moving," he said.

"Don't shoot it," Cutter said urgently, raising his hand. He edged forwards.

Scavengers were at work on the dead Hadrosaurs. Grunting, snuffling Didelphodons and other small, whiskery mammals were feeding on the carcasses, and so were some small, darting modern birds.

Then Abby spotted something else.

Three delicate, slender bipedal dinosaurs, each one no taller than a man's waist, were picking meat from the corpse of a large adult Hadrosaur. The creatures were sinuous, with powerful hind legs, long, whip-like tails and narrow skulls. They were well equipped with cutting teeth and claws. At first, Abby thought them alarmingly similar to the Raptors she'd encountered inside an anomaly on a gruelling trip to an island off the coast of Ireland, but these were less fearsome. Their large, golden eyes were alert, and faced somewhat forward, fringed by bushy eyebrows of feathery fronds.

They clacked and whistled at the approaching humans, darting back, tails lashing, heads cocked, staring with fiercely intelligent gazes, unwilling to abandon their meal.

"Troodons," Cutter whispered to Abby. "Oh, they're amazing. Look at the eyes."

The eyes were following them keenly. The Troodons chirred and piped, lowering their necks to look inquisitively at Yushenko and his purring camera.

"Are they Troodons?" Suvova asked, stealing up beside them. "Nicky, are they Troodons?"

Cutter nodded. "Look how smart they are. They're watching us as much as we're watching them."

The Troodons continued to snap and warble, warily skirting the human audience, taking morsels of food from the dead Hadrosaur as often as they dared. Their very deliberate gaze seemed to want to engage in a way that Abby had seldom seen except in primates.

"Just think what they might have become," Suvova sighed.

"What do you mean?" Abby asked.

"If it hadn't been for the extinction event, who knows where evolution might have taken them," Cutter explained.

One of the Troodons suddenly yapped loudly, like a monkey. It raised its head and stared off into the denser undergrowth.

Its two companions stopped feeding and did the same. All three noses turned in exactly the same direction. All three sets of eyes stared, unblinking. All three creatures froze, as attentive and indicative as pointing gundogs.

Then they were gone. At some subtle signal too small for human senses to detect, the three Troodons took off in a pack, and sprinted away through the trees, their thin tails high and waving.

"What made them start?" Yushenko asked, lowering his camcorder.

Cutter waited, staring into the trees.

"I don't know, but there's a lot of meat here if anything was hungry."

"Baba Yaga?" Abby suggested with a cheery smile that took some effort.

Cutter shrugged, still watching the treeline.

"Let's put it this way: the Troodons are smart. If they didn't want to stay around here, they'd have a good reason."

"Here! This way!"

Koshkin had gone on ahead. They could see him through the trees thirty or forty metres away. He was calling back to them.

"What's he found?" Suvova muttered.

He called again, and waved at them to join him.

"Koshkin! Stay close!" Cutter yelled back. The Russian turned, waved again and pressed on through the forest, moving further away.

"We should stay together," Abby said anxiously.

"Koshkin's armed," Yushenko replied.

"Koshkin's a fool," Suvova said in an undertone.

With the soldiers lagging after them, Cutter, Abby and the members of the science group scrambled through the forest to catch up with the vanishing FSB specialist. Though the rain was still dismal and the light poor, it seemed somehow to be getting brighter.

They clambered a little further and saw why.

"Oh my God," Abby said in surprise.

A great deal more of the wan Siberian sunlight was reaching the ground because the tree cover was gone. Ahead of them, a broad swathe of the ancient forest had been demolished. Hundreds of trees had been felled, and the canopy had been torn down.

Yushenko muttered a curse as he was forced to stop and load a fresh memory card into his camcorder.

Koshkin was picking his way out into the ravaged, open space. Heat and pressure had reduced the ground and pulverised the plant life. Splintered tree trunks lay everywhere, most of them blackened and smouldering. A fug of steam and slow wood-smoke hung over the landscape, filtering slowly up into the frail sunlight.

Cutter surveyed the scene. A circle of scorched and ruined destruction had been planted in the woodland, as if seared by a branding iron a kilometre in diameter. The intact trees of the forest ringed the scorched circle like mourners.

Koshkin had found the impact site.

THIRTY

As she walked out to her car at the end of a particularly long day, Jenny was aware that her briefcase felt depressingly heavy.

It was late afternoon, drearily overcast, and the ARC building behind her resembled an alien mothership that had settled gently on the English landscape.

She wondered how much longer she'd stay working there. She'd spent most of the day arguing heatedly with Lester — more heatedly than she'd ever dared before — and in the end, the arguments had stopped because she'd realised he was, in fact, being reasonable, no matter how unreasonable he sounded.

Cutter, Abby and Connor were gone. The ARC operation was entirely powerless to find them or rescue them. The best anyone could hope for was that quiet but steady pressure could be applied to the Russians through diplomatic back-channels, in an effort to get them to admit they had Cutter and the others, and then release them.

Lester didn't hold out much hope. Even if it was ultimately successful, the process might take months or years, but the chances were that the Russians would *never* acknowledge what they had done. There were, Lester had explained, too many secrets involved.

In the meantime, the work had to continue. ARC missions had effectively been suspended when Cutter disappeared, and Lester had been told that the entire project would be shut down — mothballed — unless operational activity resumed. His superiors considered it a strategic flaw that so much depended on so few key personnel.

"We need to get moving by the end of the week," Lester had told her, "or our program will be cancelled and responsibility handed to the Ministry of Defence. I'm sorry, Jenny. I'm quite aware that there is a significant personal component to this problem. The three of them were close colleagues, and it seems callous to just give up on them, but we must get our act together. I'm hoping you can cast a professional eye over these."

These were personnel dossiers, a stack of manilla folders that contained the intelligence briefs and résumés of several dozen individuals vetted by the government. Every single one of them had the potential to make a valuable addition to the ARC's multi-disciplinary team. They were replacements for Abby, Connor and even Cutter.

She'd stuffed the clutch of dossiers in her briefcase, adding considerably to its weight, and told Lester she'd be going home for the rest of the day to review them. On her way out, she wondered if she *would* review them, if she could even bring herself to open any of them. She suspected she might spend most of the evening preparing her letter of resignation.

She also suspected that if she resigned, she'd never, ever find another job that was quite so marvellous.

She unlocked her car, threw the heavy briefcase onto the

passenger seat and got in. She sat for a moment staring at the ARC building. Maybe she could learn to be as pragmatic as Lester. Maybe she'd feel different about things in the morning.

She put the key in the ignition.

"Where's Nick?"

Jenny froze. The voice had come from behind her. There was somebody in the back seat, somebody who'd been lying in wait for her like an ambush predator. She could smell a soft, primitive fragrance, a mix of fresh air and volcanic dust and wildflowers.

"Where's Nick?" the voice asked again.

She looked in the rear-view mirror. The dark eyes of Helen Cutter stared back at her.

Jenny paused a moment and collected herself. She felt trapped.

"I don't —" she began to reply.

"Don't waste my time," Helen said quickly. "I need to speak to Nick. I've been waiting for an opportunity. But there's been no sign of him. Where is he?"

"You're asking the wrong person," Jenny answered.

Helen breathed a perfunctory, exasperated sigh.

"Okay, fine. I'll find him myself." Jenny heard her move to open the rear door.

"Why did you come to me?" she asked.

"What?" Helen paused.

"Why me? Oh, wait a minute, is it because your usual line of communication isn't there any more?"

Jenny turned in her seat and looked back at Helen. The expression on the face of Nick Cutter's estranged wife was unreadable. She couldn't tell if Helen was angry or sad.

"If you mean Stephen —" Helen began.

"I do mean Stephen," Jenny acknowledged.

"Don't you dare taunt me. I didn't want Stephen to die." She hesitated for a moment. "You know nothing about it. You know nothing about our relationship, and —"

"I don't think Nick knew much about your relationship, either," Jenny said. She didn't care what reaction her words might provoke. Helen Cutter's eyes had grown so hard, it seemed possible that she would attack her.

"I need to speak to Nick," Helen said. "It's very important, to everyone, all our futures."

She reached again for the door handle.

"He's missing," Jenny said.

"He's what?"

"He's missing. He's gone. He's not here."

Helen stared at her. There was a fragment of shock in her face that made her seem surprisingly vulnerable for a second.

"Missing? You mean lost? Lost through an anomaly?"

"I wish it was that simple," Jenny said.

"*Tell* me what happened!" Helen demanded.

"As far as I know," Jenny said, "he's been kidnapped by a foreign power."

Helen blinked.

"He's been what? *What*? That's ridiculous. You're lying."

"Why did you want to speak to him?"

"You're lying!" Helen spat, and then she froze suddenly, and looked around sharply.

"I know what you're doing. Very clever."

"What am I doing?" Jenny asked curiously.

"Keeping me busy. Keeping me talking. Sorry, but it won't work." She threw open the rear door and scrambled out.

"Funnily enough, it will," Jake Hemple said. He was standing beside the car, aiming a nine-millimetre automatic in a double-handed grip. Helen came to a halt, and sagged slightly in resignation, a sneer appearing on her face.

Jenny got out of the car.

"And funnily enough," she said, "it was the truth, too."

THIRTY-ONE

"Thanks," Jenny said.

Hemple smiled. "No problem."

He was unloading the clip from the pistol, and returning both to a gun locker in Prep.

"Ever since Cutter and the others got snatched, I've been trying to raise my game," he admitted. "I can't keep letting ARC staffers get pounced on by strangers. It really doesn't do my rep as a protection officer much good."

Hemple slammed the locker shut and looked at her.

"I saw you leaving on the monitors. I saw you in the car park heading for your car. Then I realised you'd been sitting in your car for quite some time, so I cranked up the magnification. Bingo."

"Well, thank you anyway," Jenny said. "What do we do with her?"

"We find out what she knows," Lester said, appearing beside them.

***

"What did you want to talk to him about?" Hemple asked her.

"Whatever I like," Helen replied, toying with a plastic cup and staring at the middle of the table. "He's my husband, after all. I have the right."

"You said it was important," Jenny put in, "for all of us."

Helen arched her eyebrows and said nothing.

Lester pursed his lips and sat back in his seat. He smoothed his silk tie, stared up at the ceiling of the ARC's interview room, and then brushed an imaginary crumb off the polished top of the table around which they were seated.

"Well, I can't stay and chat like this all day," he said. He pushed his chair back. "If she's got nothing interesting to contribute, I suggest we get her carted off to somewhere secure, where she won't be our concern any more."

He looked down the table at Helen, who held his stare with a steady, perhaps even *superior* gaze.

"We don't even need charges for you, you know? The Official Secrets and National Security Acts alone give us enough scope to hold you without charge or process for an unimaginably long time. Until, for example, you decide to be useful."

Lester paused.

"And I have a feeling," he added, standing up, "you know better than most people what an unimaginably long time feels like."

Helen raised her eyebrows again, and remained silent.

Lester turned towards the door.

"Okay," he said, "I've tried. I've played good cop, bad cop, and best cop in a supporting character role. I've got things to do. Get her off the property."

"Who kidnapped him?" Helen demanded steadily, her voice echoing around the interview room.

Lester turned back and looked at her.

"Why should you care?"

"Because I don't believe you," she snapped. "When *she* —" Helen aimed the words at Jenny. "— said he was missing, I presumed he'd come to a sticky end in some primeval era. Very sad, but only to be expected. But... kidnapping. It's like Yuri Gagarin dying in a plane crash."

"Or Al Capone getting done for tax fraud," Lester said.

Helen smiled wryly.

"Who kidnapped him?"

Lester leaned on the back of the chair he had vacated.

"At first, we suspected a malicious ex-wife," he replied.

Helen kept smiling and gave no reaction.

Lester sat down at the table again.

"The Russians," he stated.

"Russians?" Helen repeated. "Interesting."

"Russian agents, we're fairly sure," Lester said, in an off-hand way.

Helen's smile slipped slightly, her eyes calculating.

"Why?"

"We're guessing they've got the same problem we have," Jenny said.

"*Why did you want to talk to him?*" Hemple demanded more fiercely this time.

Helen glanced at the alpha team leader, unruffled by his tone.

"There were certain things I wanted to discuss with Nick. Certain concerns."

"It must have been important," Hemple echoed.

Helen just ignored him.

"Do you know where they've taken him?" she asked Lester.

"Yes," he said.

"You know where they're holding him?"

"We've got a pretty tight fix."

"Can you get him back?"

"No," Lester said. "They've taken him overseas. The location is far, far too remote for us to have any access whatsoever."

"But you know where?"

"Yes."

"Where?"

"I'm not just going to tell you —" Lester began.

"Do *you* know where?" Jenny interjected.

Helen looked at her.

"Do you know where?" Jenny repeated. "You suspect, don't you? What do you know? Where do you *think* he is?" Helen seemed to hesitate for a moment, as if marshalling her thoughts, as if what she was contemplating saying was vastly consequential.

"Are the Russians detaining him," she asked at last, "at a place called Tunguska?"

"She knew!" Lester said. He was pacing.

"Of course she knew," Jenny countered.

"I mean," he went on, "at first, she didn't know. She thought he'd be here, but when she found out that he wasn't, she knew where he must be. I mean, spot on."

There seemed to be a growing danger that Lester's office wasn't going to be large enough to accommodate the sort of agitated pacing he had in mind.

"It rather nicely confirms our theory that the kidnapping is anomaly related," Jenny observed. "That's the only way she could have known."

"Yes, yes," Lester agreed.

"She's scared of something," Jenny went on.

"She should be scared of *me*," Lester said.

"With respect, I think it's something else."

Abruptly he stopped pacing and faced her.

"Something's up, isn't it?" he said. "I mean, the Russians, and now... *her*. This is not business as usual, is it?"

"It doesn't feel like it."

"Suggestions?"

"I think we need to give her something."

"Such as? Truth serum? A hard slap?"

Jenny shook her head.

"No, I didn't mean that. But I'm convinced she knows a great deal more than she's letting on. She'd trust Nick with it, but lord knows she's got no reason to trust us. So we have to give her something. We have to make some kind of concession and meet her halfway in the hope that she'll give us something back."

"Could we not just tie her to a chair and aim a spotlight in her eyes?"

"I don't think that's allowed any more," Jenny replied with a smile, as if the thought appealed. "And I don't think it would work anyway. Helen Cutter is a real piece of work. She's harder than steel. She's harder than you or me and I think she'd give Hemple a run for his money. She's lived wild and alone for longer than we can imagine in some of the most dangerous and inhospitable eras in Earth's history. Tough questions and a lamp in the eyes isn't really going to cut it."

"You make her sound like Tarzan," Lester said.

"I think she makes Tarzan look refined and civilised," Jenny responded.

"So what are you suggesting?" he asked.

"We have to make a concession. We have to give her something that matters to her."

"Like what?"

"Freedom," Jenny stated. "I think that's the only thing she's interested in."

"And how do we do that? Open the cell door? Let her out? She'll vanish, and that won't really get us anything, will it?"

"No."

"No, I didn't think so. So what do we do?"

"I don't know," Jenny said. Lester resumed his urgent pacing.

Hemple tapped on the glass door and entered the office. The bustle and hum of the main control chamber followed him in through the door before he closed it.

"What is it?" Lester demanded, still pacing.

"I've talked to her a little more," Hemple said. "She's a tough one, all right."

"And?"

"She wants to make us an offer."

Lester frowned.

"What kind of offer?"

"If we let her go," Hemple said, "she'll take us straight to Cutter."

THIRTY-TWO

There were no birds singing, not even in the nearest trees that had survived the impact. A haze of ash and smoke overwhelmed the mist and lay in a broad slant across the burned circle that had been, until the middle of the previous night, dense Siberian forest.

The site was at least a kilometre across and seemed almost perfectly circular. Abby followed Cutter out into the smouldering emptiness of the circle's heart. She could feel heat radiating from the burned stumps and charred, shattered tree trunks around her. It was even throbbing up out of the ground.

Around the circumference of the huge impact zone, hundreds of blackened tree trunks were laid out lengthways along the line of the blast, arranged like petals around a flowerhead in a pattern that looked deliberate and artificial. The fringes of the standing forest around the site were seared and caked with white dust. Some of the trees around the rim were perfectly intact on the sides that faced away from the impact site, and stripped bare to the heart on the blastward side.

As Cutter had predicted, there was no crater.

"It's huge," Yushenko said in disbelief, clambering across the still-burning debris and filming as he went.

"It is," Cutter agreed, "but nowhere near as big as the 1908 event. A fiftieth of the size. Less than that, perhaps."

"Still no more than base-level radiation," Bulov reported. "It's elevated, but not greatly." He adjusted the geiger counter and then coughed.

The smoke and ash was getting in their throats.

A wind was picking up. The rain increased in intensity again. They could hear it sizzling as it fell on still-glowing logs. And it was becoming more difficult to see.

"The light's going early today," Koshkin observed.

"We're not going to get back to the advance camp tonight, are we?" Abby asked.

Koshkin shrugged, as if it didn't matter.

"I suggest you get your men to set up a secure camp around the vehicles in the trees," Cutter said.

"I know what to do," Koshkin replied tersely.

"After dark, this area isn't going to be especially safe," Cutter said. Then he peered around. "Not that it's especially safe now," he added.

"I agree with what Bulov said," Yushenko called from about twenty metres away. "I'd really rather not spend the night out here." He was moving around the edge of the impact site to make a visual record of the damage sustained by the standing trees.

"I don't think we get a say in it," Suvova said quietly, staring at Koshkin.

"As usual," Bulov muttered. Koshkin ignored the scientists and strode away to instruct the soldiers.

"So?" Abby said to Cutter.

"So?" he replied.

"This is what you were expecting, isn't it?"

"Yeah," Cutter admitted. "It's like standing in the middle of one of the old photographs Kulik's team took of the 1908 impact. They didn't get to it while it was so fresh, though."

"Lucky us," Abby said. "What are we learning, then?"

"I don't know," Cutter answered frankly. "You ever try to figure out a puzzle where you had plenty of clues, and they linked up too well?"

"What do you mean 'too well'?" she asked, a confused look on her face.

"Too obvious. Too *crashingly* obvious."

"Didn't Sherlock Holmes have some kind of rule about the obvious answer being the... um... obvious one?"

Cutter grinned and shook his head.

"It's just the way it adds up. Tunguska. Impacts. The K-T boundary event. Late Cretaceous dinosaurs. Every time I put those elements together, I get an answer that scares me."

"Go on," Abby prompted.

He sighed and continued.

"Somewhere here there's got to be an anomaly or anomalies that open into the very, very end of the Cretaceous. We know that for a fact, simply by the nature of the creatures we're encountering. They're all Late Cretaceous. They're all examples of the very last types of dinosaur that ever existed. And the end of their existence was caused by just about the biggest impact event in the history of Earth as a living planet."

"And it's happening here," Abby said. "It's happening at a place that's famous for impact events."

"Notorious," Cutter agreed. "The Tunguska strike is special.

It's the biggest one in recorded history. I don't know how they can be connected. One massive impact sixty-five million years ago, another a century back, and another last night. I don't know how they can be connected.

"But, Abby, I also don't know how they can't."

It was getting darker more quickly, now. Koshkin reappeared in the impact circle with several soldiers in tow, and ordered the scientific team back to the ATVs.

"I want to get on the radio," Cutter said to him. "I want to know if Connor's had any luck rebuilding the ADD. We could use it up here."

Koshkin nodded.

"Where's Yushenko?" Abby asked.

"He's over at the rim," Suvova replied. "He's still filming."

"No," Abby said. "He was there five minutes ago. He's not there now."

They all looked around. There was no sign of the gangly botanist. Bulov and Suvova began to trudge back towards the place they'd last seen him, calling his name.

"If that idiot's wandered off into the forest…" Koshkin said.

"He hasn't," Abby replied, glaring at the FSB specialist, "because he's *not* an idiot."

Koshkin didn't acknowledge that she'd spoken.

"Find him!" he ordered three of the soldiers. "He's probably found some kind of fern or moss that's taken his interest. But we can't afford to have him go missing."

Bulov cried out.

He'd reached the edge of the impact zone, the spot where they'd all last seen Yushenko. He was holding something up for them to see.

It was the camcorder. He'd found it on the ground, still running, its strap broken.

Aside from the device, there was no evidence that Yushenko had ever been there.

THIRTY-THREE

"Either being run over by a Torosaurus has made me forget how to build one of these things," Connor grumbled irritably, "or there's something funny going on."

"Still no luck?" Medyevin asked.

Connor sat back from the bench, put down his screwdriver, and eased his throbbing arm.

"There's something up," he said. "The signals are totally nuts. I suppose it could be the atmospherics."

"Could be," Medyevin agreed. He glanced up at one of the windows of the medical shack. Rain was beating heavily off the canvas roof, and the yard of the camp outside was swathed in grim mist. Much of the time it was pouring straight down, but occasional gusts of wind threw it sideways and shook the tents. The weather had been rolling in all day, and the advent of night seemed to signal an out-and-out storm.

"The radios have been playing up since whatever it was happened last night," he continued. "And one of the patrols this afternoon reported seeing lightning, uhm, clinging like rook's nests in the tops of some trees."

"Ball lightning?" Connor asked.

"Like that — what is it called? — St. Elbow's fire."

"Elmo," Connor corrected.

"Sorry," Medyevin said.

"I like elbow better," Connor said, and he smiled.

"What is wrong with your elbow?" Antila asked, wandering in from the triage room with blood on her latex gloves.

"Nothing," Connor said.

"I should know of any new symptoms you are experiencing," she insisted.

"We were talking about something else entirely."

Antila sniffed, her expression doubtful, and started to look for a fresh packet of swabs. That afternoon, three soldiers out on patrol had been hurt when their 4x4 had rolled, trying to swerve around a Hadrosaur that had appeared out of the rain in front of them. She was patching them up in triage, and they were complaining loudly as she stitched their lacerations. One of them kept calling for a drink to soothe his pain.

"Speaking of the radio," Connor said, peering into the exposed innards of his half-built ADD, "anything from Abby and the professor?"

Medyevin shook his head.

"They should be back by now," Connor said uneasily.

"They will not be back tonight," Antila assured him. "Not now. It is too dark. They must have made camp."

"That's not good," Connor said.

"It is what it is," Antila replied, and she went back into the triage area.

"I think maybe it's time for some more coffee, and maybe a plate of supper," Medyevin suggested. "What do you think?"

"Sounds good," Connor agreed, nodding. "This might work better on a full stomach. See if you can get me some of that stew with the pieces of sausage in it."

"That wasn't sausage," Medyevin replied.

"Yeah, well, don't spoil it."

Medyevin grinned and got to his feet. "I'll be back in five minutes," he said, and he dashed out into the rain.

Connor waited for a moment, and then scooted his chair over to the end of the bench where the laptop sat.

He opened it, and got to work. Though he didn't expect much, he was keen to discover if there had been any response to his efforts of that morning. He was also hoping to send another message, maybe even set up some kind of mailbox that would keep sending the same message automatically.

He'd been working steadily for a few minutes when he glanced up and found Umarov staring right at him.

Connor jumped.

"Jeez!" he exclaimed. "I didn't know you were awake…"

Lying on his cot, Umarov continued to stare at him. His face was drawn with pain, and he was as motionless as he had been when he was unconscious, but there was a fierce light in his eyes.

"I'm not doing anything!" Connor cried. "Honestly! Nothing at all! Nada! Nothing! *Zip!* Stop staring at me like that!"

Umarov didn't even seem to blink.

"I was just playing," Connor admitted. "I was just playing with it. Okay, I was fooling around, and I may or may not have considered sending a message, but you can't blame me for that, can you? I mean, you would, in my position, wouldn't you?"

Slowly, Umarov nodded.

"Exactly," Connor said. "Who wouldn't? I tell you what: we'll just forget it, shall we? You and me? No harm, no foul? I'll leave it alone. I won't touch it again. Look, I'm shutting it down, right? I'm closing it?"

Connor quit the aps and closed the laptop.

"See? All good? No harm done. You and me — tight. Okay?"

Umarov stared at him a little longer, and then settled his head back on his pillow, closed his eyes, and appeared to drift away out of consciousness again.

Rubbing his sore arm, Connor sat back in his chair and exhaled loudly.

Too close. Way, way too close.

He tried to slow his racing pulse. Medyevin would be back any moment. He didn't want to look guilty.

But I guess it's too late for that, he mused. *I've been busted.*

The shack door squeaked open on its hinges. Connor looked up, expecting the palaeontologist.

A man had come in out of the rain. He wasn't particularly tall, but he gave the impression of being astonishingly fit. He had a wide, boxer's nose and his hair was so fair, his eyebrows were virtually invisible, as if he'd had it all shaved off.

He was wearing a set of black BDUs.

"Evening," Connor said warily.

The man wiped raindrops off his face, and walked over to the bench where Connor was working.

"We haven't met," Connor said. "I'm Connor."

"You think we don't network our computers?" the man asked in heavily accented — but precise — English.

"Sorry?" Connor responded, hardly breathing. "What are you talking about?"

"You think we don't network?" the man repeated. "You think we don't monitor user activity?"

Connor realised it was a good time to shut up.

"Koshkin said it was a mistake to let any of you have access to communication equipment. The radios. The laptop. He was right to be concerned, wasn't he?"

"You're KGB, aren't you?" Connor asked in spite of himself.

"It's FSB," the man corrected. "Federal Security."

"They said there were three of you here."

"I was out in the zone, supervising the patrols," the man said, "while Koshkin and Umarov ran things here. Then I heard Umarov had been hurt, so I came back in. Just in time, it seems."

"Have you got a name?" Connor asked.

"Shvachko," Antila said from the doorway. She glared across the room at the FSB specialist.

"Your presence here is not required, medical officer," Shvachko told her. "Go and get on with your work."

"The infirmary is *my* command area," Antila replied. "This man is my patient. I will not have you harassing my patients."

"Go away now, Natacha," Shvachko said.

Antila stared at him for a moment, as if weighing her options. Reluctantly, she withdrew back into the triage area.

Shvachko turned to look at Connor.

"You think we're idiots, don't you?"

"I didn't say anything," Connor replied. "And I don't think anything of the sort."

"Yes you do, it's written on your face. The primitive Ruskies, with their funny fur hats and their borscht and their Volga boatman's song. You think we're backward idiots. No sophistication, no modern technology..."

"Really," Connor said, "you're imagining stuff that's not in my head at all." He was beginning to sweat. There was something terribly menacing about the specialist, a quality not even the brutish Koshkin possessed. Connor had never felt so threatened by someone who was putting himself down.

"I can see it. I've seen it before. Your kind. It didn't occur to you that we would notice you using the system."

"Far from it," Connor replied. *Might as well come clean.* "I just thought it was worth a try. And I thought I'd done a decent job of covering my traces."

Shvachko nodded.

"Well, at least you're not insulting me by denying it. And you hid it well. You might have got away with one try. But to try again, just now? That wasn't a smart move."

Connor swallowed.

"On a scale of one to ten, how much am I going to regret it?"

Shvachko scratched behind his ear thoughtfully.

"This is a state of national emergency, and I have full and binding emergency powers. I can shoot you right there in that chair if I want, and dump your body in the woods for the wolves."

"That's not..." Connor said, very quietly. "That's not quite how I was planning to spend the rest of my day."

"There is one little factor in your favour," Shvachko told him. "We're in the middle of Sibir. The Krasnoyarsk Krai. Even if someone — your friends back home in the West, anyone — had recieved your little call for help, it wouldn't matter. No one would ever come and find you here."

"Good point," Connor agreed. There was a slight break in his voice. "Silly of me to even try. No harm done, then, eh?"

Medyevin returned to the infirmary hut. He was carrying a tray of food and drinks covered with a soaking-wet tea cloth.

"What's going on?" he asked, looking warily at Shvachko.

"We're just getting to know one another," Shvachko said.

Medyevin hesitated in the doorway, the tray in his hands.

"Bring that over and put it down," Shvachko said. "I need to make a radio check with Koshkin, and he's asked for an update on the device you're constructing."

"We're not there yet," Connor said. "There are some problems."

"What kind of problems?" Shvachko asked.

"Atmospherics, we think," Medyevin explained.

Shvachko nodded. "I'll tell him so."

"We might have something by the morning," Medyevin added.

Shvachko walked to the door. Pausing, he turned and spoke.

"I'll check in in the morning, then. Doctor?"

"Yes?" Medyevin said.

"Don't let him use the radio unless it's part of the work you're doing. Don't let him touch the laptop at all."

"Okay," Medyevin said, looking puzzled.

"I mean it, Doctor."

"Okay," Medyevin said more emphatically.

Shvachko went out into the rain and the dusk.

Connor breathed out.

"Why did you tell him we'd have something by the morning?" he asked Medyevin. "He'll kill us when we don't."

"Because he scares me," Medyevin said. "It's all I could think to say. He... that man. You think Koshkin's bad. Shvachko is a *real* psycho."

THIRTY-FOUR

"I don't understand how he could just vanish," Abby said. "We were all there. We were *right* there. How could we not notice he was gone until he was gone?"

Cutter shook his head. Yushenko's disappearance had really upset her.

"Try not to think about it," he said, putting his arm around her.

"Something took him, didn't it?" she asked.

He nodded.

"So why didn't we see it? It must have been big. It must have been *right there.*"

"We didn't see it because it was fast," Cutter said.

Night had fallen, and the soldiers had rigged up canvas shelters around the ATVs, a short distance into the forest and away from the smouldering impact site. Fires and lamps had been lit, and moths were whirling in out of the darkness and the drizzle. The T-90s were monstrous silhouettes in the dark beyond the limits of the firelight. A slow wind was creaking the trees around the site.

Abby could smell food cooking over the camp stove. She could hear the huddles of soldiers chatting, laughing and complaining.

"But why *him*?" Abby persisted. "Why not any of us?"

"Yushenko cut his hand during the stampede, remember," Suvova explained, bringing them cups of coffee from the stove.

"He was bleeding. It could smell him," Abby finished in a small voice.

"It could smell all of us, but Yushenko was the most appealing. Or he had the strongest odour," Suvova added.

"I don't think it was just that," Cutter said. "He was away from the group. He was close to the trees. It was an opportunity."

He was about to say something else when Koshkin approached.

"I've been on to advance," he said. "Your boy is still working on the detector. It's not finished. He is complaining about atmospherics, apparently." His expression in the dim glow of the lamps said that he wasn't convinced.

"Are you still having problems with the radios?" Cutter responded.

"Yes. On and off," Koshkin replied. "It's been a little worse since nightfall, actually."

"Then it's atmospherics, almost certainly," Cutter told him. "Connor doesn't lie."

Behind them, Bulov let out a cry of surprise and horror. They all turned to look at him, and the huddles of soldiers fell silent. Bulov looked up at Suvova. For all that he and Yushenko had liked to bicker, they had clearly been close friends, and Yushenko's disappearance had shaken him.

"Grisha?" Suvova asked. "What's the matter?"

Bulov held Yushenko's camcorder out to her with trembling hands.

"I was just playing back the footage he took," he said.

Professor Suvova realised what she was being offered. She hesitated, reluctant to accept it. Cutter took the camera out of Bulov's hand. He adjusted the flip-out screen and pressed rewind for a moment. Then he selected play.

The flip-out screen cast a luminous glow like a magic lantern into Cutter's cupped hands as the footage began to play. He watched jerky, handheld tracks of the impact site as they had seen it that afternoon. The view panned across to show him, Suvova, and then Bulov in the smouldering circle. Then Abby was on-screen for a moment, throwing a little wave and a grin.

A shot of the overcast sky.

A shot of the smoke rising.

A wide-angle shot of the trees. Then Koshkin, talking to Suvova. Then Abby and Cutter, from a much greater distance.

The camera work wasn't great. The autofocus slid in and out as the image moved around. There were snatches of voices on the soundtrack, pieces of conversation from Cutter, Suvova and Koshkin that the built-in mic had picked up. Most of it was filled with the rustle of Yushenko's waterproofs and the sound of his own breathing, magnified.

Every little while, Cutter heard Yushenko's voice, captioning the record in Russian.

"What's he saying?" he asked Suvova, who was standing next to him, peering nervously at the screen.

"He's saying... 'this is the impact site'. Now he says, 'observe the aspect of the fallen trees'." Suvova paused. "Now he just said, 'this is film of the edge of the impact area'."

Cutter kept watching. The view on the flip-out screen, still wobbly, moved away from the main group, who by that time were just figures in the middle distance. The viewfinder tracked across the trees at the limit of the crater burn: tree trunks, still standing, scorched and burned, tangles of slumped foliage, charred and coated with ashes.

The camera moved steadily to the left, then suddenly began to pan back the way it had come. On the soundtrack, Yushenko could be heard saying something.

"What was that?" Cutter asked.

Suvova shrugged.

"I don't know what he said. It was too fast."

In an instant the view on the screen scrambled. There was a burst of unintelligible sound that overwhelmed the mic for an instant, a flash of sky, jumbled motion, a jarring impact. Then there was just a resolutely steady view, looking sidelong across the ground in close-up, flecks of dirt and ash on the lens.

Nothing more.

"What did you see?" Abby asked.

"Nothing," Cutter replied. "Something hit him, and he dropped the camera."

"No, you're not looking properly," Bulov insisted. "You're not seeing. He didn't see it either, not right away. That's why he went back."

Cutter peered at him for a moment, then pressed rewind. The screen images raced backwards. The camera's POV leapt up out of the dirt and started to track backwards along the treeline.

"There," Bulov said, leaning in past Cutter's shoulder. "There."

Cutter ran and re-ran the brief sequence at half-speed, and then at an almost dead crawl. The viewfinder tracked again across the trees at the limit of the burn: tree trunks, still standing, scorched and burned...

Except they weren't all tree trunks.

Cutter tried to freeze the image, but it was so blurry and quick.

What appeared to be two larch trees, close together, scorched and half-peeled to a pale, patchy lime-and-grey pattern, weren't trees.

They were legs.

They were the rear-jointed legs of something large, something bipedal, something so big its head and body were out of the frame above Yushenko's head. They were the legs of a Carnosaur, a hyperpredator, standing just outside the ring of destruction.

Silent, still, waiting.

He could just make out the edge of one of the feet, what appeared to be three toes, like a chicken's foot, yet massively, insanely enlarged.

"Can I see it?" Abby asked.

"There's not much to see," Cutter said.

"Let me see," she insisted. "I'd rather see it. Imagining what you're looking at is worse."

He pressed freeze-frame and handed the camcorder over to her.

She looked at the image. Then she looked up, and her eyes were wide.

"So that's Baba Yaga, is it?"

When the storm broke, it took them completely by surprise. Past midnight, the rain had eased to almost nothing, and the wind had stilled. In the spaces between the tops of the tall trees around the camp, it was possible to see patches of stars in an ice-cold, crystal-clear Siberian night sky.

A titanic peal of thunder woke them. Lightning flashed so brightly every other second, it looked as though the campsite and the ATVs had been lit by strobing searchlights. There was no delay between flash and boom. The storm had appeared right over them.

There was panic and confusion, most of it born out of the fact that they had been shocked awake. A strong wind drove through the forest, shaking the trees and swirling up leaf litter, but there was no rain.

"Are you all right?" Cutter shouted at Abby.

"Yeah!" she yelled back. "But what *is* this?"

There was a tingle in the air. Everything was charged. Cutter could smell ozone. The metal wires used to hold the shelters were live with static. He could see blue snakes of electricity twitching around the UHF aerial on top of the second ATV.

There was an explosion. Sixty metres from the camp perimeter, lightning had struck a fir tree. The top third of the tree came ripping down in an incandescent shower of sparks.

As fast and as violently as it had begun, the freak storm ceased. There was a breathless moment of total stillness, and then the rain began to sheet down with renewed fury as if the thunder had shaken loose the entire contents of the clouds.

The rain was so heavy, it made Abby and Cutter laugh at each other. Soldiers scrambled around them, trying to secure shelter lines that had been freed by the wind.

Then something else came out of the trees.

THIRTY-FIVE

There were several shouts of alarm. For a brief but terrifying moment, Abby thought that Baba Yaga had paid them a visit, but it wasn't a Carnosaur. A massive quadruped loomed out of the rain and ploughed through the centre of the camp area.

Soldiers scattered.

The creature was eight or nine metres long, and must have weighed in excess of five tons. It had a small, wedge-shaped head fringed with pyramidal cheek horns, and a wide, thickset body with a domed back that was armour-plated with enormous scutes of bone.

It was an Ankylosaurus.

In the hard, local light of the camp, it appeared to be black and white. Its eyes were bovine and lugubrious, and its plant-cropping beak of a mouth kept opening to unleash braying, rattling barks of alarm.

"Get clear of it!" Cutter shouted. Abby backed away. Floundering in the darkness, a couple of soldiers fell over in the rain-slick mud.

Since Yushenko's disappearance, Bulov had been carrying a powerful CO2 pistol that he'd taken from the ATV's locker. Abby saw him struggling to load it with one of the darts he was carrying in a small shoulder bag. His fingers were slipping in the streaming rain.

"Don't shoot it!" Abby yelled, trying to steer Bulov clear of the creature. "Just get out of its way!" She wasn't sure whether he had heard her or not.

The Ankylosaurus lumbered straight through the camp area, dragging down the awnings of shelters and snapping guy-wires across its huge bulk. The stove went over, and sparking hot coals tumbled out of the metal fire basket the soldiers had set up. A line parted, and two suspended lamps thumped into the mud. The Ankylosaurus brayed again. Abby could see its tail, long and powerful, held up off the ground, twitching. The mace-like ball on the end was made out of fused osteoderms, and looked heavy and lethal.

Trammelled for a moment by the trailing shelter lines, the creature became panicked. It brayed and struck out defensively. Its tail lashed like a whip, moving with an incredible speed that belied its size and weight. The tail muscles drove the bone-club into the side of the lead ATV, a significant section of the hull caved in, and the vehicle was almost knocked over.

"Wow!" Abby yelled.

"Stay away from the tail!" Cutter shouted at the Russians around them.

"Oh, no kidding!" Suvova shouted back.

Bulov finally got his CO2 pistol loaded. He aimed it at the mighty armoured dinosaur, and fired.

"No!" Abby yelped.

The dart spat out of the pistol and ricocheted off one of the creature's bone scutes. It rebounded with considerable force, and punched into the side of one of the ATVs about ten centimetres from Cutter's face.

Abby snatched the pistol out of the Russian scientist's hands.

"Give me that before you hurt someone!" she snapped.

Tearing free, the Ankylosaurus barged on, flattening a shelter and bringing down several more cables before it cleared the edge of the camp area and vanished into the blackness and the heavy rain.

"It's as if that thing came out of nowhere!" Suvova exclaimed breathlessly.

"Like the storm," Abby said to Cutter. "And like the northern lights." She pointed. "They're back."

He looked up at the sky behind the trees.

"Come on," he said.

They moved back through the forest, making their way by torchlight, heading towards the impact site. Koshkin and the soldiers followed them. Dozens of torch beams danced and swung in the driving rain.

"What are we doing?" Bulov complained. "We should stay in the safety of the camp!"

"Where's your sense of adventure?" Abby asked him.

He glared at her.

"Give me the pistol back."

"No," she said flatly.

"What are we doing, Nicky?" Suvova asked.

"There's something I need to take a look at," Cutter replied. "It can't wait until morning."

Despite the rain, the flicker of the sky lights was bright. Ghost colours formed and merged, dragging and slipping across the sky.

They had an oddly luminous effect on the rain.

"Moonbows!" Abby declared delightedly.

Cutter nodded. Radiant arcs of silvered colour glowed in the downpour. Everything seemed unnaturally lit.

They came out into the open, into the great burned circle. At night, in the rain, it smelled of cold air and damp cinders.

The sky over the circle was rippling with light and colour, forming a patch of luminous, shivering distortion that was at least three or four kilometres wide. Beyond the circle, the swirling coloured lights extended down into the Siberian forests. Like will-o'-the-wisps, they were dancing and shining out between the distant trees. Sheet lightning grumbled and murmured in the distance, around the edges of the extraordinary show.

"It's huge," Abby said, awestruck.

"It is," Cutter agreed. "It really, really is."

"Is this some kind of lightning?" Bulov asked.

"No," Cutter said. He looked at Koshkin. "Radio the advance camp. You can tell Connor we won't need that detector after all."

"Why not?" Koshkin asked.

"There's your anomaly," Cutter announced.

THIRTY-SIX

"I swear I'm talking to myself," Lester sighed. "You are absolutely, definitely, unequivocally *not* going."

"Except, I am," Jenny replied. "It's not up for debate."

"I'm not debating," Lester said. "Am I debating? Did I *sound* like I was debating? I'm in charge. I say things and they happen. I don't call for a popular vote. You're not going. I say so."

Jenny smiled and gave him a peck on the cheek.

"It's very sweet of you to be so worried about me. But I am going. Why else would I be dressed like this?"

Lester looked her up and down. Jenny was wearing a set of khaki weatherproofs, gloves and a pair of expensive hiking boots.

"Someone's got to keep an eye on her," Jenny said. "Someone with seniority. That's you or me, James. Are you going to go?"

"I wasn't planning to, no."

"Do you *want* to go?"

"Not even slightly."

"Then it's going to be me," Jenny concluded. "Either that, or you take a resignation letter from me, and I look for a job in media."

Lester shook his head.

"This is a ridiculously hazardous thing you're doing," he said.

"Well I'm not about to send Jake Hemple and his men into any situation I wouldn't go into myself," she said.

"Really?" he replied. "I thought that was why we paid them."

"You have an almost adorably medieval view of employment law, James," she said. "I'll see you when we get back. Wish me luck."

"She can't be trusted," Lester said. "You realise that?"

Jenny nodded.

"Oh, I know."

The black Land Rovers with tinted windows were ready and waiting in the ARC's underground loading dock. Garney and Redfern had just finished loading the last of the packs.

"Ready?" Hemple asked Jenny as she walked up.

"Absolutely." She sounded as if she meant it.

"Lester not coming to wave us off?" he added wryly.

"I think he's rather preoccupied with the stack of employee life assurance certificates he's got to fill out."

"You haven't got any ID on you, have you?" Hemple asked.

"No."

"Good. We can't carry any ID, just in case..."

"I understand," she replied.

"I mean, the Russians... the diplomatic scandal would..."

"It's okay. I get it — I was there when we established that rule in the first place. Anyway, we've got to reach Russia first, remember?"

Hemple grinned.

"She tells me that's the easy part."

A side door that led onto the dock opened, and Mason

entered, escorting Helen Cutter. Mason, like Hemple and the other alpha team members, was wearing black battledress and field kit. The teams' weapons had been loaded into Land Rover One in strong boxes.

"A six-man team?" Jenny asked.

"Yeah, for the insertion," Hemple said. "Mason, Redfern, Jenkins, Garney and Murdoch. Plus me, of course."

"Of course. Can't have you missing out on the chance to shoot some monsters."

"They were fighting for places, you know."

"Who were?" she asked.

"The boys. Alpha team, plus the reserves, plus beta team. They all wanted to make the cut. I had to limit it to the senior ten men, and then draw straws."

"That's devotion to the cause," Jenny said, smiling.

"Everyone wants a chance to do this," Hemple explained. "And everyone wants a chance to put this right. We're protection duty. Cutter, Abby and Connor should never have been taken. It was our watch. We want to put things right."

Mason brought Helen over to them. Her hands were secured in a set of plastic cuffs.

"Are these really necessary?" she asked.

"From what I've heard about you," Hemple said, "it's the very *least* precaution we can take. I'll cut them off you when we get in."

Helen shrugged. "It's nice to know that my reputation has preceded me."

"So where are we going?" Jenny asked.

"It's a three-step journey," Helen replied. "You'll stay close to me and you will do *exactly* as I tell you, or you'll end up in more trouble than you can imagine." She looked at Jenny. "As it is, this is very dangerous. Are you sure you should be coming?"

"Don't *you* start," Jenny cautioned. "Where are we going?" she asked again.

"The west side of the Bairstow reservoir, just off the A163," Helen replied.

"And how do you know the anomaly will be open?" Jenny demanded.

"The ADD picked it up," Hemple interrupted, quickly. "Now, let's go," he added. "No time like the present."

"Indeed not," Helen agreed, and she smiled in a way that made Jenny nervous.

They gunned along a cycle track on the west side of the reservoir. It was mid-afternoon, breezy, sunny. Some people were walking dogs and flying kites in the park on the other side of the water.

The cinder track was flanked by chainlink fencing where litter had collected. Away from the track was a wide patch of waste ground, thick with brambles and reedy saplings.

"Here," Helen said.

The ominous vehicles pulled up. There were two Land Rovers for the alpha team, and another two for the back-up detachment who were going to take watch.

The men got out and began to unload. A member of the back-up walked along the cycle path and signalled to two cyclists to find another route.

Still cuffed, Helen strode up into the waste ground with Jenny and Hemple. About a hundred metres from the cycle track, in a ditch where the undergrowth was particularly dense, they saw the unmistakable twinkle and flash of an anomaly.

"As promised," Helen said.

"Where does it go?" Hemple asked.

"The Permian," she answered, "but we won't be there long. Just long enough to make a connection."

They went back to the transports. The back-up team members had taped off the entire area and set up electric lamp stands ready for nightfall. Alpha team was ready. They ran a quick equipment check, and hoisted their packs onto their backs.

"Shall we?" Jenny suggested. She was getting impatient, though she was sure that it was just a coping strategy for her nerves.

Escorted by the members of the back-up, alpha team went back to the anomaly with Jenny and Helen. Hemple nodded to the back-up leader, raised his weapon and led the party, single file, into the anomaly.

Jenny felt a faint tingle, nothing more. The metal clasps and buttons of her clothes and kit twitched at the pull of the anomaly as she went through.

What she noticed next was the air. She went from warm breeze to raw, bright cold, several degrees cooler. She went from a fresh, suburban air to something that tasted very different. There was something in it, some trace element, and a hint of sulphur. There was also a pressure differential that made her ears pop.

It was very bright. A hard-edged sun, still low in the sky and rising, blazed out of a gigantic pale blue sky. Alpha team spread out around her, weapons raised. Helen stood at Jenny's side.

"You've taken a step back 280 million years," Helen said.

"280..." Jenny murmured.

"Give or take." Helen raised her hands to shield her eyes. It was an awkward gesture with her wrists cuffed together. "We'd better move," she said. "It's not far, but this sun is pretty fierce. You won't feel it because of the air temperature and the wind, but you'll burn badly before you know it."

She looked at Hemple and held out her arms. He pulled out a combat knife and sliced her cuffs away. Helen rubbed her wrists, and then diligently picked up the cut strips of plastic and put them in her pocket to take with her.

"Which way?" he asked.

Helen pointed.

"About three kilometres in that direction," she said.

The landscape was lunar. Dunes of grey, volcanic sand filled the spaces between dry crags and long run-offs of loose scree. Gnarled, dead trees, like pieces of driftwood, clawed up out of the barren soil. In the distance, through a smear of heat-haze, Jenny could see glowering mountains. One of them was an active volcano, flaring sooty smoke up in a great, black stain against the blue.

They set off at a good march, raising thin grey dust from their boots. Jenny quickly felt the promised burn of sunlight on her skin, and the raw, cold air began to make her lungs ache. She was annoyed to find Helen Cutter so fit that she was in danger of leaving the alpha team boys behind.

"Not far now," Helen announced, leading the way up a steep escarpment of flaking black rock. Mason and Redfern raised their eyebrows at each other as they followed her up.

She came to a standstill at the top of the scarp.

"Ah," she said, and Jenny noted surprise in her voice.

"What?" she called. "What's the matter?"

Hemple stuck out a hand and helped her to clamber up onto the top of the scarp. She saw the next anomaly immediately. It was about half a kilometre ahead of them in the middle of a huge field of grey volcanic scree.

But they were no longer alone. Between them and the anomaly, several hundred large sailback reptiles were basking like giant iguanas on the dusty dunes.

THIRTY-SEVEN

"Damn," Helen said.

"They don't look very friendly," Jenny observed. She couldn't believe how many of the creatures she was looking at. It was like a colony of sea lions, densely packed along a rocky beach.

"Dimetrodons," Helen said. "Predators, and as such not the friendliest creatures in this particular era. It's just our luck they've decided to take the sun here."

The reptiles ranged in size, but generally they were as massive as large alligators and every bit as unfriendly. Their heads were heavy and deep, with blunt snouts and very powerful jaws. Many of the creatures were basking with their jaws wide open to reveal the extent of their jagged dentition.

A huge, semi-circular fan of skin, supported by elongated spines, rose from the back of each reptile. The creatures were a mottled grey-green colour, but their sails were tipped with streaks of russet and yellow.

None of them was moving. The wind made some of the sails nod gently. Occasionally, one of the creatures would open or close its mouth, or rise up off its belly and take a few steps forward to a new position. Every single one of the hundreds of reptiles in view was facing in the same direction.

"They're side-on to the sun," Jenny noted.

"It's fairly early in the day," Helen responded, "and they're cold-blooded. They've come up here to bask and warm up. The sails are regulators. They increase their body area by about fifty percent."

"They're catching some rays," Redfern said.

"Precisely," Helen agreed.

"We need to get through that anomaly, don't we?" Jenny said, gesturing.

Helen nodded. "Yes. It's the only way."

"Well, I don't really see these chaps letting it happen without wanting to eat us," Hemple said. "And they would eat us, wouldn't they?"

"Oh yes," Helen concured, "like a shot. But I think we're okay. It's early, as I said. They're still in a state of torpor. They're sluggish. If we don't make too much of a fuss about it, I think we can pick our way over to the anomaly before they get too interested in us."

"Oh, that sounds like a brilliant plan that's bound to go wrong," Jenny said.

"We don't seem to have much of an option," Hemple pointed out, though he sounded unsure. "Are you sure this will work?"

"I've done it before," Helen said mildly. "But we have to do it now, while they're still more interested in getting warm than their next meal. Right now, they won't feel much like moving."

"Why don't you show us how it's done?" Jenny suggested.

Without any hesitation, Helen turned and started to walk into the colony of sailbacks. One or two spun their heads slightly as she moved between them. Hemple nodded to Jenny and the members of alpha team, and started to follow her.

They threaded their way between the Dimetrodons, edging between open snouts and slack tails, their boots crunching on the loose grey scree. Sails nodded in the wind, and some of the creatures were making hissing sounds in their throats.

Jenny could smell them. It was a dry, dusty scent mixed with a bad smell of decay that emanated from their huge, wide-open, pink mouths. Some of the creatures had terrible scars on their snouts and necks, evidence of brawling and sparring, possibly as part of dominance contests or mating rituals. Jenny really didn't like the look of all the teeth she could see. Pairs of eyes, like glittering honey marbles, seemed to follow her as she gingerly made her way through the host.

If they wake up now, she thought, *and decide they're hungry, we're stuffed.*

THIRTY-EIGHT

"This is your hole in time?" Bulov asked. There didn't seem to be as much scorn in his voice any more.

"Yes," Cutter replied.

"How do you..." Suvova began. "How do you go through?"

"You just walk," Cutter said. "Look, Professor, I've never seen an anomaly this big before. It's not a standard form at all. I'm learning as much as you are."

"We go through," Koshkin announced.

"Yes," Cutter agreed. "I think that would be the best thing to do."

"Shouldn't we wait for dawn?" Bulov asked, tentatively. He glanced up at the dark and the rain. Sheet lightning continued to murmur and flash around the edges of the vast anomaly form.

"No need," Cutter said.

"We go now," Koshkin stated. "We'll bring the tanks down here and —"

"No, no, no," Cutter interjected, stepping forward. "You're not taking armoured vehicles into the past."

"I'll do what I want," Koshkin retorted.

"There are strong magnetics at work," Cutter said. "Can't you feel the tug on your buttons? On your weapon? You do *not* want to be bringing large metal objects anywhere near this thing, especially not ones with magazines full of high explosives and electromagnetically sensitive firing systems."

Koshkin stared at Cutter for a moment, and then shrugged and nodded.

"Very well," he said.

"And if you're going to bring any of your men with you," Cutter added, "you need to warn them. The experience could freak them out."

Koshkin quickly decided to go through with the scientific group, and take just a couple of men for protection. The others would remain on the Tunguska side of the anomaly.

"Let's move," he instructed.

Pelted by the cold rain, the scientific group crunched forward across the impact site and into the curious half-light of the anomaly effect.

It was suddenly warmer. Abby could smell a strong scent of wildflowers.

They stepped through…

…and entered a balmy summer afternoon. The air was humid, and it was about fifteen degrees warmer.

A great rift valley lay ahead of them. Swathes of temperate woodland covered the landscape, and Abby could see the distant glitter of a river or a coastal inlet. There was an abundance of brightly coloured flowering plants, and the summer air was thick with pollenating insects.

In the far distance, rising out of the lush green woods, craggy hills became snow-shouldered mountains. The sky was banded with white clouds, and its dark blue was beginning to flush a darker pink.

"Oh my God," Rina Suvova murmured. "I believed you, Nicky, I believed what you said, but still, to see it. It's too much."

Bulov opened and closed his mouth several times, and then sat down on a boulder, gazing into the sky. The two soldiers stopped in their tracks and stared in disbelief.

Koshkin looked at Cutter and Abby. He seemed almost angry.

"Please don't ask me if this is some kind of trick," Cutter said. "I've been honest with you from the word go. I told you this is what you could expect."

"This is... the past?" Koshkin asked, but the anger seemed to go out of him.

"Yes," Cutter said, taking it in for himself.

"The landscape and the flora," Suvova said, "they are certainly contiguous with the fauna we've encountered. This is the Cretaceous, isn't it?"

Cutter nodded.

"The endless summer," he said. He shielded his eyes with his hand and looked towards the sunlit mountains. Far away, bird-shapes that were not birds were turning slowly and majestically on the thermals.

Abby wandered ahead a little way.

Cutter went to join her. In the dappled shade under nearby trees, an adult Ankylosaurus and its calf were grazing. By lamplight in the Siberian night, the Ankylosaurus that had lumbered through their camp had seemed to be black and white, but in the softness of the afternoon sun, they could see the creatures to be cream and yellow on their legs and underside, with dark, almost chocolate-brown colouration on their domed backs. Where the yellow and brown-black patches mingled, the hide looked like the skin of an overripe banana.

"Did you notice?" Abby asked quietly.

"Notice what?" Cutter answered.

She turned and looked back at the glimmering arch of the anomaly. Koshkin, Suvova, Bulov and the soldiers were milling about in front of it. The anomaly was far less visible in the strong sunlight than it had been in the inky Siberian night, but it was still plainly much larger than usual.

"Look at the ground," she said.

Cutter did as she suggested. When they'd stepped through the anomaly, they'd all been too busy looking at the landscape around them and the bright, beautiful splendour of the world. Now he noticed something else: a broad area of earth around the anomaly was scorched and mangled, too, matching the impact area on the other side.

"The damage isn't as considerable on this side," she said, "but it's definitely the same. Whatever hit Tunguska, hit here too. I mean, it hit exactly on top of the anomaly. How is that possible?"

Cutter looked up at the sky. It was going a deep rose colour as the sun began to set. Little blemishes of white cloud speckled the air.

"I don't know. I suppose the question is: which sky did it fall out of? This one, or ours?"

Before Abby could respond to this ominous remark, a deep and utterly chilling roar echoed through the woodland. It seemed to come from quite a distance away, but that didn't diminish its effect.

"What was that?" she asked.

"That was a good reason not to hang around here much

longer," Cutter replied quickly. They hurried back towards the others. Suvova and the rest had heard the roar, too.

"We'll go back now, I think," Cutter said.

Koshkin nodded.

But it wasn't going to be as easy as that. The silvery shimmer of light had softly and silently faded away.

The anomaly was gone.

THIRTY-NINE

They almost made it.

They were so close to the anomaly, Jenny could feel its magnetic buzz. She could also feel the roasting burn of the sun on her shoulders, and knew that it was rapidly warming the swaying forest of sails.

They almost made it.

One of the basking sailbacks let out a long, pneumatic hiss, like a kettle coming to the boil, and lunged with the ambush speed of a salt-water crocodile. Its sudden motion and astonishing agility made Jenny shriek.

The cry uttered by Jenkins was equally involuntary, but it was triggered by excruciating pain, rather than surprise.

The massive jaws of the four metre-long Dimetrodon had closed around his right knee. He slammed down onto his back as if a rug had been snatched out from under his feet. Jenny heard bone crunch and grind.

"Go!" Hemple yelled. "Go for the anomaly! Go!"

Helen needed no encouragement. She began to sprint the last

of the distance through the field of basking sailbacks. Mason and Garney went after her. Redfern grabbed Jenny's arm and started to run with her towards the glittering hole.

"Get them through!" Hemple shouted. He and Murdoch had turned back for Jenkins. The man was still howling in agony.

Other sailbacks were starting to stir. A chorus of squealing hisses began.

"We can't leave them!" Jenny exclaimed. Redfern was almost dragging her along.

"Please, miss," he replied, "just *move*."

Hemple ran to where the sailback was dragging Jenkins backwards across the scree. Jenkins was writhing and flailing, trying to reach his sidearm. He'd lost his submachine gun when the creature tackled him.

Another sailback swung its heavy head around to menace Hemple. It snapped at him. Hemple clicked off his weapon's safe toggle and sprayed the sailback with bullets. It thrashed away from him violently, its body and tail jerking in fierce convulsions. Hemple had to jump back to avoid the whipping, spasming tail.

Murdoch had reached Jenkins. He pulled his MP53 up to his shoulder and fired two controlled bursts into the back and spine of the big Dimetrodon. The bullets did serious damage. Blood splashed, and the sail partly collapsed like a broken paper fan.

"Get it off me! Get it off!" Jenkins yelled.

The sailback that had seized him was dead, but its jaws had locked shut. Murdoch and Hemple fought to pry them off his leg.

There was a general motion all around them.

The sea of sails was stirring.

Redfern had got Jenny to the anomaly. Helen and the others had already gone through. Jenny looked back and saw the army of reptiles waking up.

Hemple and his men were never going to make it.

"We've got to do something!" she yelled at Redfern.

He looked at her blankly.

"Any ideas?" he asked.

Hemple and Murdoch had got Jenkins free. His knee was a terrible mess. They hauled him up between them and started to carry him towards the anomaly.

Sailbacks were closing in on them from all sides. Animated now, the reptiles were scrambling and slithering over and around one another to get at the men, crawling over backs and legs and tails. Reptilian heads butted. Jaws snapped and nipped at each other. One Dimetrodon locked its teeth around the front of a rival's sail.

Looking over his shoulder, Hemple saw that the hungry carnivores had already begun to tear into the bodies of the two reptiles he and Murdoch had shot. But that wouldn't distract them all. He struggled with his weapon, one-handed, and opened fire at some of the monsters lunging and flopping into their path.

He mortally wounded at least three more, and the sailback host fell on their twitching, shuddering bodies in an eager and bloody feeding frenzy.

Several large sailbacks went for Jenny. Redfern grabbed her, and shoved her through the anomaly. She heard gunfire. She fell as she went through, and sprawled on the ground on the other side. She was suddenly in a warmer, lusher place, where the sun was giving a softer heat. There was grass under her hands and knees.

She looked back at the anomaly she'd tumbled through, and saw Hemple and Murdoch dragging Jenkins out of its mirrorball flicker.

Then she realised it wasn't the only anomaly she could see.

Redfern helped her to her feet. He seemed rather bashful.

"I'm sorry about shoving you, miss," he said.

"It's okay," Jenny said. "That was rather close."

Helen was standing nearby, with Mason and Garney. Hemple and Murdoch were kneeling on the ground beside Jenkins.

The Dimetrodons didn't seem to be inclined to follow them. Once their prey had disappeared, they may have simply lost interest.

"How is he?" Jenny asked. She kept getting glimpses of his ugly wound between Hemple and Murdoch as they worked, and it wasn't something that she really wanted to look at.

"The bite force will have crushed his knee," Helen said, matter-of-factly. "It may have punctured a major artery. It's not a good wound."

"We're pretty experienced in battlefield trauma, ma'am," Mason told her. Hemple was cutting away the leg of Jenkins's fatigues, and Murdoch was unpacking sterile field dressing packs for swift application.

Helen shrugged.

"What?" Jenny asked her.

"The issue isn't really the bite-force damage. That's bad enough. That'll hospitalise you. But a Dimetrodon's mouth is full of microbes and bacteria. It's pretty grim, actually." She looked at Jenny intently. "It won't be the wound that kills him, it will be the infection."

"Nothing's going to kill him," Jenny growled.

Helen shrugged again and looked away.

They waited while Hemple and Murdoch got the wound cleaned and dressed. Hemple shot Jenkins with a high-dose painkiller from a disposable injector. It calmed his groans and yelps.

Jenny took stock of their surroundings. They were standing on a broad, grassy plain that swept away to the horizon in a gently undulating series of broad ridges. It was like a piece of American prairie, or Asiatic steppe, or even a wilder part of Salisbury Plain. The sky was blue, and busy with healthy white clouds. A trace of mumbling thunderstorms were chasing along the horizon.

Hundreds of anomalies glittered in the air around them. They were lined up across the rolling grasslands, almost evenly spaced, as if they had been propagated. Jenny felt as if she was standing in an orchard of the things.

"This is Spaghetti Junction," she said.

"What?" Helen stared at her.

"That's what Connor called it," Jenny replied. "It's a hub, a nexus where anomalies connect."

Helen nodded. "It's one of them. I've seen several."

"Where is it?" Jenny asked. "*When* is it?"

"I don't know." Helen shrugged. "Honestly, I don't. I've only ever used this nexus to connect one time to another. I've never had the opportunity to explore it. For all I know, twenty-first century Kansas City could be just over the horizon. Alternatively —"

"Alternatively what?" Hemple asked, rising to his feet and wiping Jenkins's blood from his hands.

Helen smiled. Her smile was always disconcerting.

"Alternatively, who knows?"

Redfern snorted.

Jenny stared at her, trying to work out if she'd simply said what she'd said for effect. It was impossible to tell, but she had a gut feeling that Helen was using every psychological weapon in her arsenal to exert dominance over the group. Helen had travelled more than any of them, so she knew more about these places.

They were obliged to trust her, and they were being forced to trust the information she gave them.

It was galling, and it was troubling. She was sure Lester had been right. They couldn't and shouldn't trust Helen Cutter any more than they absolutely had to.

"So this is the point of connection?" Jenny asked her.

"Yes."

"You know which one? Which anomaly?"

"Yes," Helen said.

"And it will take us to Nick? It will take us to this place in Siberia?"

Helen nodded.

"We've walked around the world outside of time." Jenny found the concept mind-bending. "We just come back in at a different place."

"Yeah, very zen," Hemple said. He reloaded his MP53 and took a swig of water. Then he turned to Helen. "Show us where to go, please."

She glanced at Jenkins. He was out of it, virtually unconscious on the grass. Her gaze was hard.

"What?" Hemple demanded.

"Nothing," Helen replied. "Just... nothing."

"Helen wants to leave him here," Jenny said, "but she knows we won't like the idea."

"I'm not leaving *anyone* anywhere," Hemple stated.

"Of course you're not," Helen said. "You believe in loyalty to your men. That's fine. It's an ideal that works where you come from." She began to re-roll the sleeves of her shirt. "However, it would be better for him and for us if you left him here."

"I am not leaving anyone anywhere," Hemple repeated, taking a step towards her.

"Fine," Helen said, raising her hands. "I told you to stay close to me and to do exactly as I told you, or we'd end up in trouble. It seems you don't intend to take that advice."

"Tim Jenkins goes with us!" Hemple exclaimed. "We're going to get him home."

"Please try to grasp what I'm saying," Helen said, apparently unfazed by Hemple's aggressive manner. She went back to re-rolling her sleeves. "The eras we are attempting to traverse are utterly unforgiving. One slip, one mistake, and you're dead. You have to learn to be ruthless. Completely ruthless."

"Like you?" Hemple asked.

"Yes, like me. Ruthless. Unsentimental. Pragmatic. That's the only way to survive. If you attempt to save this man, you will doom us all."

"But I can't send him back," Hemple said.

"No," Helen agreed, "in which case the kindest thing you could do for him is to inject him with three or four more of those painkiller shots so that he goes to sleep and doesn't wake up. Failing that, a bullet is quick and clean."

"You're unbelievable!" Hemple snapped.

"I am a realist," she replied. "If you don't give him a kind death now, he will get us all killed, and he will also suffer a far, far more unpleasant fate later."

"How?"

She shrugged. "I don't know. There are so many ways. That's what I'm telling you. The only sane thing to do is to cut your losses and minimise your risks. When this man dies — not if, *when* — you will wish you had listened to me and shown him some mercy."

"So noted," Hemple said. "The funny thing is, I'm a human being. When did you resign from that club?"

Helen glared at him.

"The only 'club' we all belong to is the animal kingdom," she replied.

Garney and Murdoch carried Jenkins between them. The party walked through the twinkling orchard of anomalies. Jenny noticed that Helen seemed to be counting them off.

"This one," she said finally.

"You're sure?" Jenny asked.

"I'm fairly certain," Helen replied.

Hemple and Mason led the way through. Jenny felt herself pass from warm, fresh open space to a much more humid world.

They had arrived in the evening somewhere. The sky was the colour of pink icing, and decorated with little curlicues of white cloud. The pink warmed to an amber glow along one horizon, and darkened to deep plum at the other. A few trembling stars had come out.

They'd come through on an escarpment overlooking green woodlands. Hills — and, beyond them, snow-capped mountains — rose in the middle distance. There was a pungent scent of flowers. Jenny could hear bird calls, and the stray sounds of other, unidentifiable creatures. She could hear the buzz of insects. From far away, briefly, came a hooting racket, like a brass band tuning up.

"This is the place?" Jenny asked.

"Yes," Helen replied. "This is the connection we needed." She was staring up at the evening stars, as if anxious about what she might read there.

"So where do we go?" Jenny asked. "Which way is Siberia from here?"

Helen stopped looking at the sky. She turned, took her bearings and pointed.

"That way," she said. She looked at Hemple, and then at the men supporting Jenkins. "It's about twenty-five kilometres that way."

Hemple clenched his jaw. He looked at Garney and Murdoch. Both of them nodded.

"We'll take it in turns," he told them.

"Yes, chief," Garney said.

"We'll take turns to carry Jenkins," Hemple said to Helen.

"Of course you will," she agreed sweetly, "but perhaps you're beginning to appreciate the tough wisdom of the advice that I offered, and you oh-so-pointedly ignored."

Helen turned and began to stride away down the slope.

"On the subject of mercy killings," Redfern said to Hemple, "can I shoot her?"

"Get in line," Jenny said.

FORTY

"So you know this what's-his-name Shvachko, then?" Connor asked Antila.

She scowled at him.

"He is FSB. I have no desire to talk about him." She picked up her coffee and went over to check on Umarov. Connor resumed his work. His arm was killing him. It was cold.

It was just after dawn, and he'd been awake and working most of the night. Medyevin yawned.

"Medical Officer Antila had flick with specialist Shvachko when the Spetsnaz first arrived here at the advance camp," he explained.

"A what?"

"A flick."

"A fling?"

"Is what I said."

"No, you said a flick," Connor said. "You mean fling. We call it a fling. The word is fling."

"Fling," Medyevin said to himself. "Fling, fling, fling," he

251

repeated. "Anyway, they broke up. It was messy, so I hear."

"Really?" Connor asked.

"Oh yes." Medyevin looked thoughtful. "Fling? Really, that is the word?"

"It's a fling," Connor insisted.

"What it is," Antila announced, coming back over to them, "is none of your business! How dare you? I didn't give you permission to discuss my private life!"

"Sorry," Connor said meekly.

Antila slapped Medyevin on the shoulder.

"Ow!" he protested. Then she turned to glare at Connor.

"And a slap for you, too, when your arm is healed better!" Antila told him.

"It's obviously a sensitive subject, Natacha," Connor said. "Shvachko clearly didn't treat you very well."

"That is understatement," Antila snapped.

"You don't like him?"

"He is pig-man," Antila seethed, "with trotters and snout and small curly tail!"

There was a brief pause. Connor tried to bite his lips together, but the laughter burst out anyway. Medyevin began laughing, too. After a moment, Antila's ferocious expression melted, and she started to *giggle*.

"Sorry, sorry," Connor said. "It's just that 'pig-man' sort of took me by surprise."

Medyevin said something to Antila in Russian, and she replied, causing them both to laugh even more uncontrollably.

"That was something even worse and much funnier in Russian, wasn't it?" Connor asked.

"It was," Antila said.

"Could you share it?" Connor asked. "Because he's going to

come back and shoot me any minute now, and I'd like a decent laugh as my last request."

Before either of them could answer, the door of the medical hut swung open and Shvachko walked in.

"Something is amusing you all this morning?" he asked.

The merriment died away. Antila straightened up and glared at him. Medyevin shrank back nervously. Connor just tried to pretend he wasn't there.

"How is the device progressing?" Shvachko asked.

"Well, it's a game of two halves," Connor said.

"What?"

"It's swings and roundabouts," Connor added.

"I don't understand you," the FSB specialist said irritably. "Make sense!"

"Uhm, well it's sort of very good news wrapped up in not quite such good news," Connor stammered. "It's getting there, everything's looking good, we're well on the way, it's just not quite... what's the word?"

"Finished?" Shvachko suggested.

Connor held up an index finger, opened his mouth, paused and then shrugged.

"Yeah. It's not quite finished yet. But it will be soon."

Shvachko turned away. He looked out of the hut's window at the grey morning drizzle.

"There have been reports overnight," he said, "from the expedition team. The reports have conflicted somewhat."

He looked over at Connor.

"First report, from Koshkin, announces that work on your device is no longer a priority. He says they have located this anomaly."

"They've found it?" Connor exclaimed, jumping to his feet,

jostling his arm. "Ow ow *ow*! They've really found it?"

"This is what first message said," Shvachko replied. "Second message was sent about half an hour ago, from commander of escort troop. He says that during the night, Koshkin, your two British friends and all other members of the scientific group have vanished."

FORTY-ONE

"We're trapped here!" Bulov wailed. "We're stranded in the past! We're stranded sixty-five million years in the past!"

"Shut up!" Koshkin snapped. He shoved Bulov so hard that the scientist fell over.

"Hey!" Abby protested.

"That's not helping," Cutter said.

"Is he wrong?" Koshkin asked.

Cutter sighed. "It's possible that we're stranded sixty-five million years in the past, yes," he said.

Koshkin snarled a loud curse. Bulov sat on the ground, whimpering. The two soldiers exchanged uneasy looks that said they didn't entirely understand what was going on.

"We just have to wait," Cutter said, "wait and see. There's really no alternative."

"These things come and go sometimes," Abby added.

"Come and go?" Koshkin asked.

"They close, but they open again," Abby explained. "It's not always a one-shot deal."

"Abby's right," Cutter said. "And I think it's especially true of this anomaly. If my ideas are correct, the Tunguskan anomaly has been opening and closing on a regular basis for over a century."

"But why, Nicky?" Suvova asked.

"Because it's a damn great hole, Rina," he replied. "It's a great big tear in time, a major fault! And I believe it's a major fault either because of what happened in Tunguska, or what's happening here."

"Meteor strikes?" Koshkin asked, looking around at the wounded landscape.

"Impact events," Cutter nodded. "Extinction events. Heat, shock, pressure, electromagnetics, radiation... huge releases of dynamic forces that tear the Earth apart, and maybe space and time, as well as the physical world. If this is a fault line — a fault line that runs through time between the here and now and Tunguska in our era — maybe impact events have blown it wide open."

Everyone was looking at him. He shook his head.

"I don't know," he sighed. "But I think we can get back. I think this hole will open again. All of the indications point that way. We just have to watch it, and wait for it. Let's not go wandering off. We have to stay at this location."

Another brutally deep and reverberative roar shook the evening.

"Staying here may not be such a good idea," Abby pointed out. Koshkin and the two soldiers raised their weapons and were scanning the nearby woods for signs of movement. The woods had gone quiet. Birds had stopped singing.

Something was out there, hunting.

"Okay," Cutter said, taking charge, "we need to move to a more secure location, maybe high ground. Everybody take your bearings.

Remember the landmarks, the trees, each outcrop of rock, the direction of the mountains."

"But the blast area is huge," Koshkin said, pointing to the massive patch of scorched landscape where the anomaly had been.

"It may look huge," Cutter said, "but if we wander away from it, we may not find it again." He turned. "Rina, give me your kit."

Suvova handed Cutter her bulky knapsack of equipment. He fished around inside it, and came out with an aerosol can of blue dye.

"I use it for marking erratics in herd situations," she said.

"It'll do." Cutter spray-marked a boulder and two tree trunks.

"Come on," he told them all.

They hurried after him through the lengthening shadows. It felt as though the night itself was coming in on their heels. As the rose-red dusk faded to a deep maroon, the colour washed out of the flowers, and the woods became gloomy, grey caverns of tree trunks and canopy, lit mainly by their torches. At intervals, Cutter used the spray can to mark tree trunks.

They tried to stay quiet. It felt as if the world was going into hiding. Blooms were closing their petals. The deepest shadows were as black as ink.

As they hurried along, Abby remembered the CO2 pistol she'd confiscated from Bulov and pulled it out of her waistband.

"Give me the bag of darts," she whispered to the scientist.

He hesitated, his hand on the strap of the small shoulder bag.

"If we run into trouble," she said, "wouldn't you like this to be loaded and in the hands of someone who knows how to use it?"

Bulov handed her the bag. Abby pulled out a dart, slung the bag over her shoulder, and loaded the pistol as she hurried after Cutter.

"What are the darts filled with?" she asked Bulov in a low voice.

He answered with the name of a fairly basic barbiturate.

"How strong's the dosage?" Abby asked.

"Quite strong," he assured her. "In fact, we had to stop using the capture gun, because we got the sedative balance wrong. It tended to overdose and kill creatures outright with a fatal reaction. Yushenko was intending to adjust the dosage levels and reload the darts."

Bulov paused.

"He won't be doing that now," he added.

Yet again, a penetrating roar throbbed through the closing darkness.

"Look on the bright side," Abby told him. "The way things are going, we might be glad of something with a lethal kick."

They covered another half a kilometre or so, marking trees as they went, and came out on the bank of a strong river. Trees overhung the far shore, but on their side, there was a broad curve of shingle beach. Cutter led them along the shoreline. Twilight had settled around them. The sky had turned deep purple, and the stars looked like a scatter of glitter dust. Without competition from artificial light, their glow was surprisingly strong.

Cutter had been moving fast, but now he slowed and held up his hand. They could sense movement, and feel the faint tremble of the ground. Snuffling and grunting sounds came from the vegetation above the river.

"Quiet!" he hissed. "Stay still."

A huge shape loomed out of the darkness ahead of them, sliding out of the woodland and onto the shingle. It was moving on two legs, its head down and its tail raised out behind it. Another one came into view behind it, silhouetted against the starlight, and then another.

Abby heard Bulov gasp in alarm. She looked behind them.

A dozen more huge creatures had emerged from the trees and onto the shingle behind them.

In the half-light, she recognised them. They were big duck-bills, perhaps some more Anatotitans or a similar genus. The herd was moving down to the water's edge, quietly and tentatively, as if they were skulking or creeping. They issued the occasional low communicative snuffle or grunt, but it was quite obvious they were trying not to draw attention to themselves. In the starlight, they looked like large shapes carved out of pale marble.

Cutter noted their behaviour too. The herd was travelling quietly, making reduced signals. The creatures were aware that there was danger around, and perhaps they even felt as if they were being stalked.

Their motion became very slow. They kept stopping, freezing like deer, listening for the slightest warning sound, trying to pass unnoticed.

The herd surrounded the stationary humans, ahead of them and behind them on the shingle of the river bend. Others were still emerging from the trees alongside them. One adult appeared from foliage that shivered as it was brushed aside, and crept down the shore less than five metres away. They could smell its coarse vegetable odour, a mix of sap and dung and cellulose. They could hear its slight nervous sniffs and grunts.

"Stay still," Cutter whispered.

The duck-bills halted, too, more like statues in the starlight than ever. Several had their heads raised, as if they were listening. The silent tension was almost unbearable.

The hunter made its move.

A hundred metres behind them, back along the shoreline,

something huge and dark broke cover and charged into the motionless herd. It was too far away and too dark for Cutter or any of the others to see it clearly, but the consequences of its ambush were more than obvious.

It selected one of the creatures. There was a thunderous squealing and bellowing from the prey. It hooted and blew like a broken tuba connected to a pressurised air pump. The noises were appalling, brassy booming mixed with terrible, high-pitched squealing. Cutter could see the stricken duck-bill, a large, pale shape, thrashing and crying at the water's edge, held in the grip of a massive black shadow. He heard a rumbling, predator's growl overlapping the piteous shrieking.

The rest of the duck-bill herd broke and fled in instinctive panic. Every single creature rose up on its hind legs and started to run, kicking up stones from the shingle beach and hooting their frantic alarm calls.

The victim managed to drag the hunter that had seized it into the river shallows, churning up sheets of spray as it fought and twisted and lashed its tail to break free.

But without success. The huge black shadow hung on to it.

The herd rushed into the river. Cutter and his companions were drenched by the violent spray. They tried to shield themselves from the whizzing riverbank stones that were being scattered by crashing feet. Bolting duck-bills erupted out of the trees, threatening to trample them underfoot in their panicky surge to reach the water.

Cutter grabbed Suvova and pulled her aside before a galloping Anatotitan could crush her. Bulov screamed and covered his head. Abby flinched and tried to dodge the creatures that came close.

In the river, kicking up volumes of water, the duck-bills struck out for the far bank. The water was full of them, wallowing down, heads raised, tails going, hind feet kick-paddling. The cacophony of hooting and splashing sounded like a colliery band going through a car wash.

Holding tight to Rina Suvova, Cutter looked back down the bank. As far as he could see, all the Anatotitans were in the water and crossing the river now, all of them except the prey creature. Cutter could see its pale shape in the gloom, struggling at the water's edge. It was still squealing, but its cries were weaker, and its struggles far less strenuous. The great black shadow still had hold of it.

Cutter heard the crack of major bones finally breaking under titanic pressure. He saw the starlight glistening off black wetness. Even from a hundred metres away, he could smell the blood and the stench of ruptured innards.

"Let's get into the trees," he urged the others as quietly as he could. "Find some cover."

Koshkin nodded, and led the way. Bulov followed him in something of a daze. One of the flying stones kicked up off the shore had cut his scalp. Another had badly bruised the shoulder of one of the soldiers.

Cutter brought up the rear. He took a last look back along the shore.

The ghost-pale shape of the victim had stopped moving. Something was slowly, ponderously dragging its slack shape up the shingle, away from the river.

It was too dark — too frustratingly dark — for him to see the predator properly. He could just sense the shape of it, the sheer size, the power.

For a fleeting moment, he felt its eyes on him, as if it had raised its head from the kill and turned to look his way. He felt it see him, and know him, and — in that passing moment — he realised he ought to be profoundly grateful that, by the grace of God, it had enough food in its mouth not to care about him at all.

FORTY-TWO

The moon that rose over the Cretaceous forest was a monster, too. It seemed many times bigger and brighter than any moon Abby had ever seen at home, just as the stars seemed far more numerous and livid. It was more than just the absence of light pollution. There was something unearthly about it, something magical.

In the moonlit woods, away from the river, they rested for a while. Nocturnal sounds resumed. Insects clicked and whirred, night birds called, and larger animals roaming the woodland left whoops and hoots and long, strangled bellows in the air. The hunter had made a kill: everything else was safe for a while.

"We'll rest for ten minutes, and then try to make our way back to the anomaly," Cutter said.

"We hide, and we wait until dawn," Bulov contradicted. He mopped at the blood that was seeping out of his hairline from the cut on his scalp.

"There's no point waiting," Cutter insisted. "If the anomaly's re-opened, we need to get back through it."

"Can you find the way?" Koshkin asked.

"Yes, I think so," Cutter replied. He took the spray can out of his pocket and looked at it dubiously. "Even though blue's going to be hard to see in this light."

"We really didn't go that far, did we?" Abby offered.

"No, we didn't," Cutter agreed.

"It's sort of that way," she said, pointing, "and less than a kilometre."

Cutter agreed, nodding.

Bulov threw his hands up.

"I have no idea any more. I am lost," he said.

"The girl is right," Koshkin said. "That way, less than a kilometre."

"And if it's reopened," Cutter said, "we should be able to see it a lot more easily in the dark."

They waited for a little while longer. The two soldiers sat under a tree and watched the dark, warm sky, brimful of stars. The one with the bruised shoulder nursed his arm. The other one exclaimed a couple of times, and pointed at the heavens.

"What are they saying?" Abby asked Suvova.

"One is saying, 'make a wish'," Suvova replied. "They have seen shooting stars. You make a wish when you see a shooting star."

Suvova paused as she realised what she had said. She looked over at Cutter.

"Nicky?"

Cutter had already got to his feet and was staring at the sky. Abby joined him.

"There!" she cried, after less than a minute. A sharp little line of yellow-white light had cut across the sky for a second, a fleeting back-slash amongst the multitude of stellar full stops.

"Shooting star," Cutter breathed. They saw two more almost at once, quick flashes that were there and gone, as if they'd glimpsed them in their peripheral vision. A minute later, a bigger, more spectacular slant of light lit up and disappeared.

"The Earth's passing through a meteor shower," Cutter said. "Probably one of the periodic ones. Most of the objects are tiny. They're just burning up."

"But some might be big enough to reach the surface," Abby suggested, "or at least detonate in the high atmosphere?"

Cutter put his hands to his mouth, deep in thought.

"Oh my God," he murmured, and then laughed grimly.

"This is the very end of the Cretaceous period. We know that from the creatures. I think..."

"What do you think?" Suvova asked.

"I think this is *literally* the end of the Cretaceous. This is *it*. The last years, the last weeks, maybe..."

He looked at the sky.

"Maybe the last hours."

"That's one hell of a coincidence," Suvova pointed out.

"Well, that's been my point all along," Cutter said. "All of this fits together for a reason. I think we're right on the threshold, right on the K-T boundary. It's about to happen, and the age of reptiles, the Mesozoic Era — a magnificent period more than 180 million years long — is about to come to an end.

"Look there." He pointed at the sky.

"I thought it was a cloud. Earlier on, I thought it was just a cloud in the evening sky, but it's still there. It's not shifting like a cloud at all."

"It's just a smudge of light," Koshkin said dismissively. "Just a smear. Are you sure it's not a cloud?"

"It's not a cloud," Bulov said quietly. "When you look at it, you can see that it's not. You have sharp eyes, Professor Cutter."

"Is that really it?" Abby asked.

"I think that's what we'll call the Chicxulub impactor one day," Cutter replied softly. "I think that's it, on its way in. It's a long-period comet, and its just days or hours away. When it hits, the dinosaurs and two-thirds of all species on the planet are going to die."

"The meteors, then," Abby asked. "What are they? Pieces of it?"

"Out at the edges of the solar system," Bulov said, "there is the Kuiper belt, and also the Oort cloud. Both of these regions are packed with dust, volatile gas, and rock and ice. Once in a very long while, the gravitational effects of the solar system cause objects in these regions to become disrupted, to collide. It is possible then for some of these objects to be deflected in towards the inner planets, as a swarm of Oort cloud comets, for example."

Bulov got to his feet and stood beside Cutter, staring up at the blur of light.

"This could be just such a swarm. It has been travelling in towards us for thousands of years. Smaller objects are already arriving, and burning up as shooting stars or striking like the Tunguska event. Behind them comes the big one, the main event, the killer, the ice in it heating as it approaches the sun, subliming, forming a glowing tail behind it, the coma of the comet."

"Let's head back," Cutter said suddenly. "Let's see if the anomaly has reopened."

"Let's hope it has," Suvova said. "After all this talk of the sky falling, I don't feel much like staying here."

"I hate to disagree," Cutter said, "but I kind of hope it hasn't."

"What?" Suvova laughed. "Are you mad, Nicky? You want to stay here?"

"Not at all," Cutter replied. "But if the anomaly is open when that thing hits, it won't just be *this* world that dies."

FORTY-THREE

"Do you know where we are?" Jenny asked.

"Do you mean specifically, or generally?" Helen replied.

They had stopped to rest yet again. The members of alpha team were slowly wearing themselves out carrying Jenkins. The night was humid, and a huge moon was up. Insects were thrumming in the deep woods around them.

"Try generally," Jenny said.

"The very late part of the Cretaceous."

"That means... dinosaurs."

"Very much so," Helen said, as if humouring a child. "But not for much longer. Do you see? Up there, that scar of light. There, just above the line of the trees. That's a world killer, coming this way. A comet. When it hits the planet, it will cause a mass extinction, leaving the Earth crippled for hundreds of thousands of years until life begins to restore itself."

"That's what wipes out the dinosaurs?" Jenny asked.

Helen smiled. "Absolutely. It's a sobering thought, isn't it?"

"It's a comet? Life gets wiped out by a comet."

"Not for the first time and not for the last," Helen said. "The history of life on Earth is punctuated by great extinction events. The cosmos wipes the slate clean, so that other strands of life can try their luck. At the end of the Permian, which is about 250 million years before you were born, there was an impact event that left less than ten percent of species alive. In fact, of the twenty-five major extinctions known from the geological record of our planet, at least seven were the result of large impact events."

"I can't wait to go home," Jenny said. "I can't wait to go home, and have a bath and cup of tea, and surround myself with normal things."

"Of course you can't. That's only natural. Then again, impact-based extinction events only take place once every several tens of millions of years. When you're having your bath and your cup of tea, bear in mind that by 2009, the next one will be really very overdue."

"You're a barrel of laughs, you know that?" Jenny told her. She walked off towards Hemple. Redfern was leaning against a tree nearby, keeping an eye on Helen.

Hemple was standing over Jenkins as Murdoch cleaned and re-dressed his wound.

"How is he?" Jenny asked. In the moonlight, she could see for herself. Jenkins was delirious and sweating badly.

"His wound's already infected," Hemple said grimly. "He's slipping in and out. There's nothing we can do."

"Not here maybe, but when we get him back —" Jenny began. Hemple looked at her.

"That look on your face had better not mean you don't think we're getting back, sunshine," Jenny said.

Hemple laughed, despite his mood. He motioned to her to follow and walked a little way away from the other men.

"I thought I was pretty well prepped," he said to her quietly. "I didn't think there was much I couldn't handle if I had to. But I already feel out of my depth. This is tougher than I was expecting, which is stupid of me."

"Why?" Jenny asked.

"Because it means she might be right, and I don't want her to be right," Hemple said, glancing across the clearing at Helen.

"I'd better not tell you what she just told me then," Jenny said.

"Go on."

"Apparently, on top of everything else, the world's about to end."

"Oh, great," Hemple said. "We'll get some beers in, make a night of it."

She was about to respond when Hemple raised a quick hand to shush her. Across the clearing, Helen had just ducked down low, and Redfern had followed suit. Hemple prowled across to join them, keeping as low as possible. Jenny followed him, dropping into a crouch.

"What's going on?" she whispered.

Helen looked around at her, her eyes hard in the starlight.

"Everything just went quiet," she whispered. "Can't you feel it?"

Jenny realised then that the nocturnal sounds had fallen off. Animal and bird calls had faded to nothing.

"So what is it?" Hemple said quietly.

"Something's hunting," Helen whispered back. "An apex hunter, a hyperpredator. I've felt this before. It's like the whole world goes quiet when the killer's about to strike."

"Oh fantastic. What do we do?" Jenny whispered.

"Well, we shut up for a start," Helen hissed back.

They waited. Even the insects seemed to have stopped

stridulating. Then Jenny felt it: a thump, as if something heavy — but muffled — had hit the earth. There was a pause, and then another thump. She heard a swish and rustle of foliage.

They were footfalls, the steps of something very big and very close, stalking through the woodland.

It went quiet again, and then Jenny almost jumped as dreadful, frantic shrieking and squealing split the night air. It sounded like a pig being slaughtered. A frenzy of activity was taking place in the stand of trees nearest to them. Undergrowth ripped and shook. She could hear crashes and thumps, and the splinter of wood.

An creature burst out of cover, scattering leaves and twigs. It was the source of the ghastly squealing sounds. It seemed huge to Jenny, a bipedal dinosaur nearly five metres long, sprinting on its hind legs and squealing like a butchered hog. She could see its small mouth, like a sheep's snout, open and braying, the tongue sticking out, the small eyes wide with anguish. The creature's skull was crowned with a great knotty mass of blunt spikes and knobs.

"We've got to move!" Helen cried. "*Now!*"

The shrieking creature was coming straight towards them. Blood was jetting from a series of awful gouges just above the base of its tail.

"*Move!*" Hemple yelled.

Helen was already moving. Redfern darted in the other direction. Hemple grabbed Jenny's hand and they began to run.

The stricken creature was fleeing an attacker, blinded by panic and pain. It ploughed through the undergrowth that had been concealing their group, shredding leaves in all directions, and then crashed into a tree, splintering the trunk. It staggered back, began to run again, and piled into another tree bole. This time it went over onto its side, kicking and thrashing.

The air was full of leaves flying like confetti.

Hemple pulled Jenny down into a thick bed of ferns for cover. The creature was still squealing and braying.

More branches splintered. Wood cracked. The attacker thumped out of the trees, crashing aside low-hanging boughs. It was significantly bigger than the wounded creature. Its huge legs propelled it, and the weight of its steps made the ground shudder. A seismic growl thundered out of its throat like a fierce roll on a kettle drum.

Jenny only glimpsed its huge form. She saw the immense, strutting legs, each one the size of a tree trunk. She saw the vast body and tail, striped black on black, as it slid past. She saw a flash of teeth that looked like swords. She willed the ferns to hide her and Hemple.

It strode past them, and reached the wounded creature, which was still making its abominable bleating noises and pinwheeling its legs. The predator dipped its massive head, and sank its teeth into its helpless prey. The creature's noises became more frantic for a second, and then withered away to nothing. The sour stink of blood was suddenly so powerful that Jenny almost retched.

The hyperpredator's tail, held high, lashed to and fro. Its head was still down. Bones cracked and shattered. The killer uttered another growling roar that was half-muffled by its mouthful of kill.

It scooped the dead creature up in its jaws and carried it away. The prey creature's bone-crowned head lolled out of one side, and its long hind limbs and tail dragged slack out of the other. Blood streamed off the killer's chin.

It moved away, leaving a trampled track of blood-flecked undergrowth in its wake, and vanished into the trees.

Hemple sat up. He was breathing hard. He let go of Jenny's hand, and she slowly heaved herself into a sitting position.

"Oh my God," she murmured, and shook her head.

"My thoughts exactly,"Hemple said.

"That was ridiculously close," she added. "I've had some close calls, some properly close calls, several times since I met Nick Cutter, but that... that was..."

"Tell me about it," Hemple agreed.

Something moved nearby. Hemple snatched up his weapon.

It was Garney.

"Only me, chief," he said. "You two all right?"

"Yeah," Hemple said.

"Thank you for asking," Jenny said.

"Where are the others?" Hemple asked.

"We all kind of scattered when that thing showed up, chief," Garney said.

"Round everyone up, can you?" Hemple ordered. He got up and helped Jenny to her feet.

"Damn," he said suddenly.

"What?"

"I bet she's gone."

"Helen?" Jenny asked.

"She was always going to ditch us, first chance she got. She wanted an escape," Hemple said. "This was the moment, I guess."

"Which leaves us where exactly?" she responded, trying to stop herself shaking.

"Up a well-known creek, minus the recommended equipment," Hemple replied.

Garney returned with Mason and Murdoch.

"Make sure Jenkins is okay," Hemple told them. He turned back to Jenny. "I can't believe we let that woman give us the slip," he said.

"Good thing you've got me to cover for you then, isn't it,

chief?" Redfern said. He walked into the clearing with Helen Cutter in front of his MP53. She looked as unimpressed as usual.

"She's got some legs on her," Redfern said. "But I've got a Heckler and Koch, and a commanding voice."

"That thing," Hemple asked Helen, "was it a Tyrannosaurus?"

"My, my, Hemple," she replied. "How clever. Did you have a Ladybird book of dinosaurs when you were a little boy?"

"Answer the question, please," Hemple said patiently.

Helen nodded.

"Yes. It was a Tyrannosaurus. Quite magnificently scary, aren't they, especially that close up?"

She looked at Jenny, who was still a little pale.

"Just so you know, judging from its limb-length and stride, that was a young adult. Not a really big, mature creature. The females tend to be the biggest. And the most dangerous."

"No change there, then," Hemple said, straight at her.

Helen sniffed.

"It was just unfortunate that the Pachycephalosaurus tried to escape in our direction," she said. "It rather brought disaster down on top of us."

"That was the creature it killed?" Jenny asked.

"Yes. A herbivore. Fantastically bony skull, domed and spiked. For years, it was thought the Pachycephalosaurus used their heads for butting, like rutting stags, a mating thing. But it turns out it's just display. They're very famous, though. That amazing skull. Kids love them. There was probably a Pachycephalosaurus in your Ladybird book as well, Hemple."

He ignored her. Garney had reappeared, and he looked anxious.

"What is it?" Hemple asked him.

"Jenkins has gone," he replied.

***

They'd only left him alone for the two or three minutes when the Tyrannosaurus appeared and they had scattered, but Tim Jenkins had vanished. There was a little trace of blood, and some torn shreds of field dressing.

"Maybe he woke up?" Mason said, hopefully.

"Come on," Hemple said.

"If the fever broke, and he woke up, and he didn't know where we were…" Murdoch offered.

"He couldn't walk!" Hemple exclaimed.

"He might have crawled," Redfern said. "He might be close by, in the thickets, in the undergrowth."

"Spread out. Find him," Hemple ordered.

They drew out their flashlights and began to section the area, probing the wild shadows of the undergrowth with their powerful torch beams. They called his name several times, but only the ticks and hoots and calls of the forest answered them.

They'd been searching for twenty minutes when Hemple sensed movement and small sounds in the nearby thickets, and pushed in with his torch and gun ready. Helen and Redfern were close behind him, with Jenny at their heels.

"Here's something!" he called. "Tim? Tim Jenkins?"

Chittering, yapping voices answered him. His torch beam illuminated six small, bipedal dinosaurs. They were slender and avian, with long, whip tails. As the torch found them, they hunched warily, and looked into the light with alert, golden eyes that were fringed by feather eyebrows.

One of them barked at Hemple. A second twitched and cocked its head. A third took another peck at their kill.

"Troodons," Helen said. She stamped forward and clapped her hands to drive them off. The small creatures scurried backwards, hopping and twitching, reluctant to leave. They barked some more, and stared at the humans, defiantly wishing to keep hold of their feast.

Hemple pushed past Helen and fired a burst with his MP53. The noise was deafening, and the muzzle flash bright hot. The Troodons bolted immediately, skittering and chirring as they dashed away into the woods.

Helen looked down at the bloody remains.

"They carried him here to feed," she said. "They're smart. They pretty much ate him alive. I wonder how much he knew about it?"

Jenny looked away.

"Bury him," Hemple said to his men.

"There's no point," Helen said. "They'll simply dig him up again and finish the job. Like I said, they're smart."

"Bury him," Hemple repeated.

Helen shrugged, and walked away. Redfern followed her.

With a sick feeling, Hemple realised she had been right after all. Jenkins had gone to a far more unpleasant death than the compassionate one Hemple had been in a position to offer, and he wished he hadn't thrown away the chance to afford his friend some dignity at the end of his life.

She had been right. He hated her for it. She had been right about both things.

He was damn well sure she wouldn't be right about anything else.

Especially the idea that in trying to save Jenkins, he had signed a death notice for them all.

FORTY-FOUR

The first light of dawn was appearing by the time Cutter and his group returned to the site of the anomaly. He followed the trail of blue dye marks he'd left the previous evening, and easily relocated the colossal patch of burned and seared earth, but there was still no sign of the glittering portal.

"What do we do now?" Bulov asked.

"We wait to see if our luck'll change," Cutter said.

They waited on the edge of the woods overlooking the impact site. The sunrise was spectacular. It was warm, and the air was crystal clear. The sky was flamingo pink chased through with brilliantly white clouds. The morning trembled with a dawn chorus that sounded both familiar and fundamentally alien to them.

Huge dragonflies like glass ornaments zipped through the dawn air, and darting flocks of birds flitted in silhouette against the pink sky. From the deeper woods, they could hear Hadrosaurs sounding and blowing.

They'd been there an hour when Cutter noticed the first distortions.

Small shivers of light, like fragments of the characteristic anomaly pattern, began to appear above the impact site and in the area of woodland around them. It was as if twinkling Christmas decorations were being switched on and off repeatedly amongst the trees.

"What is that?" Suvova asked.

Abby looked up.

"Is this the anomaly coming back?"

"I think so," Cutter said, watching the intensifying lightshow. "It's definitely anomaly activity of some sort. Maybe it's gathering power, preparing to reopen. These could be the first few ripples."

They watched and waited. The glittering lights grew bright for several minutes, as if the anomaly was about to swirl open, and then, frustratingly, died down again. Then the pattern repeated.

Abby went and sat on the ground with her back against a tree trunk. Bulov and Suvova came and sat near her.

Cutter paced.

The two soldiers wandered around, pointing and laughing as the lights came and went. Koshkin kept watch on the forest.

Abby was exhausted. She leant her head back against the trunk for a moment and closed her eyes.

A hand touched her arm. She opened her eyes.

A face was very near. She saw a fingertip pressed against lips. "Shhhh!"

Ten metres away through the trees, Koshkin could see the rest of the group at the edge of the impact site. He wondered where his two men had gone.

What are those idiots doing?

Then he froze. Some sixth sense — a potent blend of extreme training discipline and honed gut instinct that had seen him safely through many hazardous circumstances over the years — was telling him something was wrong.

He turned, his AK in his hands, fully expecting to see some kind of prehistoric threat within striking distance. He certainly wasn't expecting to find himself looking down the barrel of a special ops soldier's gun.

The British soldier kept his aim steady.

"Toss the gun, comrade," he said.

Koshkin lowered the AK-74 and threw it to one side.

"You are very good," he said with a nod. "I did not hear you until it was too late for me."

"Less chat." The man gestured with his weapon. "Let's join the others. Hands nice and high."

Koshkin turned, his hands half-raised. Somehow, he managed to transform the passive, obedient turn of his body into a savage sideways kick, which smacked his captor's aim up and back, on its way to connecting with his left hip.

The man grunted, tried to bring his weapon back true, and simultaneously locked his left arm around the ankle of the kicking foot to twist Koshkin off his feet.

Koshkin rolled backwards instead, clawing at the strap and muzzle of his opponent's MP53 as he went. The British soldier sailed right over the top of the Russian, and landed on his shoulders. Koshkin flexed his hips and arms violently, and bounced back onto his feet.

The man scissor-kicked Koshkin's legs out from under him, rolled in, and pinned him in the hardest, tightest straight-arm lock he could manage.

Koshkin's scarred lips peeled back in pain as the British soldier tugged a little tighter.

"Have you quite finished?" he hissed.

Koshkin coughed out a chuckle. In the course of the very quick, very savage bout, he'd drawn a little survival knife from a concealed sheath. With his free hand he was pressing the sawtooth blade of the knife against the side of his neck.

"Bravo, Hemple. You must both be feeling very macho," Helen Cutter said. She was standing over them, aiming Koshkin's AK-74 at them both.

"Hello, Nick," Helen said.

She walked into the clearing at the edge of the impact site and stood facing him, looking him up and down.

"What, no hello back?" she asked.

They were all on their feet. Garney and Redfern had the two Russian soldiers covered. They stood with their hands on their heads, looking sheepish and confused. Murdoch was watching Bulov and Suvova, and Mason had his MP53 pointing at the glowering Koshkin.

Helen had surrendered the AK to Hemple, once he had let Koshkin up and the knife had been disposed of.

"Good to see you," Cutter said to Hemple, ignoring Helen. Hemple nodded back.

"And you," Cutter said to Jenny, who had just finished giving Abby a big hug. Jenny smiled broadly at him.

"I've got to ask though," Cutter added, "what *exactly* are you doing here?"

Jenny looked offended.

"We've come to rescue you," she declared. "Isn't it obvious?"

"Well, that sounds pretty crazy," Cutter replied. "You must have come the long way round."

"If that means through the anomalies, then yes," Jenny said, "that's exactly how we got here."

"Did she show you the way?" Cutter asked. He gestured at Helen.

"Yes, 'she' showed them the way," Helen said. "You can address me directly if you like, Nick."

Cutter stared at her.

"You know what? Right now, as far as I know, there are only fourteen human beings on Planet Earth, and I still don't have much desire to talk to you, Helen."

She stiffened. It was the first time since they'd set off that Jenny had seen anything really get to the famous Helen Cutter.

"Is that the lovely Helen?" Suvova asked, stepping forward. "Helen, my dear?"

"You remember Professor Suvova?" Cutter asked.

"Of course I do." Helen smiled and embraced Rina Suvova as if they were in the midst of a polite social gathering.

"What are you doing here?" Suvova asked her.

"I came looking for Nick," Helen told her. "He may not want to talk to me, but I really want to talk to him."

"What happened to you two?" Suvova frowned. "You were such a lovely couple, but now I can feel the resentment between the pair of you."

"Unfortunately, relationships change over time," Helen said.

"Isn't that the truth." Cutter said.

"Well, I didn't travel sixty-five million years to watch a marital dispute," Jenny said, "so could we get going? It's a long way back."

"You've got a route out?" Cutter asked Hemple.

"Would we have come in without one?" Hemple replied.

"I don't know. Your mission plan hasn't shown much trace of common sense so far," Cutter said.

"Oh, there's gratitude!" Jenny exclaimed.

Hemple grinned.

"Extraction's the way we came in," he said. He looked at Helen. "I'm presuming it is, anyway," he said.

She nodded.

"Yes, it is. Not withstanding the Dimetrodon problem, it's still the most direct route out of here."

"Well, I'd like to get moving," Hemple said. "It's quite a march."

"I'm not entirely sure I'm going anywhere," Cutter replied. He looked at Jenny. "Don't get me wrong. I'm not only grateful, I'm touched that you'd all take so many risks trying to get us back, but there's something going on here, something that makes everything else seem pretty unimportant."

He turned to face Helen.

"I think you know a good deal about it, too," he said.

She nodded.

"You wanted to talk?" he said. "You've got five minutes."

FORTY-FIVE

"How long have you known?" Cutter asked.

"Only a few weeks," Helen replied. They'd walked about thirty metres away from the others. She leaned against a boulder. He stood and studied the glittering lights as they came and went, rather than look at her.

"A few weeks?"

"I began to notice a change in the way the anomalies were behaving," Helen said. "There was an increasing lack of stability, and a good deal of electromagnetic variance."

"We noticed it, too," Cutter admitted. "Connor did, anyway. He called it eccentricity."

"That's an accurate term."

"He also called it 'well-strange', so don't let's give him the Nobel yet."

She smiled. "What did you think was causing it?"

He shrugged. "We had no idea, but we knew it was affecting the whole network. It's this, isn't it? It's what's happening here?"

"Yes," Helen said. "The causal relationships are difficult to explain, because depending on your viewpoint, it will seem as though time paradoxes are involved, but —"

"Just give me the short version, Helen."

She stood up. "The fault line running between Tunguska in our era and this place, right now, is particularly weak and particularly volatile. It's the San Andreas Fault of time anomalies."

"I know it's much, much bigger than any I've ever seen," Cutter said.

"Or me," she agreed, "and much less stable. It's periodic, too."

"It's going to open again?" he asked, gesturing towards the will-o'-the-wisp lights flashing in the woodland canopy.

"Oh yes," Helen said. "Definitely. Maybe another hour or so, and you'll be able to go back through. It's so unstable and so big, it's spreading symptoms of... what was it? Eccentricity?"

"That's Connor's word."

"It's spreading symptoms of eccentricity throughout the anomaly network. Worldwide, all time periods, the effects are showing up."

"Why is it so bad here?" Cutter asked.

"That's a chicken versus egg question," Helen said. "Despite my meanderings through time, I am still a linear being, Nick. So are you. Neither of us is capable of perceiving true cause-and-effect in time's fabric. The rift may have been critically damaged and enlarged by repeated meteor impacts. Alternatively, the electromagnetic vortex of an enlarged rift may have *caused* repeated meteor impacts."

Cutter shook his head.

"Coincidence alone would seem to support the latter. This precise spot has been hit several times that we know of. That's a wild improbability, except that we know that the Earth's magnetic field has an effect on the behaviour and trajectory of collision objects. You put a massive magnetic anomaly here, it's like painting a bull's-eye on the planet."

"Except that's linear thinking," she said. "The K-T event is so huge, so catastrophic, it will send shockwaves up and down the time stream from the point of impact. This anomaly may have been damaged and enlarged, not because of what's happened here, but because of what's going to happen here."

Cutter looked up at the sky. The sunlight was glaring and it was, for the moment, impossible to detect the sinister smudge of light.

"Okay," he said after a thoughtful pause, "the bottom line is that there is an enlarged anomaly here, linking the last days of the Cretaceous with the twenty-first century, and it's likely to be wide open when the Chicxulub impactor reaches Earth. The collateral devastation could be enormous. It could wipe out life on Earth in two entirely separate eras. At the very least — in the very best-case scenario — it's going to be a bad day for mankind. We could lose vast areas of Russia and continental Europe."

"That's a pretty fair assessment," she said.

"So, how do we stop it?"

Helen stared at him. Then…

She began to laugh. It was the most laughter, and the most *genuine* laughter, he had heard from her in years and years.

"What?" he asked indignantly.

"I'm sorry," she said. "I'm not mocking you. It's just that I suddenly realised you were serious."

"Of course I'm serious."

"You actually meant that. You honestly think there's something we can do."

"Yes," he said.

"Nick, it's already happened," she said. "It's history. We just happen to be seeing it first hand. You can't *stop* it happening."

"So why are you here, if there's nothing we can do?" he asked.

"I wanted to see you," she said. She smiled faintly, an old smile he had once adored. "I wanted to talk to you before it was too late. To apologise, perhaps, for everything."

"In the face of imminent disaster you undergo a change of heart, do you?" he asked.

"I obviously still have feelings for you, Nick," she said. "I came to the ends of the Earth to find you, after all."

"Funny," he replied, not laughing.

"Look, I don't miss the world I left behind," she said. "I like my life. I wander through the ages, and I get to see things no one has ever seen. I wouldn't go back, but I have always been comforted by the idea that I could if I wanted to. I'm going to miss the world I came from when it's no longer there."

"So you came to say goodbye, did you?" he asked.

"I wanted to warn you, Nick," she replied. "I wanted to warn you about what was coming. I hoped you might —"

"What? Hoped I might what?"

"Come with me," Helen said. "Escape the end of the world and come with me. There are lifetimes to live. I could really use your company."

He looked into her eyes.

"Sorry," he said, "I just don't have the time."

The glittering fragments of energy finally seemed to cohere, and the anomaly reopened. Its gigantic structure ignited across the Cretaceous forest, seething and rippling with silver light and rainbow colours. It made a noise like a heavy, metal ingot being dragged across paving stones.

Cutter left Helen, and walked back to join the others.

"What's going on?" Hemple asked.

"Cutter?" Jenny said.

"We're going through," Cutter told them. "I'd tell you to go back the way you came, but I don't think it's going to be any safer that way in the long run. We've got to go through and see what we can do."

"Like what?" Abby asked.

"Right now, I have no idea," Cutter replied, stony-faced. He glanced at Hemple. "I think you should stop pointing your guns at Koshkin," he added.

As alpha team lowered its weapons, the Russian eyed Cutter doubtfully.

"I'm going to need your help, Koshkin," Cutter said frankly, "and you're going to need mine. You'll have to get your people on-side for me. We've got to trust each other — and fast."

"What about Helen?" Jenny asked.

"Oh, she's coming with us," Cutter replied. "She's got music to face, when all this is done with."

"Tiny problem," Abby said. She gestured. They looked around.

There was no longer any sign that Helen Cutter had ever been there.

"Where the hell did she go?" Redfern snapped.

"Dammit!" Cutter snarled. He shook his head wearily.

"Spread out. Find her," Hemple told alpha team.

"Don't bother," Cutter said. "We haven't got time to waste. We've got more important things to think about."

"What, like the world ending?" Abby asked.

"That kind of thing," Cutter agreed.

He turned, took one last look over his shoulder, and led the group towards the anomaly. One by one, they vanished into its shimmer.

***

Helen Cutter watched them go.

She stood alone for a long time after they'd gone. Then she turned and walked away into the past.

FORTY-SIX

Siberia was a step away.

They came back into the scorched circle of the impact site, and into a howling gale and a snowstorm. The wind, cold and hard, was lashing the trees around the rim of the blasted zone. The sky was white, and the snow was flurrying. Thunder was booming overhead. Every few seconds, lightning seared the flat, white sky like the element of a giant light bulb.

"Oh my God!" Jenny cried. "This is horrible!"

"It wasn't like this when we left," Cutter replied.

"To be fair," Abby shouted back over the noise of the wind and pealing thunder, "it was pretty nasty! It was just differently nasty!"

"Even for Sibir, this is unseasonal weather, Nicky," Suvova told him, raising her voice to be heard.

"It's the anomaly," Cutter called back. "The weather's getting screwed up."

They struggled towards the treeline. There was no sign of anyone.

"Maybe they all went back to the advance camp," Bulov suggested, hugging his arms around his body to keep warm.

"They would have left someone posted here," Koshkin replied. "They would have known better than to abandon the position."

They headed into the treeline. The trees shielded them from the worst of the wind. Snowflakes danced and swirled through the forest air. Overhead, the canopy rocked and thrashed.

"There! Over there!" Hemple called out.

Lightning flashed. A sizzling crack of thunder followed. They could see figures through the trees ahead of them. Three men, in Russian uniform, had spotted them.

Abby laughed.

"It's what's-his-name," she said. "It's Torosyan."

Yuri Torosyan and two other troopers ran through the forest towards them. One of them blew repeatedly on a whistle. The soldiers slowed down warily when they saw Hemple and the rest of alpha team.

"Make it clear you're friendly, or there'll be trouble," Koshkin said to them.

"Do it," Cutter added.

Hemple and his men slung their weapons on their backs so that their hands were free and open.

Torosyan led the three men closer. He was so puzzled and excited that he gabbled at them in Russian.

"English!" Abby shouted.

"Where did you come from?" Torosyan asked.

"A long way away," Koshkin said, pushing forward. He began to speak with the soldiers in rapid Russian.

"What's he saying?" Cutter asked Suvova.

"Koshkin is asking where the others are. Young Yuri is saying that everyone is out searching the woods for us."

"If Koshkin decides to sell us out, you will let me know, won't you?" Cutter said.

The Russian troopers led the group back through the woods, away from the impact site. Torosyan's companions blew on their whistles again to attract attention.

"What's wrong with radios?" Cutter asked.

"They've been in and out since the storm began," Torosyan replied.

"How long's that?"

"Three, maybe four hours."

The campsite established around the ATVs had been expanded since they had last seen it. Though the tanks had moved away, several more trucks and ATV vehicles had arrived from the advance camp, and a number of modular tents and weather shelters had been staked up. They were quivering in the fierce wind.

The alarm whistles had attracted the attention of the sentries. Troops in gloves and heavy overcoats appeared, clutching weapons. Other personnel emerged from the tents and shelters to find out what the commotion was about.

"Shvachko," Bulov moaned.

"Who?" Cutter asked.

"The other FSB specialist," Suvova answered. "He's bad news."

Shvachko, wearing black battledress and a fur-trimmed coat, walked towards them. He met Koshkin and they began to talk. Shvachko kept glancing at the alpha team members.

"Ever get the feeling you're not welcome?" Redfern asked.

"Never mind him," Abby said. "Look who else is here."

Connor hurried towards them from the tents, one sleeve of his overcoat empty around his strapped arm. Medyevin was with him.

"You came back then!" Connor exclaimed. Abby gave him a hug.

"Steady, ow, steady!" he said. "Arm, remember?"

He hugged Abby a little more anyway. Then he looked over her shoulder and frowned.

"Hang about," he said. "Where did Jenny and the ass-kickers come from?"

"It's a long story," Jenny said.

"And we don't have time to tell it properly," Cutter added. "I need to pick your brains."

"Shoot," Connor said.

"What would you do," Cutter asked, "if you wanted to close an anomaly?"

FORTY-SEVEN

Shvachko's expression was hard to read.

"You look like you don't believe me," Cutter observed.

"I am vouching for him," Koshkin said.

"I know, I know," Shvachko replied. "It is, I suppose, that this entire situation is casting up many things that strain one's credibility. I am trying to keep my priorities straight."

The three of them, along with Connor and Medyevin, were crowded into Shvachko's command shelter. A rattling fan heater was running off the power plant of an ATV that had been backed up to the shelter wall. The light of the suspended lamps shivered as the building shook in the wind. Outside, the noise-shock of the savage lightning strikes continued to blast the air.

Koshkin had sent Abby, Jenny, the ARC's alpha team members and the scientific group — along with the two bewildered soldiers who'd been through the anomaly — to be thoroughly checked out by the medical staff.

"I will need to examine you and the British professor, too," Natacha Antila had told him. She'd come up from the advance camp with the reinforcements to run medical operations at the site.

"We need to speak with Shvachko," Koshkin had said. "Then we'll submit to your exam."

Antila had sent them on their way with an admonishment to Connor not to over-exert his arm.

"I'm wondering what your priorities are, precisely," Cutter said to Shvachko in the command tent.

"The continued security of the Russian Federation," Shvachko replied smoothly.

"Well, this is a pretty big threat to it," Cutter said. "We need full cooperation. I'm not sure what will make you grasp the gravity of this. If we don't stop wasting time, there won't be a Russian Federation to secure."

"Is that some kind of ultimatum?" Shvachko challenged, leaning forward, his piercing eyes on Cutter.

"Now you're annoying me," Koshkin announced, with a weary shake of his head. "What's wrong with you, Shvachko? I'm telling you how it is, and I have final authority."

"Not actually," Shvachko replied, turning his attention to his colleague. "When you disappeared, situational command passed to me."

"I've returned," Koshkin growled.

"I can no longer attest to your psychological fitness," Shvachko said mildly. "Your tale speaks to a distinct fantasist mindset."

Koshkin shoved his folding seat back, and started to yell at Shvachko in Russian. Shvachko rose to meet him and shouted back. They were nose to nose. Connor flinched, fully expecting the specialists to come to blows.

"Hey! Hey!" Cutter shouted, and bashed his fist down on the camp table.

The men stopped and glared at him.

"How much more proof do you want?" Cutter demanded. "You've been working out here for some time, Shvachko, and you've seen — first hand — creatures that *should not exist in this time*. We're sitting about half a kilometre away from the physical evidence of a collision impact. What else do you need, exactly, before you admit that our story is pretty well corroborated?"

"Just because one impossible thing turns out to be true after all," Shvachko answered, "it does not automatically follow that all impossible things are true. The erratics, they are quite extraordinary I grant you, but as I understand it, the received scientific view is that they are survivals."

"We have moved on from there, actually —" Medyevin began.

Shvachko pointed a finger at him, and he stopped.

"You, you do not speak." He looked back at Cutter. "I was set against recruiting your expertise in the first place."

"That's one way of describing our kidnap," Cutter fired straight back.

"I believe your ideas, your very presence, is polluting the integrity of this situation. It is a federal problem, and it should be contained and dealt with by federal agencies. *Not* foreign nationals."

Shvachko looked Koshkin straight in the eyes.

"My recommendations, supported by General Markov, have been endorsed overnight by the government executive. Your actions in this matter have been officially disavowed, Koshkin. The instruction is that, should you reappear, you should be stood down. Authority has passed to me, and I intend to use it to pursue other, more rational remedies to this situation."

"Disavowed?" Koshkin echoed.

"You brought foreigners here, Koshkin," Shvachko sneered. "You risked igniting a major international incident — with Great Britain, of all places. You broke most of the international rules governing the extradition and securement of prisoners in custody. If that wasn't enough, you started to listen to their wild theories, and ended up colluding with their fantasies. You let this boy strip down field equipment, and use a secure laptop to build some kind of magical dinosaur scanner."

"It was an anomaly detector," Connor said quietly.

"Do you know what he actually did?" Shvachko asked Koshkin. "He used the laptop to send an email for help."

Koshkin glared at Connor.

Connor shrugged.

"Hey, you kidnapped us. Sorry."

"Good God," Cutter said. "I understand that this is a difficult situation, but can we try and stay on topic? A bigger problem than dinosaurs is heading this way. If you want proof, come with me to the anomaly. Come through, and see for yourself. See with your own eyes."

"Would I be able to trust them?" Shvachko answered.

"What?"

"First I'm told this problem concerns a prehistoric survival," Shvachko said. "Then I am told it's a hole through time. As I said, there are other, more rational explanations that I intend to investigate. I'm having new scientific groups flown in from universities in Moskva and Novgorod."

"What are their areas of specialty?" Cutter asked.

"Psychological warfare, behavioural stimulation and suggestion patterns," Shvachko replied.

"This is psychological warfare?" Cutter asked with an incredulous laugh. But the FSB specialist remained firm.

"Perhaps drug-induced, possibly through the use of psychotropic agents in the air or water, or even through microwave broadcasts," Shvachko said. "There are also acoustic and infrasonic methods that will be checked for."

"So you think the dinosaurs aren't really here," Cutter said. "You think it's all one big shared hallucination?"

"I think it's possible that this remote region is having some new system of warfare tested on it," Shvachko said. "The notion that this situation is a mass hysterical hallucination engineered by foreign powers is rather more credible than prehistoric survivals and holes in time, so you'll forgive me if I take seriously the security of the Russian Federation."

"But —" Cutter began. He was cut off with the wave of a hand.

"Tell me this, Professor Cutter," Shvachko continued, "just out of curiosity: if I were to accept that what you're claiming is true, that there is a giant comet hurtling towards us through a hole in time, what would you have me do about it, exactly? What actions would you be urging me to take?"

"The anomaly has to be shut," Cutter replied. "It has to be shut to shield this era from the blast. Connor and I have discussed this. The anomaly is a complex and powerful electromagnetic phenomenon. We don't understand it precisely — of course we don't — but we think the best chance you've got is to detonate something that will emit an intensely fluctuating magnetic field. An electromagnetic pulse, basically."

"An EMP, like you get with a nuclear blast," Connor put in helpfully.

"We think a strong enough EM pulse could collapse the anomaly," Cutter said.

"So, what you're saying is that you'd like me to detonate a nuclear weapon," Shvachko responded.

"Of course they're not!" Koshkin snapped. He looked at Cutter. "Are you?"

"Of course not," Cutter echoed. "There are other ways to produce an EMP. Most of them are military applications. There are electromagnetic bombs, E-bombs, designed to disable electronic systems."

"E-bombs often use explosively pumped flux compression generator technology," Connor said, "or EPFCGs if you want to get all technical. But it doesn't have to be a transient electromagnetic device like an E-bomb, it could be a chemical or gas dynamic laser, or a maser, because microwaves would do it, or even a decent directed-energy weapon like a HERF. That's —"

"A High Energy Radio Frequency weapon," Shvachko said. "I know what HERF stands for. Are you proposing to build one of these devices, the two of you? Just knock one together quickly before the world comes to an end? What will you need? A field radio? A laptop?"

"We haven't got the time or the know-how to build anything," Cutter answered. "If we had we would have done so before — it's not as though this kind of equipment is readily available."

"Oh, what a shame." Shvachko's voice dripped with contempt.

"We don't have to," Connor said, "because you've already got them."

"I have?" Shvachko said.

"The Russian Federation has," Connor told him. "I had a couple of glances at your mate Umarov's laptop, remember? All that classified stuff. You've got all sorts of goodies available, thanks to your military satellite coverage. Russia's secret Star Wars weapons are circling right overhead. I didn't have long to browse, and I didn't have the privilege codes, so I don't know what the full potential is, but you've definitely got a HERF cannon up there, and I'm pretty sure you've got some sort of

EMP-based airspace denial system for crunching the electronics on planes and missiles."

"And that's what we should use?" Shvachko asked. But he looked vaguely impressed.

"Yeah," Connor said, and he nodded enthusiastically. "You use your authority to get one of these orbital platforms re-tasked, and you take a pot-shot at the anomaly. You can't miss it. This impact site with the radiating tree trunks makes a great big hot target that's *got* to be visible from space."

"So, what you're suggesting is... to counter the threat of this 'anomaly'," Shvachko said, making quote marks with his fingers, "we should reveal to you the nature and potential of our ultra-classified orbital weapons program, and show you how to use it?" Shvachko looked at Koshkin. "And you question why I'm so concerned with federal security?"

"You have to listen to them," Koshkin said flatly.

"No, I absolutely do not," Shvachko replied.

Koshkin went for him.

The motion was so sudden and fluid, it took everyone by surprise — except Shvachko. With equal speed his hand snapped up and pressed the muzzle of a double-action combat pistol into Koshkin's cheek.

Koshkin froze.

"Whoa!" Connor yelped, recoiling.

Medyevin squealed and dived off his stool with his arms around his head.

Shvachko shoved with the end of the gun, and Koshkin sat back down. At a brisk command from Shvachko, two soldiers hurried into the shelter. There was snow on their shoulders.

"Put them with the others and keep them secure," he commanded.

"Even me?" Medyevin yelped. "I'm not with them!"

"Cheers for the support, mate," Connor said.

"I thought you subscribed to this hole in time theory, Doctor?" Shvachko questioned the scientist.

Medyevin swallowed hard and carefully considered his options. He made another important career decision.

"Of course not," he said. "It's patently preposterous."

Shvachko looked at the solders.

"Just those three, then. With the others."

The soldiers got Cutter, Connor and Koshkin on their feet.

As they were led out of the command shelter, Cutter looked back at Shvachko.

"Looks like the end of the world is going to be on your shoulders," he said.

FORTY-EIGHT

"What's taking them so long?" Jenny asked.

Hemple shook his head. The wind was howling around the medical hut, the largest shelter at the campsite. The staggering *buzz-rip-boom!* of the lightning discharge over the forest was making Antila's instruments rattle.

They had crowded into the shelter to let the medical officer run her tests: Abby, Jenny, Suvova and Bulov, along with Hemple and his team. Redfern took off his coat and exposed his arm to let Antila take a blood sample, and the medic looked appreciatively at his bicep.

"Easy, tiger," Abby sniggered.

Jenny was perched nearest to the hut's chugging fan heater unit, chaffing her hands.

"It does seem to be taking them a long time," she said.

Hemple grinned at her. "So you keep saying."

"But it is, isn't it?" Jenny persisted. "I mean, what are they talking about?"

"The end of the world, probably," Abby said.

"Okay, listen, about that," Jenny said. "You keep saying that as if it's funny, and it doesn't sound funny to me."

"It really isn't," Bulov agreed.

"Is that why we've come back here?" Jenny continued. "When Cutter said we've got more important things to worry about, is that what he meant?"

"It's *exactly* what he meant," Abby said. "Cutter is sure that an extinction event is about to occur."

"That's exactly what Helen Cutter said to me," Jenny told her. "She said a comet was about to wipe out the dinosaurs. But that's *there*, isn't it? Back then? That's not here, surely?"

"Forgive me if I'm wrong," Hemple said, "but aren't we sitting on top of a gigantic doorway that opens right into the land of the dinosaurs?"

"Exactly. The comet strike will effect this world, too," Abby explained, "if the anomaly is open. Cutter's trying to convince the Russian dude to help him close it."

"I wish him luck," Suvova said, as she held out her arm for Antila's next syringe. "Shvachko is not the most imaginative fellow."

"Huh!" Antila muttered. "Pig-man!"

"Shouldn't we just evacuate this area, then?" Jenny asked.

"I think you're underestimating the effective range of this impact," Bulov said to her. "There's nowhere to evacuate to."

The shelter door crashed open and let in a flurry of snowflakes. A crowd of Russian soldiers stomped in out of the wind and aimed their assault rifles at the occupants of the hut. Hemple and his men leapt to their feet, but there was nothing they could do. With multiple AK-74s levelled at them, they raised their hands.

"What is meaning of this outrage?" Antila protested loudly.

"Be quiet, please," Zvegin, the adjutant, replied, entering the hut. He issued quick instructions to his soldiers. Two of them gathered up the alpha team's weapons, and then began to unclasp their body-kit items.

"You will not do this in here!" Antila yelled.

"Again, *shut up*," Zvegin told her.

"What's going on?" Abby asked. One of the soldiers with Zvegin was Yuri Torosyan.

"Yuri, what the hell's going on?" She directed her question to the good-looking soldier.

Torosyan looked awkward.

"Sorry, Abby," he replied. "Orders from Shvachko."

"Pig-man!" Antila exploded.

"Come on, Yuri," Abby pleaded, "what happened to fraternisation?"

"It is orders," Torosyan insisted, keeping a firm grip on his weapon.

At Zvegin's instructions, the soldiers herded Abby, Bulov and Suvova to one end of the room with Antila, and prepared to escort Jenny and Hemple's alpha team out of the hut.

"Hold them here," Zvegin said to Torosyan, nodding towards Abby's group.

"Where are you taking us?" Jenny demanded.

"Yeah, where are you taking them?" Abby yelled.

"Shut up!" Zvegin replied.

"Why are you separating us?" Abby persisted. "Tell me!"

Zvegin looked at her.

"Because we know who you are. We brought you here. We know where you came from. This woman and these men, they are unknown to us. This is a security issue. You will be held here. These persons will be transported immediately to the advance camp for security evaluation and interview."

"I'm not going anywhere!" Jenny announced.

"You do not have a say in it," Zvegin stated. "Move them!"

The soldiers bustled Jenny and the members of alpha team out of the medical shelter.

Abby, Suvova, Bulov and Antila were left behind with Torosyan and two other armed guards. The shelter door slammed shut.

"Oh, this is not a good development," Abby said.

The soldiers marched Jenny and the alpha team squad out through the snow towards a pair of waiting vehicles. The wind was even more fierce than before, and the forest around them was thrashing and swaying. Snowflakes dazzled in the headlights of the trucks. Jagged lightning displays tore the sky.

"Oh no," Redfern muttered. "Look at that."

The terrible weather had cut light levels badly, but beyond the camp, through the driving snow and swaying trees, they could see a broad golden glow in the distance.

"That isn't coming from the impact site," Hemple said. "What the hell is it?"

"Firestorm," Zvegin said. "The lightning has set off a major forest burn. This happens often. The wind is fanning it and driving it."

"That's a fire?" Jenny said. "It's huge!"

Zvegin shrugged.

"In Sibir, nothing is small measure. If fire continues to sweep this way, the camp will have to be abandoned. Not your concern, however. You will not be here."

The transport consisted of an ATV and a smaller, six-seater truck. Zvegin insisted that Jenny and Hemple — "the leader and the woman" — would ride in the truck with him, a driver and a guard. The others were bundled into the ATV.

The vehicles set off, slithering and revving through the fast-settling snow.

FORTY-NINE

Hunched against the snow stinging their faces, the two soldiers led the three prisoners away from the command tent and through the camp towards the medical hut.

"Forest fire," Koshkin grumbled, looking at the glow in the east. "A bad one, too."

"Something else to worry about," Connor said.

There was a vivid flash as a luminous spur of lightning hit part of the tree canopy fifty metres away. It was like a bomb going off. They all froze, stunned for a moment.

Koshkin chopped his hand into the neck of one of the soldiers, and the man crashed over into the snow. Before he'd even landed, Koshkin had grabbed the other one, kicked his legs away and thrown him over his shoulder. Koshkin landed on top of the second man, delivered a brutal punch that guaranteed the soldier wasn't going to get up again in the near future, and then tore the AK-74 off him, breaking the strap. Pivoting around, Koshkin hammered the stock of the weapon down on the helmeted head of the first soldier, who had just begun to rise.

Three crunching seconds, and both of their guards were unconscious and in need of hospitalisation.

"Flaming hell!" Connor gasped.

Koshkin got up, and aimed the captured weapon at Cutter and Connor.

"Am I a fool to trust you?" he demanded.

"What?" Cutter stared at him.

"Have you lied to me all along? Is this a trick, like Shvachko says it is?"

"No, it's not."

There was a long pause. Koshkin glared at Cutter. Flakes of snow billowed between them, and the thunder assaulted the sky.

Koshkin slowly raised the weapon so it was no longer aimed at them.

"Very well," he said. "I needed to know, to be sure, before I crossed a line I could not uncross. Help me move these men into cover."

Between the three of them, they dragged the unconscious troopers into a supply tent. The Russian helped himself to both AK-74s.

"What are we doing exactly?" Connor asked.

"We're taking control of the situation," Koshkin replied, taking some spare clips from the belt pouches of one of the men.

"What's your plan?" Cutter wanted to know.

"I get hold of Shvachko's laptop," Koshkin explained, "and I supply you with the necessary entry and authority codes. You close the anomaly."

"You reckon you can do that?" Cutter asked. Connor suddenly realised that Cutter was talking to him, not the FSB agent.

"What? Huh? It's suddenly down to me?" he stammered.

"You're the specialist," Cutter said.

"Yeah, okay, thanks for the compliment," Connor responded. "But this is the end of the world, not a high score on *Command and Conquer*, so hello? First of all, no pressure, eh? Second of all, even with the fancy secret codes and everything, you're really asking me to use a military-grade laptop that I've barely had a chance to examine to re-task a mega-classified piece of orbital weapons hardware, and then aim said space weapon platform at a specific target and fire it?"

He paused.

"And not, during the whole procedure, cock up any of that?" he added.

"Yeah, that pretty much covers it," Cutter replied. "Sound about right to you?"

Koshkin nodded.

"It's an accurate summary."

Connor looked stunned.

"Okay," he said, "you're both completely barmy."

"Probably also an accurate summary." Cutter looked at Koshkin. "Let's go."

The Russian nodded again. He had one of the captured AKs in his hands, and the other looped over his shoulder.

"One thing," Cutter said. "You don't *ever* point a gun at me again."

"That's only fair," Koshkin agreed.

"This is wrong, Yuri," Abby said.

Torosyan sighed.

"Please, Abby, you have lovely face, and I would happily listen to your sweet voice for many times, but you are going on and on."

"You should listen to her," Antila said.

"Not so much from you any more, I think," Torosyan barked at the medical officer.

"Wooo, big man," Abby said.

"Yes, indeed," Antila agreed. "Big man, threatening a female with only a machine gun to protect him."

"You're as bad as each other!" Torosyan exclaimed. "Be quiet!"

The other two soldiers shuffled uncomfortably, but they kept their weapons aimed. With an exasperated puff of breath, Torosyan reached for his cigarettes.

"Not in here!" Antila ordered. "I have that much authority left, at least. You don't smoke in here. There are volatile chemicals present."

Torosyan sighed again, and left his cigarettes alone.

"There's an awful lot at stake, Yuri," Abby said in a more reasonable voice.

"I don't care."

"You *should* care," she said. She had been crowded into a corner of the hut with Suvova, Bulov and Antila. Her shoulders were up against a support post, and the post was pressing something into the small of her back. Bulov's CO_2 pistol was still tucked into her waistband, and it was loaded.

For a moment, she considered trying to grab it. But she quickly realised that it would be an incredibly stupid thing to do. Even if she got the capture gun out, and managed to fire it, and actually *hit* one of the soldiers, it was a single-shot gun and there were three of them. She had the small bag of darts over her shoulder, but it took a moment to reload the weapon.

The soldiers had assault rifles. If they opened fire, it wouldn't just be her that got hurt.

"You really should care, Yuri," she said, trying again.

"A terrible thing is going to happen and —"

"Please, please, Abby, Abby," Torosyan said, "you make my head hurt. You don't know these things for sure. You don't know anything about —"

"I do," Bulov interrupted. "I know what will happen."

He looked at the soldiers, and then dragged out a folding chair and sat down on it heavily.

"A comet is going to hit the Earth," he said. He brushed flecks of dirt off his trousers with a slightly over-fussy gesture before continuing. "It's basically a lump of rock about ten kilometres wide, and it's travelling far faster than the bullets that come out of your rifles. A nanosecond after it hits, there will be a release of energy greater than if you exploded hundreds of atomic bombs at the same time. The blast will be hotter than the heart of a star. One trillion megatons. Seas will turn to steam. It will dig a crater in the planet's crust 200 kilometres wide, and hurl a hundred trillion tons of molten rock into space.

"The planet will convulse with massive earthquakes. The impact shockwave alone will shred the atmosphere. There will be these things known as hypercanes, which are hurricanes dozens of times more powerful than we have ever, ever seen. Nitrous oxides mixed up by the fireblast chemistry will wipe out the entire ozone layer. There will be tsunamis. They will drown continents."

Bulov paused. He fussed at a loose thread on his jacket.

"And that will be merely the beginning," he resumed. "All the rock that was blasted into space, all one hundred trillion tons of it, will fall back. Rock will rain down, irradiating the surface of Planet Earth with the heat generated by its re-entry, and turning it into a furnace, an oven that will cook pretty much anything and anyone unfortunate enough to have survived. And even then, it won't be the end.

"The grotesque amounts of sulphur added to the atmosphere will cause acid rainfall. So will the raging, global firestorms consuming all the forests. The toxic pollutants in the smoke, together with the acid rain, will comprehensively poison the oceans and exterminate all marine life. By then, dust will have blocked out the light of the sun.

"Night will last for decades, maybe centuries. Average global temperatures may drop by as much as fifteen degrees Celsius. This is the impact winter. When the sun finally returns, it will bring the ultraviolet spring. With the ozone layer depleted to nothing, ultraviolet radiation will scour the planet.

"Let's suppose, in an optimistic moment, that some few shreds of life have endured to this point. The ultraviolet radiation will cause fundamental DNA damage, producing cataracts, mutations, cancers."

Bulov looked up at the soldiers.

"This is what *will* happen," he said. "So don't tell me what I know or do not know."

The soldiers looked nervously at one another. Torosyan shook his head, a sick look on his face.

"Watch them," he told the other two. "Just watch them."

Torosyan strode out of the hut into the snow and pulled out his cigarettes. He tried to light one, but the wind was too strong, so he hunched up and shuffled around to the rear of the medical tent.

The rear wall of the tent offered a little more shelter from the wind and snow. His hands were shaking. In the lee of the tent, he lit his cigarette and took several deep drags. The cigarette smoke smelled particularly strong in the biting cold air.

Torosyan hugged himself and stomped his feet to stay warm. He'd go back inside as soon as he'd had his smoke. He'd go back inside and tell them all to shut up with their stupid stories.

He turned.

His mouth opened. His last drag of smoke exhaled in a plume as he gasped in disbelief.

How long had that been standing behind him?

Yuri Torosyan reached for his gun. He was fast.

It was faster.

Inside the medical hut, they heard a muffled impact outside, a slicing thud like the drop of a giant guillotine. Something bounced off the back wall of the tent.

"What the hell was that?" Suvova's loud voice demanded.

One of the soldiers called out Yuri's name. The soldier looked at his companion, who shrugged, muttered something in Russian and went to the door of the hut.

He opened it to look out. Outside, a head lowered inquisitively, sniffing, and Baba Yaga looked in.

The soldier slammed the door shut.

Baba Yaga opened it again for him. She did it with her teeth. The colossal jaws of the mature female Tyrannosaurus bit through the door, the tent wall and the soldier simultaneously. He didn't even have time to scream. Snatching her head back, her jaws full, the eight-ton hyper-predator ripped the front wall and roof off the medical hut.

It shook the contents of its mouth, flapping the trailing, torn canvas and severed guy wires like a dog worrying a slipper.

Inside the suddenly roofless hut, Bulov began to scream. Suvova shrieked in dismay. Antila was so stunned, she stumbled backwards into a tray of instruments.

The remaining soldier stared up in immobile dismay.

"Shoot it! Shoot it! Shoot it!" Bulov screeched.

The soldier fumbled with his AK and ripped off a couple of bursts into the air. Baba Yaga took a step forwards and closed her mouth around him with another guillotine thwack. She lifted him six metres into the air. All Abby could see of him was his legs, the boots still kicking.

"Move!" she yelled at Bulov and Suvova. "Move it! Run! *Now!*"

Baba Yaga finished with the soldier.

She came for them.

FIFTY

Across the camp, Koshkin stopped as he heard the distinct *pop-pop* of gunshots.

"Hear that?" he asked.

"I can't hear anything," Connor complained. "My ears are completely ringing from the thunder and —"

"Quiet! It's gunfire!" Koshkin snapped. They hurried past a couple of supply tents and a generator truck, until they had a view along the length of the camp.

At the far end, through the whirling snow, they could see the nightmarish shape of an enormous black Tyrannosaurus shredding its way into a hut.

"Good God!" Cutter cried.

"A decent enough distraction," Koshkin said calmly. "Baba Yaga chooses to fight on our side."

"That's the medical hut, isn't it?" Cutter snarled at him.

"Abby!" Connor cried.

Cutter looked at Koshkin. The Russian tossed him the AK-74 he was carrying, and took the other one off his shoulder.

"Go!" Koshkin said. "The boy comes with me."

"Go with Koshkin," Cutter told Connor. "Do your thing."

"But —" Connor began.

"Do it, Connor!" Cutter yelled over his shoulder.

He began to run towards the monster that was looming in the lightning and the snow.

In the command tent, Shvachko looked up from the list of new command directives he was typing on-screen. He cocked his head, listening.

"Those were shots," he decided.

"Were they?" Medyevin asked.

"Go and find the sentries," Shvachko instructed him. "Find out what's going on."

"Me?"

"Yes, you, Medyevin."

Medyevin hesitated slightly. It was unbearably cold outside, and he didn't want to leave the fan heater. Furthermore, he was no soldier. However, he appreciated the fact that Shvachko seemed to be trusting him. Shvachko was the man to impress now.

Medyevin made another crucial career decision.

"No problem," he said. He zipped up his coat and went to the door. "If it's trouble, shouldn't I have a gun?"

"Do you know how to use one?"

"No," he admitted.

"Then you shouldn't. If it's trouble, rouse the damn sentries and come and get me."

"Okay." Medyevin paused again, and made a business of adjusting his gloves.

"Oh, for God's sake," Shvachko muttered. He pulled his pistol out of its holster and held it out to Medyevin, grip first. "If it makes you happier, take this."

"Thanks!" Medyevin said.

"Safety's on the grip behind the trigger."

"Got it." Medyevin hurried out into the snowstorm.

Shvachko turned back to his laptop. An email had arrived. General Markov was questioning some of the deployment revisions he had just sent.

Useless old fool. Shvachko would see that he'd get the chop, too. He was going to clean up the Tunguska operation from top to bottom.

The truck bounced along the forest track, lurching and slipping in the snow.

"He's driving a bit fast," Jenny commented.

"He's probably keen to get home to his nice warm stove," Hemple responded. They were having to hold onto the handgrips, the vehicle was bouncing so much.

Their truck was following the ATV carrying Redfern, Mason, Murdoch and Garney. They kept getting a glimpse of its rear-end in their headlights, squirming along the track ahead of them.

It was a full-on blizzard outside. The truck's wipers were fighting the dizzy blitz of snowflakes blowing out of the night. As they crossed the headlight beams, the flakes glowed phosphor-white like tiny comets.

The truck jolted so violently that Jenny and Hemple were bumped out of their seats for a second.

"Good grief! I wish he'd slow down!" Jenny said.

Zvegin looked back at her from the front passenger seat.

"We don't want to be out here all night," he said.

"No, we don't," Hemple agreed. He pointed out of the side

window. Jenny looked.

The immense forest fire was closing in. To the right of the winding track, the entire forest was back-lit by the dazzling wall of flames. Driven by the abnormal wind and fuelled by the fury of lightning strikes, it had formed a moving front that looked two or three kilometres wide, and the line of it was less than a hundred metres from the trail.

"That's spreading really fast," Hemple observed nervously. They could smell the hot odour of woodsmoke in the air pouring through the truck's ineffectual heater vents.

"It's getting close," he said to Zvegin, leaning forward.

"We'll be clear of it soon. It won't bother us," Zvegin replied. "Rain will come overnight, or more snow. That will be the end of it."

"Never mind us," Jenny said. "The rate that fire's spreading, it'll soon be at the camp."

Zvegin shrugged.

"Maybe. But they'll have sentries and fire-spotters out. They won't just sit there."

"Even so," Jenny insisted, "I think you should warn them. You've got a radio, haven't you? They may not realise how fast the fire's moving."

Zvegin thought about it.

"Maybe." He reached for the radio handset.

"Look out!" Hemple yelled.

Something was suddenly filling the truck's windscreen. The pale bulk of an adult Anatotitan lumbered through the headlight beams.

The driver hit the brakes, and the truck went into a skid. Honking and hooting in anxiety, several of the creatures were fleeing the fire, hurtling across the track from right to left.

"Hold on!" Hemple cried. He slammed his arm around Jenny and clamped her to the seat.

The truck clipped the tail of an Anatotitan. The windscreen crazed, and the vehicle's skid became a little wider and a little more ugly. Zvegin, the driver and the guard were all yelling.

They hit something in the road, head-on, crunching the front end of the truck. The impact threw them all forwards, and stopped the truck dead.

"Jenny?"

"I'm all right!"

The driver, Zvegin and the guard were still yelling. The truck was sideways-on across the trail, facing the creature they'd hit.

It wasn't an Anatotitan, though several more Anatotitans rushed past them as they sat there, dazed. The creature was a quadruped, nine metres long, weighing in excess of five tons. It had a small head fringed with pyramidal cheek horns, and a wide, domed back that was armour-plated with enormous scutes of bone. In the light of the one surviving headlamp, it appeared to be black and white.

Sensing an assault, the Ankylosaurus turned its head away from them, flexed its tail once, and then swung it at the front of the truck.

It came at them like a wrecking ball.

Jenny screamed.

The mace-ball of fused bone, powered by stupendously massive tail muscles, hit the truck.

The vehicle flipped backwards. The cab disintegrated in a cloud of glass spray and torn metal.

The world turned upside down.

FIFTY-ONE

There was nowhere to run. The front half of the tent was ripped away, and the space left there was filled with fourteen metres of Tyrannosaurus. Abby, Bulov, Suvova and Antila were crushed frantically against the back wall of the hut.

It was only a tent wall, but it had been constructed by diligent Russian quartermasters to be strong, durable and entirely secure. There were no flaps or openings. The wall was made of a thick, weatherproof, plasticised canvas that their clawing fingers could not hope to tear.

They were trapped.

Bulov was screaming.

Suvova was yelling.

The black Tyrannosaurus swung her extraordinarily big head down into the shell of the ruptured hut and opened her jaws. The curved teeth were the size of heavy bread knives and similarly serrated. They felt the hot, acid blast of its breath.

Abby picked up one of the hut's folding camp chairs and threw it at the oncoming snout. The chair bounced off, but the advance hesitated for a moment. Baba Yaga's eyes, small and bright, and high in her skull, seemed to stare at Abby for a second. There was a manic glare to them, a crazed, feral anger.

Natacha Antila snatched up a metal tin and opened it, scattering stainless steel theatre tools in all directions. She produced a surgical scalpel, stabbed it into the back wall of the tent and forced it downwards with both hands.

The blade cut a long vertical slit in the plasticised fabric before it snapped. Antila yelled something in Russian, and pushed Suvova and then the babbling Bulov out through the vent.

"Go!" Abby screamed at her. Antila plunged through the slit and vanished.

There was no time for Abby to follow. The jaws lunged at her, blind. She threw herself flat.

The Tyrannosaurus's head went straight over her, and buried itself in the rear of the tent. Baba Yaga raised her head, uprooting the back half of the hut, and bringing it with her, hooked like a canvas bag over her head and neck. The tip of her snout was poking through the slit Antila had cut.

The tent's flooring and groundsheet were integrally woven into the tent structure. As Baba Yaga straightened, Abby felt the floor being pulled up under her. She slid forward, tumbled, and then rolled off the stretched slope of the ground sheet onto the exposed forest floor. An avalanche of camp furniture and medical equipment came with her.

She landed right next to the Tyrannosaurus's left foot. The massive toes were splayed, and the claws were digging their tips down into the loam.

Abby rolled, hit snow and leapt to her feet. The scything wind was in her face, and snowflakes were hitting her like pellets.

She started to run.

She looked back.

The Tyrannosaurus was shaking her head free of the tent sack. A profoundly deep growl was throbbing from her torso and throat, the threat purr of the super-predator.

Baba Yaga was huge. Her massive skull was thrust forwards, counter-balanced by her long, heavy tail. She stood four or five metres tall at the hip, and her hind limbs were pillars of sleek muscle ready to piston her forwards.

She was black-on-black: slate black skin laced with tiger stripes of a darker black down her throat, torso and tail. There was a slight paling of tone on her belly and the underside of her throat and tail.

The infamously puny forelimbs, though dwarfed by the creature's stupendous bulk, looked pretty big to Abby. They were more than half as long as she was, and knotted with muscle. Connor had once told her that, though they were short, the arms of Tyrannosaurids had been anatomically proven to be robust and very strong. It was possible they were used as powerful anchors to hook into struggling prey and hold it tight while the jaws went to work.

Yeah, but not on me, Abby decided.

She ran through the driving snow looking for cover. Soldiers had emerged from some of the other tents in the campsite to investigate the commotion and had started yelling. Some were running away, though Abby couldn't tell if it was to find weapons or to hide. Sentries were blowing whistles, raising the alarm.

The creature purred out a huge, bellowing snort that throbbed the air. Lightning flashed. Baba Yaga took off, her legs powering her forward.

She wasn't following Abby at all.

Abby turned. The snow was in her eyes. She ran back,

bumping into wide-eyed soldiers fleeing in the opposite direction.

Antila, Bulov and Suvova had exited the medical tent and were running away from the edge of the camp across a broad snow-field between the trees. Lightning was strobing, and the thickly laying snow made everything bright. Abby could see the three of them clearly. Antila, young and fit, was in the lead by a good measure. Suvova was struggling along behind the medic, trying to bring Bulov with her, but the plump conservator seemed too rattled by fear to move with any purpose.

Baba Yaga was pounding out from the camp after them, tail high, jaws low and open, running them down.

Abby started running towards them, even though she was fairly certain that the Tyrannosaurus, with her huge stride, was going to beat her to it.

Besides, Abby had absolutely no clue what she was going to do if she got there first.

Except, perhaps, get eaten too.

There was evidently something drastic going on. As Medyevin hurried through the camp from the command tent, he could hear whistles blowing over the noise of the storm, and he could see men milling about. Some of them were running. Some of them seemed rather alarmed.

He wondered if he should go back and tell Shvachko that something had kicked off, but he decided he ought to see if he could find out what it was first. He could imagine the exchange.

"There's something going on," he would say.

"What?" Shvachko would demand nastily.

"I don't know," he would reply reasonably.

"I conclude you are a useless imbecile and I will forthwith

see to your immediate and permanent demotion," Shvachko would finish.

Medyevin began to run.

"What's going on?" he asked several of the men. But they were too concerned with running away to frame a decent response.

That didn't bode well.

He reached the southern limit of the camp area, where it faced the thicker forest, and came out through a row of tents.

Ahead of him, forty-odd metres away, three people were running with abandon towards the treeline across the snow.

Everyone's running tonight, he said to himself.

Something went past him, shaking the ground, kicking up clouds of snow. It was a colossal black beast, with a vast tail sawing around like the bough of a giant tree. It was chasing the three figures.

Nikolai Medyevin had just enough professional detachment to identify the beast as a mature Tyrannosaurid, and just enough self-control not to wet himself. He remembered that Shvachko had given him a gun, but it seemed rather small compared to the scale of things.

Medyevin concluded — on reflection — that the most rewarding career move he could make next would be to hide.

Holding his AK upright, Koshkin slid in towards the command tent. He glanced back at Connor, who was supposed to be creeping along as well, but he was too agitated about what might be happening to Abby at the medical tent.

Koshkin glared at him and mouthed something.

"What?" Connor mouthed back.

"BE... QUIET!" Koshkin mouthed.

Connor nodded, and mimed zipping up his lips, locking them and then discarding an imaginary key.

"What was that?" Koshkin mouthed.

Connor wondered how to mime "never mind".

But Koshkin turned back to the tent doorway. He held up his left hand with three fingers raised.

"Three words?" Connor mouthed. "Sounds like?" Then he realised the Russian wasn't even looking at him.

Koshkin shook his hand with the raised fingers.

"Oh, on three. Got you!" Connor nodded. One finger lowered, then another…

When the third finger went down, Koshkin stormed the tent. Connor was right behind him.

Koshkin aimed his AK from the shoulder, but the camp table and chairs were empty. The laptop was sitting on the table, a screensaver drifting across it. The fan heater was chugging.

Concealed by the side flap of the tent doorway, Shvachko rested the barrel of an AK-74 against the side of Connor's head.

"You're getting sloppy, Koshkin," he said. "You both made far too much noise."

Reluctantly, Koshkin dropped his weapon.

"Run! Run, Grisha!" Suvova screamed.

All Bulov seemed to be able to manage was a drunken stumble. Up through the ground, Suvova could feel the shock of the huge feet thundering after them.

"Run!"

Closing for a snatch-kill, the Tyrannosaurus roared. It was a brutal, chilling blast of sound, and it wasn't just a victorious call or a triumphant announcement. A great part of the complex roar was made up of infra-sound, its frequency under twenty hertz, which generated fear and disorientation. Like many apex predators, the Tyrannosaurus used its roar to immobilise its prey with numb terror.

Suvova felt the shudder of total fear, but she managed to stagger onwards, glancing fearfully over her shoulder.

Bulov simply froze, and collapsed onto his knees in the path of the racing creature. Snow puffed into the air as his knees hit the ground.

Then Abby was twenty metres away, sprinting in across the snowfield from Bulov's left. Suvova couldn't believe what she was seeing.

"Oi!" the girl yelled at the top of her lungs. "Oi! Baba Yaga!"

It was no hyperpredator roar. There was no infrasound component to stun her target. But the Tyrannosaurus broke stride slightly, distracted by the sound and the small movement to her left.

"Oi!" Abby yelled again, waving her hands for good measure. Would it turn for her? Would she be able to outrun an adult Tyrannosaurus if it did? Both questions occurred to her at once.

She was about to find out.

Baba Yaga glanced sidelong, but she was still intent on using the defenceless, defeated Bulov as a canape. Hardwired instincts urged a big predator to take any food that was offered when it was offered, the easier the better.

Abby shot the Tyrannosaurus in the flank.

She'd remembered the capture gun in her waistband. It was powerful, with a hell of a kick. It drove the dart deep into Baba Yaga's weathered, hard skin, deep enough to sting.

The creature thumped to a halt ten metres from the kneeling Bulov, and shook her rump. She turned her head.

Abby yelled again. With freezing, snow-numbed fingers, she'd reloaded the capture gun with a dart from the shoulder bag. She aimed and fired.

Despite the crosswind, Baba Yaga was a big target. The second dart *thukked*! into the skin of her neck.

She had the Tyrannosaurus's full attention.

With an explosive growl, the creature swung away from Bulov and came for her instead.

"Drugs?" she murmured. "Taking effect? Any time soon?

"Okay, not so much."

Abby turned. And ran.

FIFTY-TWO

Jenny blinked. She shook her head.

Fragments of windscreen glass fell out of her hair. Everything was on its side and at a funny angle. She had a sudden terrifying flashback to a helicopter crash not so long ago. As much as the cold, the thought made her shiver.

Then she moved.

She was battered and bruised. The truck, destroyed by the Ankylosaur's tail, was lying upside down in a gully beside the track. Snow was gusting in through the broken windows and torn-off doors, but it was very warm, almost hot. Snowflakes sizzled and turned into dew as they hit the crumpled metalwork. Jenny could hear the plastic crackle of flames nearby. She could see the dancing orange light of the forest fire.

"Hemple?" she called. "Hemple?"

She could also smell fuel, strong and pungent.

She clambered out into the open, and walked around the wreck. The driver had not survived. He was unpleasantly mangled into the front of the vehicle.

Zvegin and the guard had pulled themselves free. Both of them were injured. Zvegin's face was badly gashed.

"Help me!" Jenny yelled, searching frantically for Hemple. "Help me!"

They ignored her. The guard was supporting Zvegin and they began trudging away along the track, as if they intended to walk back to the camp.

"Come back!" Jenny yelled. "Come back here and help me!"

"Help yourself!" Zvegin shouted back. "Come with us!"

"You need to help me!" she cried.

The blazing front of the forest fire was now less than thirty metres away from the track and sweeping towards the wreck. The heat was intense, like a hard wall. The light of the inferno hurt her eyes. The truck would soon be engulfed, and its fuel would catch.

"Come back and help me!" she shouted desperately at Zvegin and the guard, but they were already too far away, and clearly cared very little.

Jenny clambered back into the wreck.

"Hemple?"

She heard him groan.

"This isn't very clever, is it?" he murmured.

"Are you hurt?"

"Um, no. Ow, yes. My leg. Right leg."

"Let's get you out. The fire's right on top of us."

She could see his eyes in the gloom and his teeth as he smiled.

"No can do," he said. "My leg's pinned."

Jenny told him exactly what she thought of that as an excuse. She scrambled around, and got to his right leg.

"Ow!" he exclaimed.

"Try pulling it," she insisted.

"I have been," he replied. "Jenny, it's really stuck. It's pinned between the floor plate and the side of the door. It's got me like a bear trap."

"We'll just have to un-get you, then."

"You're going to bend metal, are you?"

"If I have to." She looked at him. "It's either that, or saw your leg off."

"Listen," he said, "Jenny, please listen to me. There's no time to get me free. I'll keep trying. If you can find me a lever, maybe a crowbar, I will keep trying. But you're not staying in here."

"Rubbish."

"Jenny," he said, "the fire is right on us. I'm supposed to protect you. Keeping you alive is my job, not the other way around. If you try to help me, you'll get yourself killed, too, and I'm not prepared to let that happen."

"I don't care," she said. "I'm not going to leave you in this mess."

"You are. Go. Now. I insist."

She ignored him and rummaged around.

"This might do for a crowbar," she said.

"It's a bit of seat, but it might work. Give it to me."

"You can't do it. I'll do it."

"Jenny!" Hemple was getting cross. "Give me the bar and get out. I protect you. That's the way it works. Don't put yourself at risk trying to look after me."

Jenny scowled at him.

"For a smart bloke, sometimes you talk the most ridiculous nonsense. This is no longer about job descriptions. I'm not leaving you in here to burn. Now move your arm and let me get at your foot."

She wriggled past him, and pushed the end of the metal bar

into the tight gap where Hemple's lower right leg was clamped. She exerted a little pressure.

"Is it moving?"

"No," he replied.

"How about now?" she panted, pushing hard.

He groaned.

"I'll take that as a 'no'," she said.

"Let me help you," he said. "Let me get hold of it and pull with you."

She shuffled around. Outside, the roar of flames sounded like rushing water. She was beginning to perspire. It was as hot as an oven inside the twisted metal box of the truck.

Hemple leaned over and got both hands around the end of the bar. She put her hands next to his. In the dark, she could feel the tack of blood on his knuckles.

They heaved.

She heard metal creak.

"It's no use," he gasped.

"Again!" she ordered.

They heaved again. The twisted bodywork moaned in protest. Still his leg would not come free.

"We'll just have to do it again," she told him.

"Please, Jenny..." he began.

She shushed him and looked up. She could hear a crackling sound coming from the mangled cab. For an awful moment, she thought that the flames had finally reached the truck and taken hold.

It wasn't the fire. Things were moving in the cab-end of the truck, small, slender shapes with long tails that darted and twitched like birds.

Jenny saw several pairs of big, golden eyes as they caught the firelight. Something chattered.

They were the lizards that Helen Cutter had called Troodons, the vicious, bright-eyed things that had carried Jenkins off and feasted on him.

Driven by the fire and drawn by the smell of blood, they had come to the wreck, and already they were beginning to feed on the driver's corpse.

Several of them were pushing up through the broken wreckage to get at Jenny and Hemple. They trilled and barked.

"Get out," Hemple ordered, breathlessly. "Jenny, get out."

Jenny pulled the bar out of the gap and jabbed it at the advancing Troodons. They skittered back, hissing and clacking.

"Go away!" she yelled at them. "Go away!"

The Troodons chattered again. Big, smart eyes stared gleefully at her in the gloom.

They weren't scared of her at all.

"There's a fully grown Tyrannosaurus loose in the camp," Connor said.

Shvachko shook his head. He was covering Connor and Koshkin with his rifle.

"Anything to distract my attention, eh?" he said.

"I just thought you should know," Connor remarked. "It could be a valuable piece of information to have if, for example, you were planning on getting through the day without being eaten."

"Stop wasting your time," Shvachko said. "This is over. You're both dead. This is an execution offence, Koshkin. You know that."

A deep and resonant roar split the air. It was long and drawn out, ten long seconds of booming rage that wasn't the thunder.

It made Shvachko glance away for a second.

Just a second.

Koshkin tackled him. He grabbed the rifle and twisted it through ninety degrees, so that, as Shvachko fired, the burst of rounds punched through the roof of the command tent. He head-butted Shvachko, knocking him backwards. Shvachko replied by throwing a kick that cracked at least one of Koshkin's ribs.

Koshkin tried to counter with a brutal elbow chop, but he missed. Shvachko, even with blood running down his face from his split nose, was fast and utterly focused. His fist fractured Koshkin's left cheekbone. The side of his other hand chopped down onto Koshkin's collarbone. Another high kick drove the bigger man backwards.

That gave Shvachko the break he needed. His hand snatched for his pistol to shoot Koshkin dead before he could rally.

The holster was empty. He'd given his pistol to Medyevin.

Koshkin punched Shvachko square in the face. Shvachko snapped away. The back of his head struck the main ceiling post of the tent with a loud crack.

He collapsed, overturning the camp table.

"Is this what you special forces people do all day?" Connor asked. "Smack each other silly?"

"Just get the laptop," Koshkin gasped. Blood was dribbling from his nostril, and his eye was already swelling.

The laptop had been knocked onto the ground. Connor scooped it up, braced it with his splinted arm, wincing, and jabbed a few keys.

"It's not working," he announced. "It's broken. Koshkin, seriously, it's broken."

"Let me see," Koshkin said in alarm.

"Oh, it's okay," Connor said. "Phew, I've got a wake up. Screen's back."

The Russian righted the camp table, and Connor put the laptop on it.

"What happens now?" he asked.

Koshkin began to type on the keyboard, entering codewords and working his way through a series of security screens.

"I'll get you in," he said. His fingers flashed over the keys.

Protocol barriers parted. Military-grade security software opened, stage by stage.

"Here," Koshkin said. "See? Here?"

Connor slid the laptop around to face him. He scanned the wealth of information on-screen rapidly.

"Hang on, hang on," he said. "God, this is a bit, you know, complex. Let me see. What about...? No, not that."

He typed something experimentally.

"Okay," he said, "this is looking more promising. I've got a sub-menu called 'slave platform/attitude'. Well, I've got plenty of attitude."

"That's not what it means," Koshkin said.

"I know, I know!" Connor said, typing again. "That was a joke. Note to self: don't make jokes at moments of tension. Okay, look, look. Now I've got this. What does this mean? What's it asking me?"

"I don't know," Koshkin said.

Connor typed one-handed.

"Neither do I. Let's try this, then."

He fell silent as he worked quickly, trying and retrying different approaches. Several minutes passed.

"Well?" Koshkin asked at length. "Can you do it?"

"I dunno," Connor said doubtfully. The laptop pinged. "Correction, yes I can! Alrighty, here we go. New window. It's asking me for something... blah, blah, blah... Okay, Koshkin,

I've got to enter accurate GPS co-ordinates for the anomaly. Any ideas?"

Koshkin looked over his shoulder.

"Maybe you need to switch to the map screen, and then re-select the guidance menu?"

"Good call. That makes sense." Connor worked fast, humming to himself.

"Okay," he said. "This is beginning to look the way I want it to look. Now, I did select the Siberia map screen and not the North American one, didn't I?"

"Are you joking again?" Koshkin asked.

"It seems so," Connor said. There was another electronic ping.

"What is it saying?"

Connor grinned.

"It says 'platform retasking — orbital reposition in process — stand by'."

"Stand by? For how long?" Koshkin asked.

"There's a work bar," Connor said. "The satellite will be in firing position in... eleven minutes and counting."

He looked at Koshkin.

"Is that going to be fast enough?" he asked.

Outside, above the thunder, another roar shattered the air. It sounded much closer.

"Let's hope so," Koshkin said. "In the meantime, grab the laptop. We need to find somewhere safer to wait."

Abby ran back through the camp, and the bewildered soldiers scattered as they saw what was coming after her.

She risked a glance over her shoulder.

The immense black shape of Baba Yaga was pounding through the snow behind her, head lowered. She was moving more slowly now, but it wouldn't matter. Another couple of Tyrannosaurus-size strides and it would catch her.

Abby jinked left, between two tents, and then threw herself down, rolling frantically through the snow on her side to slot herself under the chassis of an ATV.

She felt the creature reach her. Above her, the ATV jarred as Baba Yaga's snout rammed into the side of it. It rammed again, and the whole vehicle lifted off its wheels on one side for a second, before flopping back down.

Abby couldn't stay under the vehicle any longer. She rolled out on the other side, and sprang up again.

Raising her head above the ATV, the Tyrannosaurus saw her. With her prey reacquired, Baba Yaga accelerated again, barging the ATV aside, crushing its front end like kitchen foil under a massive, clawing foot.

Abby turned. She loaded another dart into the capture gun, and she fired it, but it missed. Running, she reloaded and turned again, shooting up at the breast of the oncoming predator. The dart wedged fast, just above the short forearms.

"Bulov! You told me the drugs were strong!" she yelled as she resumed her breakneck sprint.

Baba Yaga rolled out another infernal roar, and trampled through a row of tents to get at her.

Abby had faith in the idea that she was small and light and fast, and that if she kept switching direction, she might be able to out-turn the comparatively ponderous giant, despite its alarming stride. She veered around a parked 4x4, but the snow and ice were against her. As a shivering spear of lightning shattered the sky above, Abby lost her footing and went sprawling.

Baba Yaga didn't go around the 4x4, she went over it, standing on it like a steeplechaser stepping on the rail to clear the water jump. All four tyres of the 4x4 blew out simultaneously under the gross weight, and the vehicle collapsed onto its axles.

The Tyrannosaurus lunged towards Abby. She saw a gape a metre wide swinging down towards her.

A hail of automatic gunfire struck Baba Yaga, and she recoiled hard, coughing out short, deep grunts of surprise. She took a step back, her tail sweeping around like an angry snake.

"Abby!" Cutter was running towards her, firing an AK-74 up at the Tyrannosaurus.

"Get up! Get up!" he yelled. She scrabbled to her feet. Cutter fired again. The assault rifle kicked hard and squirted out a bright flare of ignited gas. Cutter knew some firearms, but not modern military weapons like this one. The AK was entirely unfamiliar. He felt as if he were clumsily hosing bullets in all directions.

Some of them were hitting, though. He could see dark, glinting wounds against the matt slate-and-black skin of the hyperpredator.

Cutter backed away with Abby, firing again.

"How many shots have you got left?" she yelled.

The AK stopped firing abruptly.

"None!" he shouted back.

Baba Yaga bellowed into the storm and swung at them, wounded and angry. They ran. Cutter threw open the side door of an ATV and dragged Abby inside. He slammed the door shut, and the door skin immediately buckled as the snout drove into it from outside. The ATV rocked. Cutter and Abby were both lurched off their feet.

A corner of the roof suddenly scrunched up — Baba Yaga was biting the ATV's roofline. Several long teeth plunged through the metal into the cabin, like swords inside a magician's trick box.

With a firm, biting hold, she began to shake and worry the

ATV. Cutter clambered forward and got into the driving seat. The keys were in the ignition, because the power plant had been left on, connected up to a heater in the adjoining tent. He started the engine, found a forward gear and put his foot down

The wheels of the anchored ATV spun in the wet snow. Neck hunched, like a dog refusing to let go of a stick, Baba Yaga held on.

Metal shredded. The ATV lurched forwards with a huge tear along its roof. Baba Yaga staggered back. The fan heater unit and its connecting vent and power cable tore out of the back of the tent and tumbled after the ATV.

"Hang on!" Cutter yelled.

Abby clung on. The ATV wasn't behaving well in the blizzard, especially not from a ridiculous racing start. The back end swung out, and they side-swiped a trunk with a tooth-jarring impact.

In pursuit, the Tyrannosaurus butted them from behind, skipping them forward. Abby fell against a seat.

Cutter cursed and hit the brakes. He selected reverse with a violent twist of the stick, and put his foot down again.

The ATV leapt backwards and hit the creature like a battering ram. Baba Yaga roared. Cutter sped forward, and then selected reverse again and rammed her a second time.

The rear end of the ATV was a mess. When Cutter pulled forward again, he could hear crumpled bodywork dragging and clattering behind him.

Baba Yaga surged back at them in a frenzied attack. Her snout crashed into the side of the ATV just as Cutter tried to turn the wheel, and that was enough to flop the ATV over onto its side with a heavy crash.

The Tyrannosaurus fell on the ATV as if it were a major kill. She lifted one hind limb, and dug the massive claws of her foot into the bodywork, squealing them into the metal. Pressing down, she hooked her small but powerful front limbs into the side door and anchored them, causing the vehicle's hull to bend outwards under the gigantic stress. Her head swung in, and she took the first of several bites at the cab end, smashing the windows and shredding the roof.

Cutter grabbed Abby's hand and kicked out the crazed windscreen in one piece, rubber seal and all. They bailed out through the empty space and started to run again.

Baba Yaga saw them, and tore away from the ATV, kicking it aside in her eagerness to seize them. They had nothing like enough of a headstart to pull clear.

He tried to shield Abby, and it was his turn to see the metre-wide gape rushing at him.

At least it was going to be quick.

FIFTY-THREE

The Tyrannosaurus's powerful lunge turned into a shivering headlong collapse. The creature's chin hit the snowy ground hard and began to slide, with its body and churning limbs following close behind.

Cutter and Abby were smashed aside by the snout and sent tumbling, as if they'd been run down by a car.

Stretched out at full length, Baba Yaga rolled onto her back. Her raised leg twitched, and she lay still.

"Abby?" Cutter murmured.

"I'm okay," she said. She rose, staring at the supine mass of the creature. "Wow," she added.

"Indeed," Cutter agreed.

She looked down at the capture gun in her hand.

"I guess now we know that an adult Tyrannosaurus takes three darts, and about five minutes for the drugs to fully metabolise."

He grinned.

"Give or take."

Suvova and Bulov came running out of the snow storm.

"Are you all right? Nicky, are you all right?"

"We're both fine," Cutter said. "We've got to find Connor and Koshkin fast. Have you seen them?"

Suvova shook her head.

"The whole place is in chaos," she said. "Men are running in all directions because of the Tyrannosaurus."

"And the fire is coming," Bulov said, pointing at the advancing inferno out in the forest. "It's moving this way really fast."

"None of that matters," Cutter replied, "not in the long run. We've got to find Connor. We've got to close the —"

He was interrupted by an enormous roar, the unmistakable bellow of a Tyrannosaurus.

They looked around in panic, but Baba Yaga was still stretched out like a small black mountain.

"Oh my God," Abby said, despair thick in her voice.

"There's another one," Cutter said. "There's another Tyrannosaurus in the forest, and it's coming this way."

"I don't believe my heart can take another," Bulov said.

"Shut up, Grisha!" Suvova snapped. "Nicky, what do we do?"

"We run," Cutter said. "We run, and we find Connor."

They started to move. Sixty metres away, on the other side of the camp, another black shape strode into view between the trees. It seemed to emerge from the raging forest blaze like a demonic beast, thick black smoke streaming around it.

The second Tyrannosaurus was a young male, six tons and ten metres long — small compared to Baba Yaga's magnificent eight-ton and fourteen-metre bulk — but he was still a huge and powerful hunting machine, and every bit a hyperpredator. He spurred forward, barking out his whooping, snarling roars.

"Go!" Cutter told the others. "Go!"

***

Hiding had its drawbacks, Medyevin decided. It was cold and uncomfortable, cowering under a truck's back axle during a blizzard in Siberia. He'd waited long enough.

There had been some terrible sounds, and fear had pinned him to the spot, but fear of sitting still was getting to him. He decided he had to find Shvachko.

Then, possibly, if he could at all manage it, a transfer back to the institute in Sankt-Peterburg.

Medyevin slipped out of cover and looked around. Snowflakes landed on his eyelashes. He could smell smoke. He started to run through the camp, a great deal of which was torn to pieces. There was a crushed 4x4 and a shredded tent-hut. He tried to get his bearings.

Where was the command tent?

Up ahead of him, he suddenly saw Abby and Suvova. They were running.

"Abby!" he shouted. "Hey, Abby!"

He started to run towards them. There was Cutter, as well, and Bulov. They were also running.

"Hey!"

Abby saw him, and shouted something. She shouted something and waved her arms frantically.

Medyevin felt the ground quiver. He looked over his shoulder.

The young male Tyrannosaurus was black-on-black like the big female, but his belly was paler and his neck was leaner. Nevertheless, to Medyevin, he looked five times as big as Baba Yaga because he was so close.

Medyevin shrieked, and ran towards the nearest tent. He ducked inside, and scrambled through the side slit into the next tent, and then through into the next. In the third tent, he cowered down and made the greatest effort of anyone in the history of the human race not to make a sound.

A split second before he died, Nikolai Medyevin reflected that, as career moves went, the extravagant application of cheap cologne had not been a wise one.

The first Troodon lunged at Jenny and she knocked it out of the wreck with a sideswipe of the metal bar.

"Awful things!" she shouted. "Go away! Shooo!"

They were getting bolder. When the next one lunged, it grabbed the end of her bar and held on.

She kicked it instead.

"Go away!"

Chattering, they lunged and snapped again.

A loud bang shook the wreck. The swirling flames had reached the trees above them, and a huge bough had come crashing down in a blizzard of sparks. It thumped off the front of the upturned truck and flared up in a burst of angry flame.

The Troodons scattered in terror. They darted away, out of the shattered doors and windows. One ran over Jenny's legs in an effort to find an exit.

"Please get out of the truck," Hemple said.

Jenny didn't bother to answer. She inserted the end of the bar back into the gap and hauled on it, bracing her feet against the doorsill for extra purchase.

There were flames all around them. The heat was stifling. The leaking tanks would catch any second.

"Jenny!"

"Now! *Now*! Drag your foot out!"

Hemple heaved and cried out in pain. His foot slid clear.

She released the bar, which dropped with a clatter, and fell on top of him.

"Come on!" she screamed, coughing as the smoke filled her lungs. "Come on!"

She grabbed his coat and began to drag him. He stuck out his arms to pull himself backwards. Flames billowed in through the shattered wind-screen and began to engulf the front seats.

Jenny hauled Hemple backwards out of the rear of the truck and onto the slushy track. She pulled him across the half-melted snow as far as she could. The track was forming a limited firebreak.

With a sucking *whooommff!* the fuel caught, and the truck went up like a bonfire. They shielded their faces from the heat.

"Thanks," he said, after a while.

"It's okay," she said. "You'd have done the same for me."

"Yeah," he agreed, "but that's my job."

They heard an engine. An ATV was coming up the trail in the opposite direction to the one they'd been heading in. Its headlights found them, helpless, in the middle of the road.

The ATV stopped, and men jumped out.

"How are you doing, chief?" Redfern asked.

"What the *hell* are you doing here?" Hemple asked. Garney and Mason were behind Redfern, and Murdoch sat behind the wheel.

"We saw that you weren't with us any more," Redfern said, "so we asked the Russian boys nicely if they'd mind turning around."

"But they didn't seem very keen on the idea," Mason continued.

"So we decided to take charge of things," Garney concluded, rubbing his knuckles.

"Where are they?" Hemple asked.

Redfern jerked a thumb over his shoulder.

"About a mile back that way, walking home in their underwear," he said.

Garney racked the bolt of a captured AK-74.

"So," he said to Jenny, "where to, miss?"

They saw the Tyrannosaurus take the tent Medyevin had been hiding in, blood gushing from the folds in the fabric, and then stride on after other prey. Cutter sent Suvova and Bulov off in the opposite direction, towards the forest to the west of the camp.

"Just keep running," he told them. Suvova nodded. Bulov ran.

Cutter grabbed Abby's hand again, and they headed into the camp. Fire had reached the first of the tents at the eastern end.

In the middle of the camp, they stopped and looked around. Most of the soldiers had fled. A couple were driving 4x4s away across the snow.

"Where could he be?" Abby asked.

"I don't know," Cutter replied.

"Do you think he's managed to do it?"

"I really don't know."

"So which way?"

They turned left, meaning to head for the command tent.

The young male Tyrannosaurus strode into view twenty metres ahead, saw them, and turned their way. It started to accelerate.

Cutter and Abby ran. As she sprinted, Abby reached into the shoulder bag for another dart to fit in the capture gun.

There were none left.

They'd set up the laptop on a tree stump just inside the treeline, away from the chaos of the camp. Snow was swirling around them, and the forest seemed as bright as day, thanks to the glow of the approaching fire.

Koshkin paced while Connor watched the work bar slowly

loading. His arm really ached. The pain was so great, it was making him feel lightheaded and even a little nauseous. Every now and then he looked up into the dark vaults of the black trees around them, and watched the snowflakes swirling into the constellations of sparks and drifting cinders.

Fire and ice, tiny worlds in collision.

"How much longer?" Koshkin asked.

"Fifty seconds," Connor replied. There was an electronic ping.

"What was that?"

"Uhm," Connor began, checking. "Battery low. That was the battery low signal."

He looked up at Koshkin.

"Not really anywhere to plug it in around here, is there?"

Koshkin looked at the power light.

"There's enough power to get us there. It'll be enough."

"I certainly hope so."

There was another chime.

"Okay," Connor said, reading the new window on-screen. "It's there. We're good to go. The platform is re-aligned, the target vectors are set, confirmed and locked. All I have to do is select the approval and confirm options, and then press, you know, *ka-powie*."

"Step away from the laptop."

They both looked up. Dried blood caked Shvachko's face. He had found a pistol, and he was aiming it at them.

"Step away," he insisted. He seemed a little unsteady.

Koshkin tensed slightly, weighing up the optimum moment to make a move and attempt to disarm him.

Shvachko shot him.

Connor yelped. Koshkin jerked as he was hit and staggered backwards. He hit the trunk of a fir tree, shaking snow out of its lower boughs, and slid down onto the ground.

"I'm taking no chances," Shvachko said.

It was Cutter's turn to fall. He caught his ankle on a loose guy wire from a collapsed tent that was half-buried in the deepening snow and crashed onto his face.

"Get up!" Abby screamed, pulling at his arm.

The young male Tyrannosaurus came bounding in, his jaws opening, his head sweeping down to striking height.

Baba Yaga slammed into him and smashed him sideways. A couple of Abby's darts still dangled from her flesh. She had just woken up, and she was in a foul mood.

Her jaws clamped around the male's throat as she brought him down. Abby and Cutter felt the serious impact of the two entangled creatures as they hit the ground, locked together.

The young male howled and spluttered, thrashing to get free. Their tails lashed. Baba Yaga held on, and tightened her bite. Her right leg came up to tear at his flank and belly. Black-on-black skin slid against black-on-black skin. Arterial blood jetted onto the snow.

Cutter got up and pulled Abby away from the mortal combat.

"Seems Baba Yaga doesn't like competition," he said.

"Seriously, I'm going to press this," Connor said, finger poised, "so you'd better shoot me if you're going to."

Shvachko laughed and took aim.

There was a solid crack. Connor winced. When he reopened his eyes, he found, to his relief, that there were no bullet holes in him.

Shvachko pitched face-first into the snow. There was a bloody wound on the back of his scalp.

Natacha Antila lowered the log she was clutching.

"Pig-man!" she declared.

She ran over to Koshkin and applied pressure to his gunshot wound.

"Tell him!" Koshkin gasped up at her. "Tell him to press the button!"

"He says you should press the button," Antila relayed.

"Okay," Connor said. He hesitated.

"Can you ask him," he added, "and I know it's last minute, but it's only just occurred to me: are we safe here?"

"What?" Koshkin wheezed. "What is he saying now?"

"Lie still!" Antila snapped.

"I was just wondering," Connor called. "Should we really be this close to the target zone? I mean, it's only just over there. Is this a good idea?"

"Is *not* pressing it a good idea?" Koshkin asked him.

"No, I suppose not," Connor admitted, "end of the world and that.

"Well, here goes everything," he said, and he pressed the button.

FIFTY-FOUR

The helicopter's giant rotors began to cycle up, stirring the cool mid-morning air.

"Of course," Koshkin was saying, "this entire circumstance is beyond secret. There will be significant exchanges between our governments at intelligence level, but nothing formal, and nothing can be made public."

"Sorry, mate," Connor said, "I'm selling my exclusive to the tabloids."

Koshkin looked at him. The specialist was pale from the painkillers, and his arm was strapped up to ease his chest wound.

"You —" he began.

"Joking," Connor said with a grin.

The Russian just scowled.

The convoy of trucks and 4x4s bumped along the airstrip and pulled up beside the transport chopper. Their passengers all climbed out.

"Are you sure you won't stay, Nicky?" Rina Suvova asked as she hugged him.

"I'm quite keen to get back home," Cutter said, smiling.

"We could really use your help," Bulov said, shaking Cutter's hand. "The anomaly may be closed, but the forests are still full of erratics."

"And you'll have years of fun finding them all," Abby said, also smiling. She hugged Professor Suvova, and then kissed Bulov on the cheek. He blushed.

"I think the EM pulse did the trick," Cutter said to Koshkin. "I think it's sealed the Tunguskan anomaly permanently. But you have to monitor the site from now on. If there's even a hint that it's opening up again, you know what to do."

Koshkin nodded.

"Of course."

"Those are some majorly scary satellite weapons you've got there, comrade," Connor added. "I promise not to tell anyone about them, ever. Cross my heart and hope to die."

He winked at Koshkin.

"Ta for letting me play with them, though."

Koshkin nodded again. His scowl seemed less severe.

Alpha team had dismounted from the truck behind them. Hemple was walking on crutches with help from Jenny and Natacha Antila.

"Are we all set?" Cutter asked.

"The flight's waiting," Koshkin said. "You will transfer to an airliner in a few hours. It should be a more comfortable trip home than the one that brought you here."

Antila came over and gave first Abby and then Connor a firm embrace.

"Ow!" Connor said.

"What?" Antila asked.

"I think," he said, adjusting his shoulder, "I think you might have pulled my arm out with that hug. It's probably best if you give me a thorough physical before we leave, you know, otherwise..."

"Get onto helicopter," she said.

An honour guard of Russian soldiers assembled at the side of the airstrip to see them off. Abby saw Vols standing in line in the front rank and ran over to him.

"You look after yourself," she told him.

"You go to be home," he said.

"That's right."

"Be good?"

"It's very be good," she said.

"As I said before," Cutter remarked as he walked towards the chopper's ramp with Koshkin, "if this happens again..."

"We know where to find you," Koshkin finished. "Yes, and thank you."

The chopper thundered westward. Abby looked down at the endless forests sliding past below.

"Any regrets at all about undertaking this ridiculous mission?" Jenny asked Hemple.

He shrugged.

"Not really," he said. "Except... I didn't get to shoot enough monsters."

"Yeah, where were you?" Connor asked. "We could have used you with Baba Yaga."

"She's still down there somewhere," Abby said. Just after the eerie flash and airshock of the EMP had sealed the anomaly, she had spotted the big female Tyrannosaurus heading out of the ruined camp. Her sleek, black shape had vanished into the trees like a forest demon returning to its lair. Behind her lay the ruined body of the male.

It was an image she wouldn't forget in a hurry.

Jenny looked over at the brooding figure of Cutter. He hadn't said a word since take-off.

"What's the matter?" she asked, coming over and sitting down beside him.

"Oh, nothing really," he said.

"Come on, I saw the look on your face just then," she said. "What were you thinking about?"

EPILOGUE

It's late afternoon on a summer's day. A hooting chorus echoes up through the woods from the bright river. Dragonflies race and dazzle through the sunbeams. Birds, and almost-birds, flit and dart in the trees. In the distance, there are snow-capped mountains under a blue sky.

Somewhere out there, there is a hunter, a killer, preparing to strike. It's choosing its moment. No one can see it, and no one knows it's there. It's stalking its prey, and its prey doesn't suspect a thing.

Silently, it comes closer. At the very end, it will rush in, an ambush predator, far faster than its prey can react to. It will rush in and deliver a terminal strike.

The Hadrosaurs commune at the water's edge. The adults are watching over the young. They have no idea what's coming.

They know to be wary, though. Experience has taught them that. They know there's always a killer out there somewhere, waiting for its opportunity. They know they have to be vigilant and ready to sound the alarm at the first hint of danger.

It's almost time.

There's a moment, an inkling. The woods go quiet. The birds stop singing. The insects hush. The Hadrosaurs stop hooting and freeze. As is always the case, a terrible silence descends just before the killer rushes into view and strikes.

There is a light in the sky.

THE END

ACKNOWLEDGEMENTS

The author would like to thank Adrian Hodges and Tim Haines for their cooperation and inspiration; Nancia Leggett at Impossible; Douglas Henshall, Lucy Brown and Andrew-Lee Potts for not being too distracted by a bloke with a notebook; and Cath Trechman for keeping track of all anomalies.

PRIMEVAL

THE SHADOW OF THE JAGUAR
STEVEN SAVILE

A delirious backpacker crawls out of the dense Peruvian jungle muttering about the impossible things he has seen... A local ranger reports seeing extraordinary animal tracks and bones — *fresh* ones — that he cannot explain...

Cutter and the team are plunged into the hostile environment of the Peruvian rainforest, where they endure a perilous journey leading them to something more terrifying than they could possibly have imagined...

PRIMEVAL

THE LOST ISLAND
PAUL KEARNEY

A trawler is torn to pieces by a mysterious creature off the Irish coast; meanwhile Connor's anomaly detector goes off the charts. Half a dozen rifts in time have appeared... all on one deserted — yet politically contentious — island.

While Lester struggles to hold on to his career as the story edges ever closer to the front page, Cutter and the team battle through a deadly storm to reach the island, only to find themselves fighting to survive amidst the terrifying creatures roaming the harsh landscape...

PRIMEVAL

FIRE AND WATER
SIMON GUERRIER

At a safari park in South Africa, rangers are inexplicably disappearing and strange creatures have been seen battling with wild animals. Danny and Lester fly in to investigate and are drawn into a dark and dangerous conspiracy which could have terrible consequences...

Back in London, Connor, Abby and Sarah have been left to cope on their own. As torrential rain pours down over the city, an enormous anomaly opens up in East London...